BURN

A NOVEL BY

Paul Slatter

This book is entirely a work of fiction. References to real people alive or dead, events, establishments, organizations, or locales are for the intended purpose only to provide a sense of authenticity, and are used fictitiously. All other characters, and all incidents and dialogue, are drawn from the author's imagination and are not to be construed as real.

Also by Paul Slatter

Rock Solid
Trust Me

For

Joy

Manus in manu

Book One:

Burn

Chapter One

Padam Bahadur hoisted the blond-haired man's body onto the small boat, covered it in fuel, lit two small fuses, placed his foot on its side, and kicked it hard into the creek's calm water.

Stepping back, he stood in silence, watching the small boat drift slowly through the reflections of the distant city lights streaming across the black water.

The air was warm and still as he walked along the seawall toward the girl's apartment, thinking now about the boat that rested somewhere out there on the creek. He reached her apartment block, stopped a moment and stared at the windows that rose up from the water's edge. Then he hit the button for number four-five-four and waited. Seconds later, she answered, her voice soft and sweet.

He smelled her perfume as she opened the door and watched her long brown hair dance across her back as he followed her along the corridor toward the main room. She was young and sexy and wore a simple black dress and heels as if she'd been about to go out.

Turning to him, she smiled and asked in a Baltic accent Padam couldn't place, "Would you like a drink?"

Shaking his head in answer, he sat down and looked around. She had a nice home—expensive, all white and glass with a million-dollar view that spread out across the water.

She looked at him and asked, "So how has your evening been?"

"Good, thank you," he said deliberately.

It had been very good so far. The blond man had not been

a problem. In fact, he'd been much easier than Padam had expected.

"So what would you like to do?" the girl smiled and asked, her voice silky, even smoother in real life.

For a moment, Padam just stared and said nothing, then he said, "I want to look at you. Stand by the window and look out for a moment."

The girl turned and walked slowly to the window, her right hand trailing by her side, gently stroking the furniture as she passed. She looked at him, smiled, then faced the window. Looking out over the lights outside and slowly arching her back, she asked, "What are you going to do to me?"

Gently swaying her behind, she slipped her dress off, one shoulder at a time, until it slid down and pooled on the floor. He stared at her, not saying a word. Her breasts were large and firm, her ass like a peach. Turning her head, she looked at him.

Padam continued to stare for a moment, thinking. Slowly, he drew in a deep breath. As his eyes began to close in resignation to something that had to be done, he said, "I'm going to fuck you."

Considering this, the girl smiled, and her voice, almost a whisper, answered, "Lucky me." She turned back toward the window. In the distance, the boat was now afire, burning brightly in the darkness and casting a shimmering golden glow across the cold, shadowy water. Without looking back, she said, "There's a boat on fire out on the water."

Padam stared at her for a moment as she stood there naked before him. He watched the burning boat on the creek below without a care. The girl no longer swayed but stood still, her naked back long and shapely, her perfect ass framed by delicate little knickers, her beautiful legs long and toned. Then he told her what he'd done.

"It is a funeral pyre."

Confused, the girl looked back at him, not quite understanding.

As Padam walked toward her, he said it again. "It's a funeral pyre—your blond boyfriend's burning out there in that boat."

The girl looked away from the water and back toward Padam to hear the last words he'd bother to say to her that evening.

"I told you I was going to fuck you."

Chapter Two

Daltrey stood at the edge of the bank, looking down at the burned boat as the sun began to break in the morning sky. There was an ambulance crew there. They'd done their work. The fire crew had done their work as well. Six cops stood around who'd so far done nothing except for the one who was wet. She knew if she told the other five to get off their asses and pan out, they could at least find where the boat had come from in a matter of an hour, but what was the point…they all hated her.

Daltrey looked around, aware she was being stared at. The rush of blood from her stomach hit her chest, and unable to hold it in, she called over to two cops sitting sidesaddle on their bikes. "Whoever did this fucked off a long time ago," she said, "so if you're waiting for him to come back, he isn't."

The cops looked at her strangely, this chick with a badge who should still be in school. One answered back, "What?"

"The guy in the boat's dead—he's not leaving."

In their eyes, they were here securing the crime scene— she'd been around long enough to know that.

"Now that the sun's up, why don't you walk along the shoreline and see if you can figure out where the boat came from," she said.

The cops looked at her, then along the seawall that ran for miles. In almost all their eyes, she could see the words *go fuck yourself* manifesting, but then one of them, whom she figured she hadn't seen in at least a year, took a deep breath, piped up, pointed back into town, and said, "I've got

4

something I need to chase up."

So that's why you've been hanging around here for an hour doing fuck all, Daltrey thought as she stared at him, knowing she could make him do what she said, or any of them for that matter if she wanted to. But what was the point? Dead wood was dead wood. And besides, there could be a message chalked on the path reading, 'Small boat with dead guy left from here,' and they'd still miss it. So instead, she just said, "Yeah, I understand. It's hard to walk when you've got gout."

Fuck them, she thought. Most had hit on her in one way or another when she first joined the force. They thought she was cute and dumb and wanted to help her on her way, would hate to see her fail. They would say, "Oh, you're so cute" or "You have lovely hair, skin, and lips." And now? They hated her mouth and the cruel words it spat out, words that flowed so freely from between those lovely lips they'd told her she had, those lovely lips they'd tried to kiss and stick their dicks into. Now it snapped back harsh and emasculating words, words that came without fear and hit home, words that cut them down like an unseen Gurkha warrior soldier wielding a razor-sharp sword.

Daltrey walked to the boat and looked at the charred remains of the body for the second time. The young kid who had used his initiative and swam out and pulled it in stood there, now dressed, with his hair wet. Daltrey looked at him. He was strong and fit with light in his eyes.

"What's your name?"

"Williams."

"Where was he when you found him?"

Williams pointed out into the creek, the tide now turning. In the distance, she could see another boat close by, its stern pulling out to sea from the anchor.

She turned back to Williams and asked, "Where was the tide when you got here?"

Williams didn't have a clue. He stared at the water, and answered, "It was dark."

Daltrey looked back to the body, now charred beyond recognition. She pulled out a pencil, and lifted a charred cream-colored man's shoe from the ashes.

She drove along through the city that was just waking with the shoe in a plastic bag next to her on the passenger seat. As she pulled up to the traffic lights, she looked at it again, lifting it and examining its white pattern and leather soles closely. One shoe was a long shot, but what she already knew from the shoe itself—and from what forensics would tell her by the end of the day—it belonged to a male, late twenties or early thirties, and six foot plus.

The shoe store opened at eight, and by nine, she knew she had a size eleven Mauri "slow mover" in light blue—not cream—retailing at around a thousand bucks a pair and sold in only three shops on Vancouver's lower mainland. By midday, she had the names of six men who had bought a pair of size elevens in the last year and had spoken to five of them, the last being a Swedish gentleman by the name of Mazzi Hegan.

It was just coming up to twelve thirty, a little over six hours since she'd pulled the shoe from the charred rowboat, and Daltrey was getting hungry. She pulled up outside Mazzi Hegan's apartment complex and walked up to the door. It was a nice place, plush, with marble columns and a fancy lobby. The building manager looked at her ID and reluctantly let her into Hegan's apartment on the twentieth floor.

Daltrey moved through the big and airy apartment. A

large dark blue sofa ran along the wall. Above it were stylish pictures on an off-white wall—pictures that meant something to someone. Watching her closely, the apartment complex manager spoke up.

"Doesn't look like he's here."

Fuck me state the obvious, you dopey bitch, Daltrey thought as she turned around and looked at the woman who was getting on but still trying to hold it together.

She carried on, ignoring her. She walked into Mazzi Hegan's bedroom, opening the sliding closet without permission then asking after, "Do you mind if I look?"

The apartment manager took a deep breath. This pushy cop with an attitude was getting on her nerves now. How would she feel if someone had been snooping around her place without permission, and what if Mazzi was to come back right now and catch them? She knew how prissy he could be, with his fancy blond hair, so she said, "Maybe we shouldn't be here. I can call you if I see him later."

Daltrey pulled the charred shoe from her bag and said, "Well, if he's wearing the other one of these, you'll be seeing a ghost."

******

Bright sun lit up the center of Main Street as Daltrey headed south toward the center of town. A wardrobe full of silk suits and alligator skin shoes gave her the impression that Hegan could very well be the man who had burned to death on the boat. It was now 3:30, and she still hadn't eaten. She pulled her car up alongside a deli and got out. After ordering an orange juice with a salad bagel, she sat down at a table by the window and watched the world pass her by. Across the road, a young kid in his twenties sat with his knees up and a 'need money for food' sign written on a piece of cardboard resting against his shins. Daltrey stared at him for a moment, then looked up at a sign positioned right above his head that read 'Help Wanted.'

Fucking idiot, she thought and mouthed it to him slowly as the kid looked back at her through the window, trying to make out her words. Looking back down at her bagel, she thought back to the charred body in the boat. She'd seen worse and crazier things, but wouldn't most people think to jump into the water if they were on fire? She looked back outside to the street kid with his cap out, begging for handouts, the lazy prick. He didn't look sick or mentally ill, and from what she could see, he had good shoes on his feet, though perhaps not the stylish and slick blue Mauri slow movers that her new friend Mazzi Hegan had worn to go boating.

Taking a bite of the bagel, she stared at the kid, who was still holding his cap out and looking up at the passersby like a little puppy. Eventually catching site of Daltrey again, the kid stared back, his eyes almost tearful. Seemingly starving, homeless, desperate, and in need of love, he held out his cap to her for help. Daltrey looked back, and holding the kid's stare for a moment, she finished chewing and then mouthed back silently, her lips so slow and precise that even Stevie Wonder could get the gist, *Get – a – fucking – job!*

The kid stared at her, still not getting what she was saying.

Fuck me, Daltrey thought. She tried again, this time pointing toward the sign above his head. *Go...Get... A...Fucking...Job!*

Getting it, the kid looked behind him, then back to

Daltrey as a stranger passing by dropped some cash into his hat.

It was around four thirty when Daltrey got back into her cubicle in the second-floor office of the Vancouver Police Department on Hastings and Main Street. Sitting at the desk, she turned on her computer and punched in Mazzi Hegan on the keyboard. Top off the line was a website for Slave Media Advertising Agency. She hit the link and opened up a glossy site.

Reach the Top with Slave

The Media Marketing Specialists

"Wow, don't you guys look fabulous," Daltrey muttered quietly as she scrolled down through the photos of commercial ads shot beautifully and fronted by models with huge attitude. At the bottom was a shot of two men standing in front of a red Ferrari, and underneath was the statement:

Impossible is Nothing

Slave—Creative Directors, Sebastian String & Mazzi Hegan

Daltrey leaned in and looked closer at the two hotshots who claimed to have so much talent. The guy on the left was older with a sweet, soft face. On the right was a tall, good-looking blond man in his thirties wearing a blue suit and brown crocodile skin shoes not unlike the burned one sitting on her desk.

She stared at the photo for a moment, thinking, as a smiling Mazzi Hegan stared back at her. She asked out loud to no one but herself, "What did you do last night, Mr. Slick, to get yourself barbecued on a rowboat?"

She printed the photo and then entered the police database. Seconds later, Mazzi Hegan's photo appeared alongside his date of birth, address, and social insurance number. She scrolled down further. He appeared to be a good citizen with only two speeding convictions and one ticket for parking badly. That was it. *Fuck all,* she thought. She hit another button, refined the search, and again nothing.

Picking up the phone, she dialed the number for the Slave website and asked to speak to Mr. Hegan. As she expected, he wasn't in. "When will he be in, please?" The receptionist was unsure. "Of course you are, my love," Daltrey said as she hung up and stared at the picture of Mazzi Hegan beaming back at her from the computer screen.

It was him. She knew it. The penthouse apartment just off Cambie, close to the creek, expensive furniture, a Ferrari in the garage. Daltrey stared back at the photo, and something inside her told her the shoe was Hegan's, and rarely was she wrong.

Chapter Three

Playing with the electronic infrared door key he'd just made in the basement where he lived in his mum's house, Dan Treedle stood waiting in front of the sandwich shop at the corner of Georgia and Richards. He quickly stuffed the last few inches of a foot-long salmon salad sandwich with extra gherkins into his mouth as he watched Daltrey pull up and open the door for him to jump in.

She was almost unrecognizable now, he thought, with her hair pulled back tight to the back of her head in a ponytail for work. Nothing like she'd looked when he'd met her at a party three months back. She'd been dancing in the living room with this woman who looked like a guy, drunk, her hair down and flowing as she flipped it around like a cheerleader at a hockey game. She'd been flipping it then, and again when she'd agreed to meet him a few days later, when he'd pounded oysters until he threw up.

Sitting down, he leaned across the center console, moving in for a kiss.

Daltrey said, "You been eating fish?"

"Just a sandwich."

Good, Daltrey thought as she put the car into gear and pulled out into traffic. She now had an out if he asked her to go for lunch.

Dan continued, "If you're hungry, though, I know a great café."

Daltrey looked at him and smiled, saying, "Don't worry, I'm good. You've already eaten. But thanks."

Once she had the infrared system needed to bypass the

security system to Mazzi Hegan's apartment complex Dan had promised her, and if it worked, there was little chance she'd ever have to see him and his food-stained mouth again—unless the system broke.

She looked into her rearview mirror and then to Dan and asked, "You got it?"

Dan reached into his pocket and pulled out an open circuit board attached by a switch to a nine-volt battery and said, "It's a bit thrown together, but it should work fine. Hit the switch, and it'll send out frequencies to open any of the doors and work the elevators in most of the new apartment blocks in town."

Daltrey smiled, it was just what she was after—and the sole reason she'd agreed to the oyster date in the first place after dancing all night with that crazy girl and then this guy after he joined in and then listening to him bang on for an hour in the kitchen as she and her friend cooled off. Daltrey remembered standing there, feeling the panties inside her jeans wet from the sweat rolling down her back, listening to him rattling off bullshit about how his mother was a dancer and how he had in-depth knowledge of modern day infrared security systems and could build custom electronic keys that could easily beat any new security system in the city.

She looked at him as she drove and grabbed his knee. "Thanks," she said.

There was something about this guy, she thought. Young, a good physique, kind of good-looking—but at the same time an absolute moron. Holding up the key with her right hand, she stared at the makeshift contraption and said disbelievingly, "This really works?"

Dan nodded. "Go ahead and try it. Try it anywhere!"

Picking an apartment building at the side of the road with

no concierge, she pulled up, got out, and tried the door. Locked. She hit the button to Dan's device, waited a few seconds, pushed the door, and it opened. *My god, the guy's a genius,* she thought as she closed the door and walked back to the car.

As she got behind the wheel, he asked, "So who lives in this apartment you need access to?"

Daltrey looked to the road and pulled away. "Lived, I think."

Dan looked at her, confused. "Someone moved out?"

Daltrey shook her head, then stopped and thought about it. "Yeah, kind of. Being dead'll do that. Well, maybe dead."

Dan stared out the window, then turned to look at Daltrey as the sun hit her from the side, lighting up her straightened brown hair that was normally wavy. She was still hot even if she was dressed like a guy. He asked her, "He or she?"

Without looking, Daltrey answered, "We found a guy burned to death on a rowboat this morning."

"Where?"

"Out on False Creek." Daltrey looked at him and frowned. "That's why I'm taking a sneak look at his stuff while he's still warm."

Dan smiled. He'd eaten a shitload of croissants that morning some guy in tight trousers had brought over for his mum, and he'd burned the third round cramming them into the toaster, so he had a rough idea of what the guy must have looked like. He asked, "You found him?"

"No, we got a call early this morning."

"I thought you police types had procedures?"

Daltrey looked at him and raised her eyebrows. She pulled her car up alongside Mazzi Hegan's apartment block and looked Dan straight in the eye.

"You going to tell on me, Dan?"

They walked to the apartment complex door as Daltrey pulled out her new makeshift electronic device. She hit the button, and seconds later the door was unlocked.

Walking inside, they stared at the marble columns as they entered the elevator. Dan took the device from Daltrey's hand and hit the button again, bypassing the security system, and then handed it back to her.

Daltrey watched as the doors closed and the elevator began to rise, leaving the ornate marble columns behind. She held up the small device, looking closely at the cheap wiring circuit.

"You're a genius!" she exclaimed.

Dan smiled. He liked this, hanging out with a cop who dressed like a guy but let her hair down on the weekends.

Her eyes were transfixed on the flashing brilliant red numbers as the elevator counted its way up to the twentieth floor. "Do you think I could keep this?"

"It depends on whether or not you let me take a look inside."

The elevator stopped, and they walked along the corridor to Mazzi Hegan's front door. Pulling a set of keys from her pocket, Daltrey lifted them up and tried one after the other in the lock. The fifth one worked, and she stepped inside.

"Was your last boyfriend a locksmith?" Dan asked.

As it happened, he was. Sandy was his name, and he was a master locksmith. He lived just outside town, and she'd met him at a bar one night when she'd been horny and out looking for an old friend. Their relationship had fizzled out a couple of days after she became bored with him and his constantly hard penis and had her hands on a set of master keys that could open almost any door.

Now she had it all, Daltrey thought as she put the keys back into her pocket and felt them resting heavily against her new electronic door-opening device.

They walked into the living room and looked out the window to the view of the city with the water below.

"I like it!" Dan said as he wandered around the place and looked inside the fridge. "Nice pad!"

Daltrey walked away from him as she began to carefully open drawers. Without looking back, she said, "Goes with the Ferrari in the garage."

She continued to look gently through things as Dan turned and called back, "Really? What type?"

She didn't know and didn't care. She'd only looked at it briefly after the manager had politely asked her if she'd like to see if Hegan's car was there in an attempt to get her out of the place. Without looking up, she answered, "A red one."

Dan stopped and stared at the place, letting out a long breath. He couldn't believe it. He'd never seen a home like this. It was a million miles away from his mother's basement. He walked around, fiddling with everything he could, then stopped at a picture off Mazzi Hegan and lifted it up.

"So this is the dead guy?"

Daltrey looked over and said. "You shouldn't touch stuff."

Dan put down the picture and wiped it with his sleeve and asked, "Do you think he set himself on fire by accident?"

Daltrey looked at him. He brought up a good point—she still didn't know what had happened. In fact, she didn't have a clue. "That's why I'm here," she answered.

Dan couldn't give a shit either way. He walked back to look out of the window.

"If it was an accident, I'd say he'd have jumped into the

water," Daltrey said.

"Maybe he couldn't swim," Dan snapped back without hesitation. He turned around to see Daltrey opening another drawer and looking inside. From afar, he could see nothing of value—old tickets, scissors, a screwdriver. He walked over, and with a huge dumb grin on his face, he said, "You know, it's a shame for an apartment like this to go to waste."

Daltrey closed the drawer she was looking through and opened the next. In it, a roll of tape, some gum, a spare set of keys. "What are you talking about now?" she asked.

Dan stood next to her now, looking down, his crotch now almost ten inches from her face. "Well, you know, we could put it to some use."

Daltrey closed the drawer and stood, looking Dan straight in the eye. "In what way?"

Dan smiled and shrugged, saying, "You know, hang out."

"You mean, like you hang out of me?" Daltrey said as she shook her head and walked away toward the kitchen. *So in his mind, it's okay to stuff his face with fish and then think he can get it on*, she thought. But she had what she wanted now. Suffering through the oysters the last time they'd been out, with him puking and all, was enough. Luckily, she hadn't had to sleep with the moron with his fishy breath to clinch the deal. Without looking back, she said aloud, "I didn't invite you along for us to party, Dan, if that's what you were thinking. I've got work to do."

Dan shrugged again and walked over to a cabinet where he looked at a few loose pictures of Mazzi Hegan on a yacht with another guy and a tall girl who looked like a model. He lifted the picture closer to get a better look at the girl's ass, then called across to Daltrey.

"You should see if there's a blue yacht moored in the

creek. If there is, I bet it's without its dinghy."

Daltrey looked at him. "Why do you say that?"

Dan walked away into the apartment's master bedroom and called out, "Because there's a picture of him on one on the dressers."

Daltrey stood and walked to the dresser and picked up the photo. As stupid as he seemed, Dan wasn't all that stupid. She turned toward the master bedroom and said, "Keep your hands off of things in there."

Dan stared at the king-size bed with its large pillows and purple silk sheets. He looked at the ceiling covered in crazy artwork of strange black-shaded lines and shapes. Walking away, he stepped into the en suite, its huge shower no doubt built for two. Reaching in, he turned on the power jets and watched, mesmerized, as the shower's pump-action jets blasted out steaming hot water from all angles.

Opening the door to the walk-in wardrobe, Dan stared at the silk suits, shirts, and ties, crocodile skin shoes, and silk socks—all lined up and perfectly labeled. He picked up a suit jacket and tried it on, looking at himself in the mirror. He saw himself again in another mirror and then, turning, caught a glimpse of himself again at another angle. It was fantastic. He looked styling. Everywhere he looked, he could see himself— back, front, side, low angle, high angle. He hadn't seen anything like it since he'd watched Bruce Lee slashed with a multi-bladed knife at the end of *Enter the Dragon*, and after he'd broken the basement window when his shoe flew off.

And then he saw it. A small drawer made of dark mahogany, varnished like glass. It had a plaque embossed with gold letters that spelled out the word - *SPECIAL.*

******

It was nearly six o'clock when Daltrey found the yacht from the photo settled in among nearly a hundred other boats just below the bridge, all moored alongside Granville Island at the mouth to the creek. Sixty feet long, sleek, finished in a light blue trim, and designed to cut through water as easily as a tailor's scissors slipped through expensive linen.

The fact that Dan had stripped and put on Mazzi Hegan's clothes, then tried it with her sexually as he had, still irked her. It was either that or the fact that she was hungry. Probably both, Daltrey thought as she climbed on board the sleek yacht with the missing dinghy. She reached the boat's door and gave it a shove. It was solid, and the lock, like the small door, was pitted from the elements.

Pulling out her set of master keys, she opened the lock and began to climb down the small ladder. The boat, which had been unused for a while, smelled more musty than damp. She walked slowly through the center of the vessel. According to the newspaper left on the countertop, no one had been around for at least a month, and from the notes on the calendar on the wall, it appeared they wouldn't be back for another two. Looking up, she opened a couple of cupboards and peeked inside. They were full of coffee and cookies, maps and booze.

She walked slowly through to the cabin at the rear. Opening the door, she saw a small bed, its pillows just peeking out from the brown woolen blankets all neatly lined up and shipshape, readied no doubt for the next voyage. Walking out again, she stopped and pulled out a map of the San Juan Islands from an upended pocket shelf. She sat down at the small kitchen table and opened it. Daltrey stared at the map and a crumpled tidal chart that had been tucked inside. She knew the area well. She ran her slender fingers through her hair.

A year back, a guy with really hairy legs had whisked her off in a forty-foot schooner around the very same islands for a long weekend. It had been fun—fun in the sense of freedom. The freedom of the sea, the wind in her hair, the surf blowing up, bubbling white froth along the wooden deck. The tiny harbors and secluded coves…it was a time of magic if you were with the right crowd or the right someone. But the right someone wasn't him, and as the days went on, and the clock began to tick slower as one hour felt like two, then three, the guy with the chunky and hairy legs had wanted sex. And the magic had begun to drift away.

Daltrey sat back and looked around and thought about how at first she'd wanted him, but when he was naked in his socks trying to stick his dick in her, she hadn't. And how she'd lied and told him she was sore down there, and had paid for a float plane to come pick her up and take her home.

Standing up, she looked around. The yacht was lovely— really lovely in fact—but as lovely as it was, it wasn't *Mazzi Hegan* lovely. It didn't have that flair she'd seen at his apartment. His yacht would be fancier, carry more of the swirl and swagger that came with a guy who'd go out and buy a pair of fancy thousand-dollar shoes. And with this sudden awareness that she was in the wrong place and that she was trespassing, the sinking feeling welled within. Daltrey headed for the galley's small door that led to the deck, with every step feeling the discomfort deep within that comes to someone who knows right from wrong saying to herself out loud, "Last time, Daltrey—last time." But deep down she knew what she was asking of herself was impossible.

Chapter Four

Dan stood in the steaming hot shower, its razor-sharp jets striking his shoulders. He squirted another dollop of aloe vera herbal shampoo on his head and rubbed it into his hair. He'd read somewhere that its prolonged use promoted hair growth, and since Mazzi Hegan wouldn't be worrying about his hair anymore, he felt it was a shame to let it go to waste. He rinsed the shampoo and turned off the water, grabbed the softest towel he'd ever felt in his life off a nearby towel bar, and stepped out onto the luxurious bathroom floor, feeling the warmth of the underfloor heating radiate into his toes.

Things were looking good, and they were about to get better. Sure, his relationship with Daltrey was over before it had begun, but fuck it. If she was freaked out just because he had been lying on the bed in a pair of Mazzi Hegan's silver underpants he'd found in the "special" drawer, that was her problem. She needed to be sexier anyway, walking about like a guy the way she did at work when she could so easily let her hair down and be sexy.

Looking at his skinny, naked frame in the mirror, he reached out and grabbed a white bathrobe with the initials *MH* embroidered on the collar.

"Tonight, Danny boy, you're going to get yourself some prime uptown pussy."

Dressed like a million dollars in Mazzi's clothes, Dan picked up Hegan's keys to the Ferrari. He pulled the car out of the parking garage and steamed it down Cambie Street toward town. It was a dream come true. How many years had he dreamt of pulling up at Mickey D's in a red Ferrari, and now, there in the distance, the Golden Arches were calling.

He dropped a gear, overtook a loser in a Ford, and pulled up sharp at the light. Across the road, a bus stop full of people were waiting. Dan stared at them, the small group there watching him as he gave the engine a thunderous roar. *You getting the bus, yeah?* he thought. *The loser cruiser. Well, that's right, I'm not—because I've got a fucking Ferrari!*

The light changed, and Dan quickly slapped the car into first and ripped away, passing a guy his age in a Hyundai. "Yeah, fuck you as well," he said out loud.

Seconds later, he swept across the road and past the Golden Arches into the McDonald's parking lot, pulling the Ferrari up longways right outside the huge plate-glass window on the side. He stepped out and stared at himself in the reflection. He looked good—a white shirt under one of Mazzi Hegan's cream silk suits, Gator shoes, a Rolex, and the Ferrari behind him. The suit was a bit big for him, but what the hell, that's how they wore them these days.

He slammed the car door, hit the button—beep beep boop—and walked through the door, stopping at the counter right in front of the girl he'd had his eye on for weeks. The name tag clipped just above her right breast read *Melissa*.

"Hi, Melissa."

Melissa stared at him for a moment, then at the car, and with a smile, she said, "How can I help you?"

Dan just stood, savoring the moment and the girl with the blond hair, standing right there in front of him in her nice striped uniform. He slowly pulled out one of Mazzi Hegan's crocodile skin wallets and checked the huge wad of one hundred dollar bills he'd found in the man's underwear drawer. He was going big tonight.

"I'd like three Big Macs and fries, please."

"Drink?"

Dan nodded and smiled.

"To go?"

Dan laughed and said, "I don't like to eat in the Ferrari."

Melissa looked back at him, this guy in the suit that didn't fit, showing off his money. Then she said, "Why, is it your dad's car?"

Dan laughed again. How ridiculous. "No, I'm in electronics, design, and development actually."

Pretending to be interested for a moment, Melissa nodded approvingly then walked away, grabbed his food, and came back. She said, "I'm surprised you came here. We don't get many Ferraris in our parking lot."

Dan looked at her, her eyes big and blue, and said, "Really? If you want, when you're finished, I'll take you for a spin."

******

Daltrey threw down her keys, unclipped her gun, and flopped down on the sofa. It had been a long day, and the early call hadn't helped. Mazzi Hegan's burned body in the boat was playing on her mind. She'd tried to be a hero and beat the system, have the mystery wrapped up one way or the other before anyone was reported missing or the people from dental records and DNA analysis got in touch.

She leaned back in the long chair and closed her eyes, knowing a glass of wine would go down well right now, but the half-open bottle of chardonnay in the fridge was too far away. Letting out a deep breath, she relaxed and thought it all through. They'd awakened her at four in the morning with a phone call. She'd been there at four twenty along with a squad car who'd taken the initial call, which had come in at three ten when the fire on the boat had been first reported. The fire crew were there first, joined quickly by another ambulance crew that had been helping with a separate incident a few blocks away.

Leaning over, she picked up the phone and called the internal number for the ambulance service. After a five-minute wait, the answer she was after came back quick and simple—the call for the other emergency had come in at almost the same time as the calls from the residences overlooking the creek reporting a fire in a boat out on the water, except for one call reporting that a girl was lying injured in her apartment on the west-facing fourth floor. The fire brigade had found the apartment and upon entering had found a girl with a severe back injury lying unconscious by the window.

******

Daltrey walked quickly along the hospital corridor. She reached the nurses' station of the ward to which the girl had been admitted and stood waiting. Her phone call to the ambulance service and the information that the same girl had remained silent since she'd arrived had aroused enough suspicion to get her back up off the couch. Why would someone who had been seriously injured not be crying out for their mother or someone near or dear? It didn't make sense.

The ward station nurse looked up. It was late, and Daltrey could see the woman was tired and had had enough. But fuck her, so was she.

"There's a young woman who was brought in this morning at around four?" Daltrey asked.

"Are you a relative?"

Daltrey shook her head and pulled out her ID.

The nurse sighed. Looking back to her desk, she said, "She was in surgery for most of the morning, and now she's resting."

"I'd like to speak to her."

After a moment, the nurse stood and walked out from behind the station, the words "Join the club, dearie" in her mind. The administration had been on her back all day, being passive-aggressive about "hospital procedures." And to top it off, her back was aching again. Normally, she would have just said, "Sorry, but the patient is in need of rest right now. Would you like to leave your number, and I'll have someone call you in a few days?" Then she'd smile and say "thank you" at exactly the same time she said "fuck you" in her mind.

It was what she liked to do.

But she needed the name of the girl as much as anyone, so if this pushy cop woman could get somewhere, then so be it. Besides, no one else had come forth saying they'd lost a beauty queen with perfect teeth, and the thought of another call from the office downstairs was too much.

She walked down the hallway, wondering why policewomen weren't feminine anymore the way Cagney and Lacey used to be. She passed three orderlies who needed to get a move on and headed toward a room at the end of the corridor. Pausing at the third from the last, she looked back at Daltrey and said, "I'll see if she's asleep."

Daltrey watched the nurse as she entered the room. She stepped forward. Reaching down, she took the girl's arm and gently shook it. The girl's pretty face was devoid of injury, and only the drip in her arm and the wires connected to her hand gave any sign there was anything wrong at all. The nurse spoke, her voice now one of an angel. "Hello, love. We've someone here who might be able to help you."

Daltrey watched the nurse, her tone now completely different from the woman she'd just encountered outside as she placed her fingers softly upon the girl's brow and began to stroke gently across her forehead. The patient was obviously not asleep, but was refusing to acknowledge their presence.

The nurse tried again. "Lovey, please, can we have a quick word?"

Daltrey stared at the girl as she lay there pretending not to hear, her eyes flickering back and forth behind her eyelids as the nurse's words rolled from her lips as soft as velvet.

Nothing.

The nurse stepped outside, and they walked back toward the nurses' station. Daltrey was confused. The girl looked so perfect and untouched lying there in the hospital bed. Turning to the nurse, she said, "She doesn't look as if she's been in an accident."

The nurse shook her head and looked to the floor for a moment, thinking. Then she said, "Don't be deceived. She may look beautiful, but if she ever gets married, she won't be walking down the aisle."

******

On first impression, most girls' opinion of Dan was that he was pretty stupid. Very few though ever hung around long enough to confirm this.

Unfortunately, an expensive car, an ill-fitting silk suit, and a pair of super-slick crocodile skin shoes had affected Melissa's better judgement, and she now sat in the front seat of Mazzi Hegan's red Ferrari, feeling the purr of the engine beneath her backside and wondering how many times she'd seen this goofy guy grinning at her from the other side of the counter each time he'd been in to buy a burger. Letting the power of the sports car pull her back into the calf leather seat, she gazed in admiration at Dan as he shifted gears, hit the accelerator, and watched as the cars disappeared behind him, fading into nothingness in his rearview mirror.

Melissa looked good at his side, Dan thought as he raced toward the next traffic jam, then used the car's formula one brakes to stop just in time and then wait for the rest of the world—in their shit cars—to catch up. Yes, Melissa, the sexy girl who always gave him those extra fries, was sitting there next to him now.

She was in the front seat of his Ferrari, her blouse slightly open, enough for him to sneak a look at her lacy bra. Leaning forward, she pushed the power button on the car's stereo, blasting Donna Summer out of the speakers cleverly hidden within the dashboard.

Looking at him, smiling, she asked, "You like Donna Summer?"

Dan shrugged. He didn't even know who she was, but agreed anyway as he put the sports car into gear and began to pull forward, "Yes, I love her. She's fantastic."

"Wow," Melissa replied, excited. "I can't believe it—I love Donna Summer, too. Let's go dancing."

Dan slowed the car. This was an interesting turn of events, and one he hadn't planned for. In his mind, they'd just cruise around in the Ferrari all evening until either one of them—inevitably him—got hungry again. Then they'd hit Mickey D's, snag a couple of triple-decker burgers and some fries, then meander all cool-like through the marble lobby and hit the elevator up to Mazzi Hegan's fancy pad to see what might happen. But dancing, Dan thought, dancing could be fun, dancing could be interesting.

Without a second thought, he said, "Sounds great."

******

Daltrey drove back downtown and pulled up outside the girl's apartment. She walked down to the seawall and looked up at the building. Fourth floor up and looking west, the ambulance guys had told her. Very nice. She walked to the building's front door, pulled out Dan's thrown-together electronic device, and hit the button. Seconds later, the door opened. Fuck, this was good.

The lobby was plush, designed with polished wood and red velvet. Daltrey hit the button and entered the elevator. She pointed Dan's device at the control panel, disabling the system's security, and hit the button for the fourth floor. The first key she tried from her ex-boyfriend's set of master keys opened the door to the girl's apartment. This was incredible—now she could snoop around anywhere.

Daltrey turned on the lights and walked into the living room. There was no sign of a struggle, no blood on the floor, just a chair that had been moved to one side for the gurney. She walked to the window and looked out. The lights from the buildings on the other side of the creek streamed back at her across the black water. The boat would have been out there ablaze, impossible to miss in the darkness. She headed to the kitchen, opened the fridge, and looked inside. The milk was fresh, and there was beer, wine, and champagne. The kitchen cupboards were sparsely filled as well—coffee cups, beer and wine glasses, barely any food.

Daltrey closed the cupboard doors and walked to the bedroom. She opened the door and looked around. There were clothes lying neatly over the backs of chairs, perfume bottles, small trinkets adorning the surface of the dressers— but no photographs or memories of mother, father, siblings, boyfriends, nieces, nephews, or anything else you'd expect in a pretty girl's room. She walked in further and carefully opened one of the top drawers. Nothing out of the ordinary. Bras and knickers. Vests and clothes in the other drawers. Sitting on the bed, Daltrey opened the drawer to the nightstand. Condoms and lube. Leaning down, she opened the bigger cupboard below—more condoms, various dildos, soft rope, and a blindfold.

She walked over to the mirror-paneled wardrobe and slid the door open. On one side was a long line of designer dresses and clothes. She slid the door shut and opened the other side. Inside hung a variety of sexually explicit outfits. Reaching in, she pulled out a black latex catsuit, took a step back, and held it up to herself in the mirror.

"You sassy girl, you!"

She placed the catsuit back on the hanger, pulled out a red corset reminiscent of the Wild West and did the same. Placing it back in the closet, Daltrey slid her hand along the shelf at the top, felt the edge of a large envelope, and pulled it down. Sitting back down on the bed, she opened the envelope and dropped out a half dozen naked photos of the girl and a man in his fifties, instantly recognizable due to his own self-promotion. She opened the envelope further, looked inside, and turned it upside down, shaking a small handwritten letter out and watching it land in the center of the photos. She picked it up and opened it.

Natasha,
Every day I dream of you. Our secret is the reason I smile, the reason I live, the reason I cry.
Love,
Patrick

Daltrey picked up a photo and stared hard at an image of the girl holding a huge dildo and working it into the man's ass.

"My god, Patrick, with the size of that thing, it's no wonder you cry!" she said.

She slipped the photos and the letter back into the envelope and stood up. So the girl in the hospital with the broken back calling herself Natasha was a whore. There was little doubt about that. And Patrick De'Sendro, one of Vancouver's top realtors who spent a small fortune on advertising his name and face throughout the city, was in love with her and, it seemed, loved what she did for him also, Daltrey thought as she rode the elevator back down to the street, carrying the envelope, the girl's laptop, and her phone.

The whole apartment, devoid of basic home essentials, was a charade obviously designed for one thing only—short-term, high-end fucking. And the girl Natasha—if that was her real name—lived someplace else. Daltrey walked through the lobby and out into the cool night air, thinking. A high-class hooker who was injured in her apartment at the same time a man was burned to death in a rowboat on the creek in full view outside the apartment window. Connected? *No doubt about it,* she thought as she reached her car and opened the door, placing the girl's laptop and phone on the passenger seat.

******

A two-hundred-dollar sweetener discreetly handed to the guys at the door ensured prime parking for the Ferrari and instant access to the Bam Bam club for the guy in the big silk suit and his girl.

Dan laid down forty bucks for two more cocktails and dropped the same again to the waitress for her trouble. He was full of it and loving every minute. In Dan's eyes, he doubted Mazzi Hegan—R.I.P.—had ever had so much fun with his money.

Feeling like a queen, Melissa raised her glass and leaned back into the VIP booth. "Cheers," she said.

Dan smiled and joined her toast, the sleeve to his jacket riding back and fitting his arm for the first time that evening.

"You really live life to the fullest, don't you, Dan?" said Melissa.

Dan laughed and, tilting his head to one side, answered back with the air of a guy who had money to burn. "You'd better believe it!"

It was true—he did. Only two days ago, he was living it up down at Subway Sandwich. Dan looked around and relaxed, listening to the music he didn't really like. This was it, he thought. This was fucking it! The high life. Fuck, he'd end up buying this place and a few others like it. He'd change the music and sit here like a real king. Then Daltrey would know what she'd missed out on. She'd come into his club one night wearing those tight jeans she had on the other day and her boots, see him sitting there at his table with his champagne and a few hot chicks, and she'd say, "Hi Dan, don't you look good?"

And he'd say, "I'm sorry, have we met?"

Play it cool, just like that. Then she'd want him, not use him the way she had tried to. If she was lucky, he'd even let her suck his dick.

Dan stared out at the lights and the girls dancing around in the weird way they did. Daltrey had been easy to fool at first, being a cop. She'd seemed interested in his electronic research and the development bullshit on their first date, and he'd have been in had he not puked up those oysters like he had.

He continued staring at the dance floor as a girl with a short skirt began to shake her bootie. Watching her every move, shifting in his seat as the lights from the disco ball and the strobes blinded him. Her thin and sinewy legs moving as they twisted, and shook, reminding him of a chicken and making him hungry again. He could do with a plate of barbecue wings, he thought. He looked around through the crowd for his waitress, trying to locate her, his head and body shifting from side to side in time to the music.

Melissa smiled as she watched him move, eventually catching his eye, she said, "You look like you're wanting to dance, Dan."

Dan leaned back in his seat and nodded. She was right. Dancing would be perfect. After he'd eaten, though. He'd take her out there on the floor, shake her up, rock it hard, and show old chicken legs out there how to move properly. He had to after all—he was still wearing Mazzi Hegan's silver underpants, and they were beginning to itch.

Chapter Five

Dennis Willis sat at the kitchen table of his basement apartment and thought of his wife as he read the headline on the front page of the *Vancouver Sun* for the third time:

Unidentified man found burned to death on False Creek

He wondered again if it could have been him.

It hadn't been long since he had thought of his wife, maybe an hour at least, but it had been a while since he'd thought about most other things. Once upon a time, he'd been on his way, and now the realization had set in at the ripe age of fifty that he was going nowhere, and he'd possibly never get going again.

Many times in the darkness of the basement, he'd wracked his brains as to how she'd been able to possess him. Was it her hair, her lips, her eyes? Who knew… What had it been that had attracted him so strongly? Day after day, she'd called to him as he'd stared at her face. Her there among so many others, seducing him, drawing him in, and making him love her without speaking or even knowing he was there.

His heart had pounded when he saw her for the first time. Shorter than expected, but still so very beautiful. He'd smiled as she walked toward him, smelled her hair and soft skin when she held him, felt the tender touch of her lips when they'd kissed and the churning of guilt within, knowing that deep down he'd cheated himself in the game of love.

He had taken her to his home, which back then had been his own—and she had cried with happiness at its size and grandeur. She had taken him to his bed and kissed his cheeks, his eyes, his lips, her loving soothing his fears. She had known him before they met, seen him in her long wonderful dreams. She knew his hair, his eyes, his smile. Age was no issue, for souls have no age. Why else would she have waited for him when she, so beautiful, could have had so many? And as the months passed, and his guilt evaporated into the truth of her words and one's own destiny, marriage came. Life couldn't have been better.

And then her brother arrived.

She had said he loved her and missed her, that she had been selfish, and it was wrong. "What harm could he do?" she had said. Nothing could challenge what was special, what was right, what was meant to be.

There was no eye contact when he met him for the first time. All that mattered to this man, this brother, was the girl. Dennis watched as he held her hand, stroked her long, wavy hair, and walked around Dennis's home as if it was his own. He was older, thickset, and incredibly strong, and Dennis could do little when he raped her, and even less when her brother raped him.

******

Illya Brakva's thirtieth birthday just happened to coincide with the day of his release from Vladamir Central Prison, which lay one hundred and eighty kilometers to the east of Moscow. Before the clock had struck midnight, he'd managed to kill a dog and break his father's fingers.

Why his parents would make him so angry during the celebratory meal for his birthday and prison release, he would never understand. Refusing to give out the address of the man in Canada his sister had married could, in his mind, only be described as ridiculous. After all, this guy was now family, and family was family. Blood was blood.

The two incidents—the one with the dog and the one with his father's fingers—were in no way connected. The dog's demise being the unlucky result of a hatred that had manifested itself in Illya's mind day by day throughout his prison term. The dispute was simple—money smuggled in and paid out for an easier ride through the Russian penal system had earned him only a damaged wrist courtesy of a pair of government-issue jack boots and a door that would not close properly. Come the end of Illya's term, death could be the only retribution for the head guard who had not delivered on promises made.

But as the doors closed behind him, and fresh air washed over him, the sight of the clear blue sky and the thought of his sister living happily without him alone in a far-off land quickly kindled the furnace of hatred to a simmering flame. The dog had taken the brunt of Illya's wrath.

The guard's house sat in the middle of a long street, away from the gray concrete communist-built slums constructed to house the masses. A place where stray dogs and lost people roamed. The house, its wooden-slatted sides painted green, tucked among many, had been given to him as a simple gift from the powers that be for following the party line throughout the long years of communist rule—years in which he'd felt privileged and elite enough to have a home. But now, beaten down and worn thin from living among the filth of humanity, he saw himself for who and what he really was.

The guard opened the door and stared at the man he'd never seen before. He was a convict, yes. He'd lived with them long enough to know their kind, their eyes, their stance. This one had the eyes, and although he couldn't see the tattoos, he was sure muted jailhouse art covered the man's body, the images all linked together, hidden just under the shirt.

Illya stared at the man, and spoke first, his face neither angry nor bitter. "Remember me?"

The guard shook his head and tightened his grip on the small gun he held behind the door. "Should I?"

"You stole my money."

The guard stared back at him, wondering who he was, how he had found his address, and what favors, monetary or otherwise, he'd given to get it. Then he said, "Prisons are full of thieves. You can't say it was me."

And Illya answered, "But you are the man who held my wrist in between the door and the frame while your friend tried to kick it closed. I swore to you both that I'd burn you."

Then the guard remembered the man who had made a fuss about his money, telling them they would both burn the first chance he got. He remembered the guy who'd worked on the wing with him kicking the door over and over while he held the man's wrist. And he remembered, years later after retirement, hearing the news about how the other guard—the one who'd kicked the door—had been found burned alive in the kitchen. He also remembered how he'd tried for an hour to remember the name of the man who now stood before him.

Then he used the words he'd said to others many times before. "If you've come here for trouble, I suggest you leave and be done with whatever grudges you harbor. Now you are free, and the consequences of your actions today will either end your life now, or worse, see you back where you've just come from. Let sleeping dogs lie."

Illya watched the older man standing in his sweater, threadbare at the elbows. He stared into his beady eyes, the guard now old, but still tough with his hand behind the door holding a weapon, playing it cool as the other guard had when Illya cornered him in the filthy prison kitchen, acting relaxed but waiting like a snake ready to strike—as this man would do so very soon. And when he did, he'd be quick, Illya thought, as are all animals who know they're about to die. That was certain. How many men, Illya thought, had this man ripped off or injured as he had Illya? How many others had stood here before him, angry and betrayed, and heard the same song?

He said quietly to the man, "Your dog's sleeping, but he won't be waking up. You'll find it burned to death in your backyard—it could have been you had I wanted it to, even with what you are hiding behind your door. Go take a look, when you find him there dead and I want you to know it should have been you."

The guard waited as the convict turned and began to leave. When he reached the road, he stopped, turned, and called back, "My sister saved your life."

The guard stared into the morning light, watching Illya disappear in the distance. Closing the door, he stuck his pistol back in his belt and walked through his house gifted to him for living with filth. He wondered what this man fresh out of jail was talking about when he said his sister had saved him and he'd killed his dog. He shook his head and walked into the kitchen. He didn't even have a dog. In fact, he hated dogs, especially his neighbor's dog that he'd sworn to kill the next time he found it in his yard. Strangely enough, Illya had saved him the bother.

******

As stupid as he was, there were two things that could never be taken away from Dan. The first was his incredible understanding of electronics. The second, his ability to dance with a pure and natural rhythm unknown to nearly all the white guys in the Western world. When those two things were joined, one could behold something that was nothing short of a miracle in itself.

He'd inherited his ability to dance from a mother who was, throughout his early days, a lonely single mum. She had whipped the nights away, spinning and twisting, waltzing and jiving around the house with Dan either watching or riding on the top of her toes. It was early training for a young boy that made for a good night out for any girl who stuck around long enough to discover Dan's natural born talent. And Melissa was no exception. In her experience, most guys fit into two categories—those who could barely dance and those who couldn't. Dan, on the other hand, was an exception to the rule. She'd watched him bumping and grinding his way around the dance floor, pissing off the guys as he rotated his groin in perfect time with the beat while still managing to eat his chicken wings. He moved animatedly across the floor, his shoulders lifting up and down, his arms and hands reaching out in exaggerated movements as he grabbed his food to the beat of the music, eating as he danced, his teeth stripping the flesh from the wing. He wowed the crowd with his fluid motion, slowly stripping off Mazzi Hegan's expensive clothes and slinging them across the floor as he dropped to his knees with his arms in the air, sweat dripping from his brow and chest and running in a constant stream all the way down to his groin.

Dan looked at Melissa as he pulled the Ferrari up outside Mazzi Hegan's apartment block. He had her now, it was certain. He could tell by the way her breathing changed each time he'd thrown a piece of chicken to her across the dance floor and smooched up on her, purposely letting the sweat from his brow drip down into her cleavage.

He walked around the car, opening Melissa's door the same way he'd seen some guy do it in a movie once. He was on his way...he knew it. Reaching down, he grasped Melissa's hand and pulled her gently from the car to him. He placed his other hand around her back, twisted his head away and gave a silent belch, and then leaned in and kissed her hard on the lips.

Melissa held Dan tightly around the neck, kissing him back with a fury. She could feel the energy emanating from this man. He was elemental, like no one she had ever met before. He had this incredible gusto and passion for life. It was almost as though he knew that his world was about to end.

Melissa pulled her head back and stared into Dan's bloodshot eyes. It had been a long time since she'd had a night out like this, and she was horny. Her lips tingled from the kissing, and she could taste the pickle from the Big Mac he'd eaten on their way back from the club.

They took the elevator up to the apartment, quickly found their way to the bedroom, flopped down onto the huge silk-covered king-size bed, and began to giggle. Trying to take control, Dan climbed on top of her and slipped his hand up her shirt, feeling her breasts. He quickly unbuttoned her blouse and simultaneously whipped off the now dirty silk shirt and trousers he'd found earlier, freshly pressed and waiting for him in the mirror-lined wardrobe, and lay back down next to Melissa wearing only Mazzi Hegan's silver underpants.

He leaned back over and began to bite at Melissa's breasts, slobbering and drooling all over them as she began to moan louder and louder. Grabbing Dan's hand, she pulled it downward and up the inside of her skirt. He could feel the wetness that was building from within and began to rub her from the outside of her panties, not quite knowing what to do now after all the hard work he'd done to get there.

Then Melissa opened her eyes and stared up at the ceiling. She gasped as she pushed his hand away from her and said, "Is this your bedroom?"

Dan nodded and, his mouth half full of nipple, answered, "Yes."

Confused, she asked again, "It's really yours?"

Dan said yes again, and Melissa sat up.

"Oh my god—are you gay?"

Dan stopped what he was doing and looked up at Melissa. "What?"

"You're gay!"

Dan sat back and kneeled before her on the bed, his silver underpants glistening in the bedside light.

"Why do you say that?"

Melissa quickly sat up and began to button up her blouse. She gently pushed Dan away from her legs and slowly eased herself off the bed. In seconds, she was down the corridor and out the front door. Gone.

Standing there in the room in his shiny silver underpants, Dan stared at himself in the mirror. "Gay? Me? Fucking gay? Jesus."

What the fuck just happened? he asked himself. Sitting himself down again, he leaned back, stretching himself out on the bed, his arms splayed out up on top of the enormous silk pillows. He stared at the door. He couldn't believe it. He hadn't gotten this far with a chick since he'd met that blind girl in the park and her guide dog had gotten angry.

Slowly, he leaned his head back and rested his neck. He was hungry again now and was thinking about finishing off the green veggie shredded-wheat-type thing he'd left in the fridge. Looking up, he saw what Melissa had seen, and only visible from the bed. Above him, the elaborately drawn ceiling artwork, it's black lines and shapes, all came together to create a picture of two naked men having sex.

Dan lay there, staring up at the drawing. He'd never seen such a thing, a portrait full of muscle, sweat, and hair. Then with a bang, the apartment door reopened. Dan smiled. Yes, Melissa was back. She'd come to her senses and was back for more. Quickly, he adjusted his silver underpants and straightened himself up. Leaning back again against the silk pillows, he listened as she walked back down the corridor toward him. He called out to her.

"Come get me, baby!"

Only it wasn't Melissa. It was Mazzi Hegan.

Chapter Six

Illya stood and looked out of the window of the girl's apartment. He was worried about his sister. She was supposed to have been there all day yesterday and the night before, but somehow she had disappeared. The math was simple—his phone had been ringing, and since he had no friends, it was money lost. He was down somewhere around four and a half thousand dollars and counting, the ungrateful bitch. He should have left her sweeping the carpet for that loser of a husband she'd shacked up with.

Illya walked away from the window, pulled a beer from the fridge, and sat down. His sister was smart, had done well at school, and while he was away, she had managed to find a guy who would pay for her to get away from the shithole they'd grown up in and bring her to this great city. Now that he'd arrived, she was happy—happy to see him and happier for him to sell her off here instead of in Moscow as he'd intended to when he'd gotten out of jail. With his sister being as pretty as she was and not too resistant to his demands, things were looking good. It was all working out. But where the fuck had she gone?

He doubted she would be back with her husband. Why would you take a vacuum cleaner and dishes as a reward for putting out when you could instead have a little money, perfume, and nice clothes that turned heads?

Illya stuck his finger into his ear, dug about, and then wiped it on the sofa. He liked Vancouver with its mountains and beaches, peculiar small dogs in coats, and the little section down by the park where men looked like women and

41

women looked like men. His sister was a smart girl and couldn't have picked a better place. The city had everything—clean air, the sea, mountains, skiing, incredibly nice and polite people, prostitution, drugs, gangs, and a police force with officers who liked coffee and were okay with everything.

Perfect.

He leaned back, pulled out a cigarette, lit it, and blew the smoke up toward the white ceiling. Fuck it, if she wasn't back soon, he'd find another girl, a real pretty one. He'd pick her up on Granville Street when the clubs emptied and bring her back here, get her high, and then hit her in the kidneys with a phone book until she got around to his way of thinking. Then he'd get another apartment and another girl, but the next whore he'd import himself. He'd get one of those hot ones from back home, the ones who suck off businessmen around the hotels in Moscow.

He'd make some calls to the guys he'd met in jail, set up someone in Moscow, give out a finder's fee, and keep them coming until he got so big that the players here started to come around and take notice. And when they did, they'd know Illya Bragin meant business.

Trouble came easy for Illya, and he'd had his first serious taste early. It was trouble born out of nothing and had started simply as a joke at the youthful age of fifteen. He'd been with his friends, hanging out at the edge of the main road that led out of Varero. Asked a hard-faced girl who waited at the bus stop every day and never left if she'd dyed her shaggy blond locks with battery acid to get them so white, and the next day he'd woken up in an alley.

Two days later, recovered from his bruising, Illya had punched the whore with no sense of humor in the mouth and waited all evening for the middle-aged man in the thick leather jacket who drove the Mercedes to come back, only he didn't. And it was Illya's mother who paid the price for not keeping her son in line.

And that's when things really got nasty.

Illya had pulled the whore with the bleach job, with her knickers down around her ankles, off the lap of a guy in a car, held her to the ground, and poured real battery acid into her hair as the guy who never knew her name sped away, spraying mud and gravel from the track at the side of the road onto her as she lay screaming in the rain.

Then Illya let her go, and screamed down at her, "Tell him I'll be waiting right here!"

And that's exactly where he was when Bogdan Banin, drunk and angry, turned his seven-year-old Mercedes quickly onto the dirty gravel track on the main road that ran past Illya's home, scaring away the stray dogs that roamed hungry along the path where his girl with the pure white hair and big tits liked to blow and fuck guys who picked her up at the bus stop.

Bogdan, at it since eleven that morning, sitting in the dark and dingy bar in which he liked to while away the day, trying to get to the football game before it started at seven that evening. He ran five girls that worked the cold, wet main road that left Varejo for Moscow in the east, and he took seventy percent from each. All for the pleasure of having to sort out their troubles with the cops and listen to them go on and on about shit like how they'd just had their hair ruined with battery acid by some young kid. But his women were his women, and the money they earned him was better than digging a ditch or a kick in the teeth, which was exactly what he was going to give this punk kid who couldn't take a hint.

Bogdan stopped the car, got out, and kicked at a dog as he walked calmly toward Illya. Enough was enough with this prick. He'd take out his frustrations on the kid's mouth, throw him in the back of the car, stick a bullet in the back of his head, then throw his body in a storm drain he knew on the way to the stadium. Then everyone would know what happened to punk kids who fucked with his girls. If he was quick, he could make the game before it started.

Illya stood and watched as the man who had caught him from behind and beaten him one day and then his mother the next walked toward him. In Illya's right hand, he held a can of hair spray, and in the other, a mug full of gasoline.

Bogdan drew closer. Seeing the hairspray, he said, "What the fuck is it with you and hair?"

Illya's heart pounded as he waited in the rain, his finger tight on the top of the hairspray's nozzle. As Bogdan closed in, he threw the mug full of fuel at him and in one swift motion lifted the hairspray and lit the spray with a lighter, sending a three-foot flame out and onto the gangster in his leather coat, catching him on fire before he could even think of drawing his gun.

Bogdan batted frantically at his flaming heavy leather jacket and threw himself to the ground, desperately rolling around and around in the dirt and rain, trying to douse the flames. Illya stood above him watching, stepping forward only to reignite the flames as they subsided, blasting his hair, his hands, and eventually his face with hot burning chemicals that clung to his clothes and melted his skin as the rain fell.

One minute later, Bogdan was dead.

Although it was the first time Illya had killed a man, it was not the first time he had killed this way. At an early age, fuel from a nearby car, a lighter, and a stolen metal bicycle pump had made short work of the rats that roamed freely through the garbage that grew on a daily basis at the back of the housing development where he'd lived as a boy.

Soon the bicycle pump was exchanged for hairspray stolen from his mother, and slowly throughout the years, cornered rats became cornered stray dogs which he goaded and poked until their tempers broke and they came at him snapping and snarling with ferocious speed. Illya twisting and turning with the grace of a matador avoiding an enraged bull until the dogs met a swift execution by fire that no overweight fuckhead pimp, dressed in leather and drunk on vodka, could ever hope to match.

******

Daltrey sat at her desk in her home, which was a lot less glamorously decorated and spacious than Mazzi Hegan's pad, and scrolled through the contents of the laptop computer she'd "borrowed" from the apartment. The girl had one email account with a picture of her standing in a beautiful gown in what looked to Daltrey like the lobby of the Grand Hotel.

Daltrey opened her emails and scrolled through. Apparently she was a busy girl and a lot of men were in love with her. She stopped at an email from Patrick and laughed. From what she could see, he was a regular—maybe once or twice a week—and had been there the same night she'd been injured. Daltrey laughed as she remembered the photo of him on all fours with tears in his eyes.

"You'll have to find another pony to ride you now, big guy," Daltrey said as she stared at the screen for a moment.

There was nothing in the email account that gave a hint as to her real identity. The apartment was the same as when she'd checked, rented out and owned by a numbered company in the Caribbean, its strata bills all paid a year in advance by company check. So far no one had come forward to place a missing person report for her or even Mazzi Hegan. Apart from a high-priced whore with no name in the hospital with an unexplained injury to her spine, Daltrey had nothing.

She sat back in her chair and continued to stare at the screen, and then she made a decision. Leaning forward, she hit the reply button to Patrick's email and wrote, *Patrick, I miss you. You are also the reason I smile…let's have coffee?*

******

Daltrey watched as Patrick pulled his expensive BMW up alongside the overpriced café that overlooked the harbor. Her eyes following the brown tassels on his loafers, swinging from side to side as he walked across the road into the café that sat on the edge of the seawall in Yaletown.

Seeing that his Natasha was not yet there, he ordered a coffee and picked a table. As soon as he sat down, Daltrey joined him, pulling out her badge as she sat.

"Sorry," she said, "Natasha can't make it." Patrick stared at her nervously as Daltrey continued. "Did you know she's in the hospital?"

Patrick didn't answer, and in his silence, it was obvious he did know.

"I know about your little secret, Patrick. She's been taking photos of the both of you playing with her toys. I think you need to talk to me because I also know you were with her on the same day she ended up in the hospital."

46

Patrick stared at her, this hot chick with a badge who knew about his little secret. He quickly thought back…what on earth was going on? There'd never been a camera involved in their games. Then it hit him. What an idiot he was! This woman wasn't a cop. She was too good-looking to be one anyway with that long hair and that nice, tight waist. This hot cop was a friend of Natasha's. She'd set it up for him as a thank you. This chick was going to arrest him and take him away and work him, just the way he liked it. Maybe if he was lucky, Natasha would be okay by now, and she'd be there waiting.

Patrick looked up from the table and grinned at Daltrey. In a hushed voice, he said, "I've been a bad boy."

It was what he'd say to Natasha, and when he did, she knew he wanted her to work him. He'd say it, and she'd say, "Yes, you're a bad boy, Patrick, a very bad boy indeed." Then she'd take him to her room and strip him.

Daltrey stared back at this guy whose eyes had just lit up and said, "If you think that at any second I'm going to whip out a set of cuffs, strip down to my panties, and wish you a happy birthday, then you've got it all wrong, mister. Now you'd better start talking—and if you leave out anything, I'll start looking into the possibility of an aggravated assault charge, and if that happens, then Natasha won't be the only person in the world who'll know your little secret."

Patrick began to panic. His mind in overdrive, he could feel the sweat begin to bead on his neck and back. If he had to explain to all and sundry about anything he'd been up to, he'd be ruined. Natasha was kind and beautiful and gave him what he needed, but who would understand that?

His face turned bright red as he began to stutter, his forehead becoming clammy. "Am I in trouble?"

"You tell me," Daltrey snapped back then kept quiet. She knew from experience that when stressed, people reveal much more than they need to when you said nothing, and it seemed to be working.

"I never hurt her—it wasn't me."

He hadn't, it was obvious, and if he had, then why would he have come to meet her for coffee? "You were with her two nights ago?"

He was. It was written all over his face.

He asked again, "Am I in trouble?"

"She was severely hurt the evening you were with her. Tell me everything you know now, and maybe this will be it." Then Daltrey asked, "So where did you first meet her?"

Someone he knew told him she was looking for a place to buy. He'd contacted her, and that's how it started, that's how they got to know each other, that's how they fell in love. Daltrey stopped him there. It all sounded like a crock of shit. "In love?" she asked.

Patrick nodded. "Yes."

"But you paid her?"

"At first, yes, but then we started to spend more time together."

"How long?"

Patrick stared off into nowhere, thinking. "You know," he said. "At night."

"All night?"

Patrick nodded. "And evenings. Then she said that I didn't have to pay anymore because she'd fallen in love with me."

"And you with her?"

Patrick nodded and said, "She's still a human being. People have met under stranger circumstances."

48

He felt better now he could read her well. This girl was a straight player even if she was a detective. It would be okay if he played out his part of the bargain.

Daltrey stared at this sap of a man who was in love with a whore who was in the hospital and hadn't yet asked why. Then she asked, "Did you buy her things?"

Patrick nodded again. "Of course."

"Jewelry? Clothes?" Patrick nodded again as Daltrey continued, "Expensive?"

The answer to that question was obvious by the look of his suit and his car. It could be no other way.

Patrick answered, "Always."

"And is Natasha her real name?"

"I'm not sure."

"And you were going to marry her, but you didn't know her real name?"

Feeling stupid, Patrick nodded again, then said, "We spoke of marriage, yes."

Daltrey stared at him. "But there's a problem—you're already married."

Patrick leaned back and shook his head and said, "No, she is."

This one stumped Daltrey. She would have laid good money down that it was the other way around. "*She's* married?"

Patrick nodded. "To a dentist, but they're not together."

"A dentist?" Patrick nodded. "And she left him because she loves you?"

Patrick shook his head. "No, she told me she left him before we'd met. She said she didn't love him."

"Why?"

"Because he was older."

Daltrey stared at him then asked, "Like you?"

"And he'd bought her."

This was getting better, thought Daltrey. "In the same way you bought her?"

Patrick stayed quiet for a moment, then said, "No, not like me—different."

"What did he do then? Go to the mall to buy her?"

Patrick shook his head. He was worried now, and visions of himself standing by a height chart having his photo taken flashed before his eyes.

"No, not like that. He bought her from the Internet. She's from overseas."

"Where?" Daltrey stared at him, waiting for the answer.

"Russia."

"She's Russian?" She stared at Patrick, and she could tell he didn't want to answer. So she said, "There's nothing wrong with being Russian, Patrick."

"I know. I just don't want you to send her back."

Daltrey shook her head, looked at him straight, and said, "I think there's something you're not telling me."

Patrick stared back at her, then looked at the floor.

Then Daltrey asked, "You keep telling me how much you love this girl, but you haven't even asked me why she's in the hospital."

And Patrick swallowed hard and said, "That's because I already know. I'm the one who called the ambulance."

******

Daltrey was still shaking her head when she drove away from the café. She thought she'd heard it all, but Patrick was possibly one of the strangest individuals she had met in a long time.

"Fuck me, Patrick, you kinky bastard," Daltrey muttered to herself as she pulled her car onto the main drag and joined the traffic.

Patrick, the hopeless romantic who was in love with a whore who worked his ass with a rubber cock. What a bizarre world it was. And to top it off, he was a big-time celebrity realtor in town.

He'd found the girl of his dreams living two apartments down from him. Through his contacts, he'd found himself a place nearer with a clear view straight into her living room and bedroom so that he could watch other guys pay to fuck her. He'd been watching her that night. A man had been there in her apartment, just out of sight. He'd made her strip down and stand at the window, but Patrick hadn't seen what had happened because, like her, he had been distracted by the boat burning on the creek. It was only later that he'd seen her lying on the floor, now alone, and had made the call.

Daltrey turned a corner and slid in behind a bus, on its back a picture of Patrick smiling, showing off his bright white teeth. The happy realtor, calling to her with his eyes, telling her to trust him and only him in this town to buy or sell her place. His slogan was printed right there under his smiling face: *Trust me—I take it all the way.*

Yeah, well, at least you're honest, Patrick, Daltrey thought as the bus pulled into its stop and Daltrey passed it, heading back toward the hospital.

Chapter Seven

Mazzi Hegan couldn't believe it. He knew something was wrong when he saw his beautiful red Ferrari parked on the wrong side of the road outside his apartment complex, then food on the floor of the elevator and his hallway and inside his doorway—and then this strange guy lying on his bed.

What the fuck was going on?

At first, he thought it was some crazy gift from Sebastian, like he sometimes liked to do, but the expression on this guy's face told him differently, and Mazzi had screamed out, "Who the fuck are you? Who the fuck are you?"

What the fuck was going on? What was this guy doing in his bed wearing his favorite designer underpants from Milan? And they looked stretched—fuck, they were ruined, the fucking prick! They were so special he'd had some hot carpenter make a special drawer for them and was tucking them away until his birthday.

He looked around and saw his crocodile skin shoes, food everywhere, his cream-colored Dolce and Gabbana silk suit lying crumpled on the floor. Jesus fucking H. Christ. Fuck, that was it. He freaked out, lost it, and came at Dan, lashing out, scratching, and slapping down with his chin out and his head pulled back. Swinging out, he corked Dan straight in the face with his man bag.

Mazzi Hegan breathed heavily as he strutted along the foot of his king-size bed, staring at this guy with red slap marks on his arms and shoulders and blood trickling from his now slightly crooked nose. He wanted an answer, and he wanted it right now. He took a deep breath, trying to calm himself, and asked, "Who are you? I need to know who you are and what you're doing here!"

The guy stared at him, and Mazzi could see he didn't know what to say. Then he answered, "You're supposed to be dead."

Confused, Mazzi Hegan lifted his hand and rubbed it through his highlighted blond hair. "What?"

"She said you were dead."

"She? Who's she? Well, let me tell you something—I'm not. I'm right here, right fucking here."

Dan stayed still, frozen to the spot, then looked to the dresser. Mazzi stormed over to it and opened his sock drawer and noticed his wad of cash was gone. He tried to think of how much was in there, but couldn't remember.

Turning to this guy who hadn't moved, hadn't even tried to run, he said, "Where's my money? I suppose it went to pay for drugs?"

"No, burgers."

That was it. Mazzi was tired. He'd had a long journey from LA where he'd been staying with a friend, and he'd had enough. A strange, hot guy naked in his bed? Contrary to all his normal bodily instincts, he was going to call the cops, and that was that. He reached into his pocket, began to dial 911, and said with his Swedish accent in full flow, "You are in big trouble! Big fucking trouble, mister!"

Then in a flash of brilliance, like a gift from God, he saw it right there in front of him and ran out of his bedroom like a demon toward his office.

Dan didn't understand what the hell was going on. All he wanted to do was get out of this place, but he didn't have any clothes on, his nose was hurting, and he could feel blood dripping into his mouth—and now this gay guy had rushed out and come back in with a huge camera and was taking pictures of him. What the fuck was going on? Jesus, could this night get any worse? He held his hand up, shielding himself from the relentless flashing from this gay guy with the camera. He tried to stand and, once upright, moved slowly along the mirrored wall, heading for the door. Fuck, he couldn't remember where his own clothes were. He looked around the bedroom, but all he could see was this gay guy's silk stuff. Fuck it. Enough was enough with this shit. He'd have to get out of there, underpants or not. Opening the door quickly, he moved out into the corridor and made a break for it. He ran down the hallway, grabbed the handle to the front door of the apartment, ripped it open, and ran for the elevator.

Mazzi Hegan followed, the camera flashing picture after picture. The elevator door opened, and Dan shot inside and stood with his back to the wall, staring out as the door closed on Mazzi Hegan as he snapped his last shots.

******

Daltrey sat at the side of the hospital bed and waited in silence for the girl to open her eyes. She'd been there a while now, sitting patiently while she slept and while the girl pretended to sleep.

Daltrey took a deep breath and asked, "If you don't want to talk to me, would you like me to call the Russian embassy and have someone come down here and talk to you?"

She knew it was utter nonsense. The Russian embassy was over two thousand miles away in the east of the country, and chances were slim to none she'd even get her calls returned. It worked, though. There was a slight movement under her eyelids, and then the girl's eyes opened.

Daltrey smiled and said, "You don't need to be afraid. I'm here to help you."

The girl lay there, not moving a muscle, just staring into nowhere as Daltrey continued, "What you do in your apartment is your business, not mine, and what you do with Patrick has nothing to do with me, either. You have nothing to fear from me."

The girl stayed silent.

Moving toward the window, Daltrey continued, "Do you have family here? Can I call someone for you?"

Still nothing.

"The night you were hurt, a man by the name of Mazzi Hegan was burned to death outside your apartment."

Hearing this, the girl's eyes blinked, and Daltrey could tell she was thinking about the name she'd just heard.

"Did you know this man? Did you know the man burning out there in the boat? Who is Mazzi Hegan to you?"

******

Daltrey walked along the corridor of the police station and entered a busy room where her desk sat in a corner by the window. The extra hour she had stayed sitting by a hospital bed had been well worth the effort. The girl had still said nothing, but in her silence, she had answered Daltrey's questions.

Each question she'd asked about Mazzi Hegan burning to death in the boat had struck a chord. There was no doubt about that. The simplest gesture—the closing of her eyes and the slightest change in breath—gave it all away. There was a connection.

55

She turned on her computer, plugged her small camera into its side, and opened up a picture of the girl sleeping. Finagling her way into Canada's immigration files, she searched through the pictures of girls from Russia of similar age who'd come into Canada over the last ten years. Within an hour, she had narrowed it down to a mere five thousand.

Within two hours, she had the number down to five hundred, and in only another hour, she was down to fifty. Things were looking good. Of the fifty, forty had married older men, and only thirteen were living in British Columbia, six of whom were close enough to Vancouver's downtown region.

Daltrey stared at the screen as each black and white photo passed before her and then stopped at one. It was hard to tell—the girl was not dissimilar to a lot of the girls, very pretty with the same high-cheekboned features, her hair was pulled back. Scrolling down, she read on. Alla Bragin had arrived on a holiday visa three years ago and never left. She'd applied for an extension, then married a Dennis Willis, forty-five years of age, now living out in Burnaby.

******

It was raining by the time Daltrey reached the basement suite that Dennis Willis now called home. She walked to the side door and knocked, waited, then knocked again. Five minutes passed before the door opened. Daltrey smiled as Dennis looked down on her and told her he wasn't interested.

"I'm not selling anything, Mr. Willis. I'm just wondering if you know anything about a girl named Alla Bragin?"

He did. She already knew this. He was married to her after all.

"Why do you ask?" asked Willis, his dark eyes squinting.

Daltrey pulled out the picture of the girl in the hospital and sheltered it from the rain so he could see. Dennis stared at the photo, then looked back to Daltrey.

"That's a hospital bed. Is she okay?"

Bingo! She had it on the first try. The girl in the hospital was Alla Bragin. Daltrey pulled out her police ID, shook her head, and said, "No, she isn't. I believe she was assaulted, and from what I can gather, her spine has received trauma."

The kitchen table was dirty, and Daltrey thought if it were her, she would have put a cloth over it a long time ago. Willis stood in the kitchenette and stirred a coffee.

Looking over at him, she said, "I used to have a table almost identical to this one. I slapped a cloth on it, you know, the same as they do in the restaurants. You get a few more years out of it that way."

Stopping for a moment, Willis looked at her. "I'm sorry, but this isn't my place."

Changing the subject, Daltrey asked, "When did you last see your wife?"

Willis held back a moment then said. "A year ago, or thereabouts." He walked over to the table and placed the coffee down. "Could I see the photo again?"

Daltrey sat down at the table in front of the steaming cup and pulled out the photo. She handed it to him across the table and waited in silence while he sat there staring at the picture of his wife.

"I still care for her, you know. I really do."

Nodding, Daltrey said, "Why wouldn't you? She's your wife."

"People told me it was never going to work, just because of the nature of how we met, but I'm telling you, she loved me. I know she did."

Daltrey nodded again, took a sip of her drink, and said, "You can tell."

Dennis took a deep breath then let it out and stared out of the window for a moment. "I could feel it, you know, inside—you can't hide that."

Daltrey gave him time to finish. He was right. She'd known a lot of guys, and she could tell the difference between the ones who just wanted to play her and get in her panties and the ones who were genuinely in love. There was a difference. "You're right," she said gently.

Dennis handed the photo back to her across the table and said, "Her hair's longer now."

Daltrey waited a moment then asked, "Where did you meet?"

"Through a dating agency."

Daltrey smiled as she lifted her coffee to her lips. "Times are changing."

Willis nodded. "My friends told me they were worried, said they thought she was a Russian hooker."

"Your friends said this?"

Dennis shook his head. "Not in a bad way, you know. They said it after she left me, but you're not wrong, because they also left me as soon as I ended up here."

Daltrey stared at him. She could taste the bad coffee in her mouth now as she held the cup close to her lips. Slowly, she moved the cup away. "Some people can be cruel."

Dennis looked at her and took a deep breath. "Maybe it's true enough, though."

Fuck me, you don't know the half of it, Daltrey thought, then smiled and said politely, "Well, talk is cheap."

Dennis looked away and stared at the coffee rings on the

table, unconsciously circling one with his finger. "Is she okay? Is she in trouble?"

"She's not in trouble with the police, but she's in the hospital because her back is broken."

Tears welled up in Dennis Willis's eyes, and for a split second, it looked as if he was going to say something, but then he stopped and asked, "Can I see her?"

Dennis sat in the rear of Daltrey's car as she headed back into town toward Vancouver General Hospital. One thing that was not right in her mind was that as shocked and concerned as he was, Dennis, like Patrick, had not asked how it had happened.

******

Mazzi Hegan had had trouble with his Ferrari, making him late for work for the first time in five years. The problem had not been that the car was broken after Dan had driven it. In fact, it was not mechanically unsound or damaged in any way at all. It was simply that the smell from all the semi-eaten Big Macs and cheeseburger wrappers and fries Dan had left on the floor behind the backseat had made him retch twice, and it wasn't going to happen a third time. That and the fact he had no shampoo and all his clothes were creased and thrown back on the wrong shelves would normally have made this the worst day of his life, but somehow it wasn't. Things were peaches and cream, and he was on cloud nine because, fuck, he knew what he had was just brilliant.

Mazzi stood in the boardroom at Slave's offices in Yaletown and reviewed the photos on the monitor of his super slim laptop for the twentieth time. *What a moment,* he thought. *Oh my god, what a fucking moment.* A man, frightened, distraught, trapped on his bed with blood on his nose and surrounded by silk—he couldn't imagine ever having seen anything so outrageously sexy before, even in his crazy days growing up in Stockholm.

Then Mazzi looked back at the photos of Dan fleeing like a desperate caged animal along the corridor into the safety of the elevator, the whole time wearing his favorite shiny silver designer underpants from Milan. It was beautiful.

As he turned off the screen, his boss and business partner Sebastian String walked into the room carrying his fluffy toy dog. Mazzi walked over to the door, closed it, sat Sebastian down, turned off the main fluorescent lights, walked down to the other end of the boardroom, turned a small spotlight on himself, then held his hands out toward Sebastian to hold his attention. In the heavily accented Swedish English he'd learned at college, he said, "Now I want you to imagine driving along the road and seeing… Bam!"

He hit the switch to the projector, and a huge image of Dan cowering on Mazzi's bed came up on the screen.

"Then you pass by another billboard and… Bam!" Mazzi shouted as the next picture of Dan creeping naked along the mirrored wall appeared. Another picture and another and another popped up as Mazzi clicked the switch, enthusiastically shouting out "Bam!" each time.

The sequential display of Dan's flight out of Mazzi's apartment revealed itself in a series of terrorized anxious movements, culminating in the shot of Dan holding his hand across his crotch in the elevator. Superimposed across Dan's knees at the bottom of that photo were the words *BlueBoy's new Bad-Boy Condoms – Don't Get Caught Without One.*

Sebastian looked at the screen, at Dan in the elevator with his blood-streaked face staring frantically back at him, and said, "That's absolutely fantastic!"

It was priceless, and they both knew it. They'd been searching for the last month for the right way to sell the new *Bad-Boy* line of BlueBoy Condoms, and this was the answer. My god, Mazzi had done it. Sebastian put his dog down on the floor and asked, "Who the hell is this guy?"

Mazzi turned on the overhead lights and looked at Sebastian and said, as camp as ever, "Yes, well, this is de problem."

******

Dan was tired and starving and could do with a Big Mac and fries to calm his nerves. He'd come straight out of Mazzi Hegan's apartment building and jumped naked into a taxi. As soon as the cab had come to a halt at the top of his road, Dan had the door open and was off and gone, disappearing into the night. Never in a million years would he ever have thought it possible that a middle-aged man in a turban could move so fast.

Fuck, he'd almost gotten him. First, the gay guy with the camera, and then the Punjabi warrior with his field hockey stick. Last night hadn't exactly gone according to plan. And it wasn't over—he'd seen the same taxi cruise past at least twice this morning, and the guy in the turban had been wandering up and down the road, still armed with his hockey stick.

He walked over and sneaked another look out the window. Fuck, this was ridiculous, being held siege in his mum's basement by Gandhi. What a fucking mess Daltrey had gotten him into, all the trouble she'd caused, telling him that blond-haired guy was dead. For fuck's sake, what kind of detective was she? She didn't even know Mazzi Hegan was a bender.

He walked back to his bed, sat down, and laughed to himself. It had been pretty funny, though. A good ride while it lasted, even if he had been blinded by the paparazzi and nearly killed by the cabbie. He'd had a good run, had driven that red rocket around for a bit, used all that fancy shampoo in the big fuck-you shower, and got a little bit of titty action in the process, but fuck, his nose was sore.

He walked to the bathroom and looked in the mirror he'd rigged up after his mum said he could stay there as long as he paid some rent and didn't bring girls back—and so far, he'd done neither. He turned to his side, then back again. Something was up. It was his nose. It was different. He walked out to his bedside cabinet and picked up the car wing mirror he used when he wanted to spy on his mum undressing and looked again.

It *was* different. Dan ran the tap and washed the blood from his lips and face and sniffed in and then breathed out, blowing out bubbles full of snot and blood. "Jesus," he said out loud as he stared at himself and his nose that was now a little off center. He turned his head again and looked at his face from a different angle. His nose was definitely broken, but somehow, he thought, in a strange way, the break really made him look good, even kind of sexy.

******

Dennis Willis stared at his wife as he walked into the hospital room. From what Daltrey could tell, it really had been a while since he'd seen her. From the way his face grew red and his breathing changed, she thought his heart must have been pounding in his chest. The only thing he said was hello, and upon hearing his voice, Alla opened her eyes.

Daltrey kept quiet in this moment of silence as she watched Dennis move forward and kneel down at Alla's side, placing his hand upon her head and kissing her gently on the cheek. Dennis Willis was not dreaming. Daltrey could tell there was a chance this girl did still love him. She could tell by the way she looked at him and the way silent tears rolled down her smooth, ivory cheeks as she spoke for the first time.

"Dennis, love, I can't feel my feet."

Dennis's eyes welled up. A year of loneliness surfacing as he held her head and her neck, his other hand reaching out and holding her hand. "You will soon," he said. "Don't worry, you'll heal."

Alla closed her eyes, his voice, soft and gentle, was something Daltrey could tell she had missed. His words, full of love and reassurance. He was obviously a good man, Daltrey thought, a man who deserved more than he was getting at this moment.

Chapter Eight

Alla Bragin lay in the bed and looked at the floor. What a mess she was in. She was happy to see her husband, and in a strange way felt secure when she'd heard his voice and felt his touch. After all, right now he was all she had. Her brother was still out there somewhere, and there was a strong chance he could end up like her—or like Sergei, if indeed it really was him who had been burning out there on the creek as the man who had put her here had said.

If that man had killed her brother, then so be it. If not, she was no good to him now anyway with her legs crippled as they were. He'd abandon her—it was the way he was made, and she knew it. Either way, she would be rid of him.

She opened her eyes and looked at her husband sitting with her by the bed, feeling the softness of his touch as he gently stroked her hair. The woman who dressed like a man was still in the room, sitting there silently and watching every move. She was trouble—Alla could feel it. She knew it the moment she walked into the room for the first time, even before she told her she was a cop and started going on about a guy called Wazzi or something.

Who the hell was the guy who'd hit her so hard, and had he really killed Sergei like he'd said? It had to be bullshit, but where was Sergei now?

Alla rolled the options around in her head. Fuck, she was frightened. She wanted to get up and run, escape this mess, head down to the States and disappear, but for the moment she'd lost control and had become a prisoner in her own body. She needed to recuperate, heal, and get her legs moving again, and find someone to look after her, care for her, and love her while her back mended. Looking up, she stared into Dennis's eyes and smiled. Through her tears and pain, she could tell that he was the one.

Alla was a survivor—she always had been—and from an early age, she'd known the world was bigger than the dark, dreary tenement block her mother had grown up in and her father had moved into when her grandparents died.

When Alla was at the tender age of twelve, her friend's older sister Eva had come home, walking with the grace of a goddess and smelling of French perfume, her nails colored and perfectly manicured and her beautifully cut blond hair soft as silk. She wore Italian clothes and stylish shoes from designer stores in New York, the quality and feel of which she had never seen or felt before. She'd known her before when they were younger as she'd sat in her friend's big sister's room, watching and listening as Eva learned a language so strange and sang along to songs Alla didn't understand. Alla there, wanting to be grown up, trying on Eva's new counterfeit clothes that did not fit and the lipstick Eva had bought with the money she earned up on the road.

Then one day, Eva was gone.

******

A year after Eva came home, Alla's brother came to her room and made her bleed and cry. As the weeks turned into months, she began to understand what Eva had sold—and the other girls now sold—up there on the road. By the age of fifteen, Alla had joined them, wearing her own new lipstick and counterfeit clothes her brother had bought her, and the men in cars became her life.

At the age of eighteen, as she felt her youth passing her by and her skin darkening from the wind and cold of life working the cars, her brother Illya was taken by the police. She knew she had five years to set herself free. The moment he was taken, Alla began to work and save, for she knew that soon another would take his place. When that man came, smelling of vodka in his flashy car, wanting to run her and wanting the money she earned and her sex for free, she took the train to Moscow. Laying her clothes across the bed of a cheap hotel, she looked in the mirror and combed her hair, colored her eyelids, and painted on a smile.

The handsome blond photographer came, and she paid him in cash and then in kind, and her day in the city became two and then three as she fell in love for the first time. Her smile became as real as a summer's day as she innocently wrote lies about her life as a student in Moscow, how she ate croissants when she shouldn't and loved herbal tea, and how she took bike rides on summer evenings. She spoke of her hopes and dreams, about how love was eternal, about the connection of souls passing through time, and how she knew her love was out there waiting. Then once everything was perfect, she paid the fee and signed up to find love.

Time passed as she waited in her room. Then the letters came, and she answered them all with hope and honesty as she worked the expensive hotels and kept herself beautiful. Before long, the proposals came from the lost and lonely in search of love. They offered lives on farms and in cities, and she accepted them all. Age, race, creed mattered not at all, for stepping stones, like the men in their cars, were soon forgotten. Then, as a hungry fish strikes the hook and can't let go, one man could write no more, and a visa was arranged, the agency paid, and a flight soon followed, and like Eva so many years before with the scent of French perfume, counterfeit clothes, and hair like silk, she was gone—off to a new life, far away from the ash grey tenement blocks with stray dogs and a brother who would soon be home.

******

With the euphoria of capturing the images he needed for his latest ad campaign wearing thin, Mazzi Hegan was beginning to feel violated.

"Jesus," he said as he watched the middle-aged cleaning lady with no style come out of the bedroom frowning, a half-eaten taco in one of her hands.

"I just found this in the pocket of one of your jackets, and there's chewing gum stuck to the inside of your shower and some more on the mirror. I'd say chances are he's also been using your toothbrush."

For a second, Mazzi thought he was going to puke. The guy was a fucking animal. Storming out of his bedroom, he went to stand on the balcony. God, he wished he hadn't lost his temper and hit the guy in the face with his man bag. At least then he would have found out who this guy was and how the hell he got the keys to the apartment in the first place. Of course, then he wouldn't have gotten the photos, so what was done was done. It was fate, pure fate—it just had to be.

He leaned against the balcony rail, wracking his brain, and looked out at the view of the city. Was this person a guy he'd picked up at a club, fucked, and forgotten about on the night he left? No. Was he an old flame? No, definitely not. Was he a friend of an old flame? Maybe. No, he'd remember.

Then he remembered that guy at the gym a month back, the plumber. They were doing squats together, and he'd had him to his apartment to help him fix the shower. They'd had a wild weekend, and Mazzi had told him he could come back anytime—but no, shit, he was Mexican. "Oh god!" he shouted out. He was just so fucked up. All he had to go on was the man's wallet, with its single six-inch sandwich voucher to Subway.

Mazzi took a deep breath and tried to calm himself down. The whole situation was crazy, and he needed to get it figured out. Once the place was cleaned, and he'd replaced his sheets, towels, toothbrush, and all his socks, shirts, and underwear, he'd find the guy, swallow his pride, and get a contract signed so he could move forward. He'd do it fair and square, even if the man, whoever he was, had left his favorite bathroom loofah in the fridge.

******

Charles Chuck Chendrill had worked for Sebastian String before. He was, in Sebastian's eyes, two things. One, he was the best private investigator he'd ever known. Two, he was the most expensive private investigator he'd ever known.

They'd all met in a coffee house, and after waiting ten minutes for Chendrill to come out of the restroom, Mazzi Hegan was already pissed. He asked his partner out loud and with enough volume for the private eye to hear through the restroom door, "Why do you hire him?"

Sebastian stared at the door and then, without looking back, he said, "Because he's the best!"

Mazzi joined him in staring at the restroom door. He rubbed his hands through his hair and looked away to the cute girl who had served them, wondering where she'd had her highlights done. "You think so? He stinks of horses. Can't you smell him?"

Sebastian looked back to Mazzi and said, "*You'd* know, dear. Anyway, I like him."

"Why?"

"Because he saved Fluffy."

Mazzi looked back to Sebastian and said, "I think you just like hanging around with straight guys."

Sebastian knew Hegan was right, but ignored him and looked to the bathroom door again. It *was* a little odd that Chendrill, as hunky as he was, had come in, shaken both their hands, got the gist of what the problem was, asked Mazzi a few personal questions, and then disappeared into the washroom for what seemed like an age. Looking back to Mazzi, Sebastian said, "Well, shoot me."

The restroom door opened, and Chendrill walked back out, rubbing the water from his hands. He sat down and said, "Sorry about that."

Sebastian smiled. "It's okay. When you've got to go, you've got to go."

Mazzi Hegan closed his eyes. Why Sebastian insisted on using this guy, he couldn't fathom. The man had no idea how to dress and always insisted on asking Mazzi too many questions about his love life. Why the fuck did he have to know how many men he'd had back to his place on a weekly basis? After all, the only thing the man had ever really done for them so far, this Mr. Fucking Charlie "Chuck" Chendrill, super sleuth, Magnum PI fucking wannabe, was to find Sebastian's dog when it'd gone missing, and even his grandmother could have done that if she'd gone to the fucking pound.

Chendrill smiled at Mazzi and said, "So let's recap everything. From what I can gather, Mr. Hegan, you came home after a week away, and when you got back, some strange guy was in your bed wearing your clothes."

"He was naked except for my silver underwear, which he stole."

Chendrill stared at the photos of Dan for a moment, then continued. "And you took these photos of him, and now you're trying to track him down."

Fuck me, Mazzi thought, then answered, "Yes."

"Okay, so you don't know this guy?"

"No."

"And you've never seen him at any clubs or parties before?"

"No."

"And do you think this gentleman could be part of the homosexual community in this city?"

"You tell me."

Chendrill looked again at the photo of Dan kneeling on the bed with blood coming from his nose and grinned. "And you struck this gentleman?"

"No, my bag did."

Charles Chuck Chendrill was already regretting taking the call. He'd had enough of this bitchy guy with the highlights and the attitude. Memories of all the hysterical screaming and crying that went on during the fiasco with the lost dog were starting to flood back. But work was work, and Sebastian paid well.

He opened his briefcase, placed the photo inside, and closed it with a snap. "Right then," he said. "Thank you. I'll go find this guy." Reaching out, he took Sebastian's hand first, then Mazzi's, and walked toward the door.

******

After he'd taken a long shower and changed his clothes, the

first thing Chendrill did was talk to the apartment manager who'd shown Mazzi Hegan's apartment to Daltrey the day after she'd found the body on the boat out on the creek. As she looked at the picture of Dan folded at the neck, she said, "The only person I saw here was the cop."

"The cop?"

The manager nodded and stepped back, resting her backside on the desk. She liked this guy's confidence and the way he wore his moustache.

"Did you get a name?"

"No, but she was really just snooping around looking for shoes."

"She?"

"Yeah, she had the same name as the old singer."

Chendrill smiled. He was on his way. He knew Daltrey and had met her when he himself had been a detective with the Vancouver police force. He liked her. She was different even then and had always thought outside the box. She'd caused a stir, he remembered, for busting a marijuana grow op in her first year when all she was supposed to be doing was school duty.

But for him, that was another lifetime, before the frustration and the politics set in and he'd switched from chasing murderers to spending time chasing married couples around, investigating insurance fraud, and searching for lost dogs.

Chendrill stepped to one side and leaned against the wall so he could see himself in the large mirror in the reception area. He looked good—everything was perfect except for his stomach. He looked back at the manager. She was kind of cute, even if she was getting on a bit.

"You look after this big place all on your own?" he asked, flirting.

The manager blushed. If she'd known she was going to get a visit from a hunky private investigator who looked like Thomas Magnum, she would have worn her new skirt. "I manage," she said and gave a little smile.

"I'm sure you do, young lady, I'm sure you do."

Then she said, "I have some stored CCTV footage if you'd like to check through it."

The sight of Dan, first in the elevator and then running through the lobby, was too funny. The manager leaning over his back in her office, accidentally letting her titties rub his shoulder, had been the icing on the cake. Chendrill was still laughing when he met Daltrey at the small French restaurant on Denman.

"I'm trying to find someone. Do you know this guy?"

Daltrey nodded as she looked down at the photo of Dan, which was now just a headshot.

"Yeah."

Chendrill carried on. "May I ask how?"

Daltrey smiled, slightly embarrassed, and said, "We kind of dated once."

"Really? I thought he was gay."

"No, he's an electronics genius."

Chendrill smiled. He hadn't been expecting that one. Most electronics geniuses he'd come across lived in their mother's basements and never went out. They weren't running around stealing Ferraris.

"Why would you think he's gay?"

"A client of mine found him waiting naked in his bed."

Daltrey stared at him for a moment. This was getting confusing. Dan gay? No. He couldn't be. Not with the way he'd come on to her like he had, standing there at Hegan's place with his cock semi-erect right in her face, looking like he'd pulled a huge pork sausage out the fridge and stuffed it down his pants.

She grinned to herself as she looked at Chendrill's big moustache and long hair. She liked him. She remembered him from her early days on the force when she'd been in trouble after skipping school duty to bring in a million-dollar drug operation she'd cottoned onto running out the back of a local car service facility. He'd come over to her in the canteen and said, "Stick up for yourself. They're jealous, and you embarrassed them. That's all."

Not too much later, the two had slept together after a night at a bar, and it hadn't been Chendrill who'd instigated things. There was just something about the man—the way he moved, his calmness, the way he listened. Then afterward, as they'd laid together on his bed, he'd asked her in the most honest and nonjudgmental of ways if she preferred girls. To prove him wrong, she'd done him again. But from then on, she'd often wondered deep down how he'd known.

Later, she heard he'd walked off the force.

"He's not gay. Who's the client?" Daltrey asked and remembered how his big moustache had felt on her pussy oh so many years ago.

"A guy by the name of Sebastian String and his business partner Mazzi Hegan own the apartment you were snooping around in." He tapped his finger on Dan's photo. "Looks like after you left, your ex stuck around and had a bit of fun, living it up and driving around in the guy's Ferrari."

Daltrey's heart almost stopped. She could feel the blood rush from her stomach. "And have you spoken to this Mazzi Hegan?"

Chendrill nodded. "Yep, today. Why?"

Daltrey rolled her eyes. She'd never felt so embarrassed. *Fuck, fuck, that fucking fuckhead Dan,* she thought. He must have stolen the spare keys that were in the drawer before she kicked him out. Nervously, she rubbed her fingers through her long hair. She leaned forward and spoke quietly. "Listen, there was a body found burned two nights ago out on False Creek. It hasn't been identified yet. I had been pretty certain it was this Mazzi Hegan you're talking about."

A certain part of Chendrill wished it was. Smiling, he looked at Daltrey and shook his head. "No, but if the condescending prick keeps talking down to me the way he does, he could be a good future candidate."

Chapter Nine

Dan was scared to go outside now, after seeing the guy in the turban for the sixth time walking up and down the street armed with his field hockey stick. There was a whole box of fresh bagels and iced buns on the kitchen counter. He sliced two bagels, covered them in strawberry jam, licked the knife clean, and stuck it back into the jar, crammed the last two iced buns into his mouth and had just plopped the last bagel into the toaster when he heard a knock at the door.

Who the fuck is this? he thought, sneaking a look through a window and relieved to see Charles Chuck Chendrill standing outside in his bright Hawaiian shirt and deck shoes and not the taxi driver with the turban. The man waiting out there, all hair and moustache, like so many idiots before him, coming around and sniffing about in the hope they could screw his mum.

Dan walked to the front door and, not bothering to open it, called through the mail slot. "She's not in…she's getting her muff waxed."

That'll do it, he thought. That'll get rid of the loser.

But Chendrill didn't flinch and said right back, "Well, all I can say is from the photos I've seen of you in those silver underpants, you'd better go join her."

Dan put the chain on, opened the door, and looked out through the crack. "What photos?"

Chendrill looked back at the guy with a broken nose hiding behind the door and smiled. "The ones of you rolling around naked in some gay guy's bed."

******

75

Chendrill sat in the restaurant and watched Dan eat. All he'd said to him to get him there was, "I'll take you for a burger, and you can eat whatever you want if you come and hear me out." And all that Dan had wanted was the Big Mac and fries he'd been craving since he'd gotten home and found himself held siege by the crazy taxi driver in the turban.

Dan watched as Chendrill stared at himself in the mirror and said to him, "Mirror, mirror on the wall, you should spend the night hanging out in Mazzi Hegan's walk-in wardrobe. You'd like it in there."

Chendrill looked over to him, the prick, and laughed. He was right, though. He was vain, and he knew it. But what the fuck. There was something about this kid he liked, although he couldn't as yet put his finger on it. Maybe it was his rawness, his openness—or maybe it was just that he was such a cheeky fucker. He looked over to the counter and saw Melissa standing at the till, showing her teeth like they'd told her to do during her weeklong training. He looked back over at Dan and said, "Your girlfriend's here."

Dan looked up at him and then to the counter and saw Melissa serving up a portion of fries. With a mouth full of burger, he asked, "How the fuck did you know I know her?"

Chendrill laughed and said, "I saw footage of her this morning getting in and out of an elevator. She was quite distressed when she passed your boyfriend in the lobby a minute before he found you in his bed."

Dan looked at Melissa and then at everyone else behind the counter. To him, they all looked the same, even the guys. How the hell had this guy spotted her among the other dozen people running around making shakes? Especially when all he had to go on was a tiny image from an elevator camera. "How'd you pick her out of that bunch of lookalikes, from a low-resolution CCTV camera picture and not a closed-circuit, digital, high-def, photographic-based system?" He liked the way that one sounded, flowing off his lips like it had and sounding cool.

Chendrill stared at him for a moment and said, "It's what I do. So how do you know so much about digital imagery?"

Dan smirked and then took another hit on his shake. "It's what I do," he mimicked. "I'm into electronics research and development."

Chendrill stared at him for a moment, working him out. Then, as he caught sight of himself in another mirror he'd not noticed before, he said, "By the looks of where you're living, you're not too good at it then."

He wasn't half wrong. Dan knew he could do more these days to apply this talent he had, but God, it just was way too much effort, and lately he could only get so far reading up on science before he switched it out for a titty site. But he'd known true genius lay within him, and when the real motivation was there, it had taken only an afternoon of research and some detailed plans taken from the Internet to put together the infrared electronic device he'd given to Daltrey.

Dan stared back at Chendrill for a second, then said, "It's still early, but I can tell you that one day you'll be saying, 'You know, I met that kid once.'"

Chendrill nodded. "You mean, like the same as if I'd once sat and watched Bill Gates stuff his face with a Big Mac?"

Dan nodded. "Kind of."

Chendrill sat back and grinned at the kid with tomato ketchup around his mouth and said, "Well, from what I know, the guys out there who have made billions from being just a bit technically smarter with electronics or computer systems than the next guy don't usually have to be tracked down by the likes of me because they get caught wearing another man's underpants."

Dan came right back at him. "How do you know?"

And Dan was right. He didn't know, so he just said, "You're right. I don't. So I wish you well, but if you keep stuffing your face with that shit, I'll be saying you know, I knew that fat bastard when he used to live with his mum."

Dan shook his head. Not him, no chance. "That's not going to happen. It can't. You see, I'm blessed with a gene that won't allow my body to put on weight."

"That's not a gene—it's called worms."

Ignoring him, Dan reached down and scooped up a handful of fries. He put them in what was left of his burger bun and swallowed the lot. "Same as my mum," he said. "You should see her. She's hot. Not an ounce of fat on her...never has been."

Chendrill stared at this skinny kid with a broken nose who was living in his mother's basement and was going to get rich from electronics. "Maybe you and your mum should patent that gene of yours, and then you'd really will be rich."

With a smirk, Dan added, "And you can be my first customer."

******

Daltrey was annoyed at herself and at the same time quite pleased. She'd gotten it wrong with Mazzi Hegan, but only half wrong. She was wrong about his shoes, but the shoes had not been her only line of inquiry, and things were moving forward.

Burn

It was the other one she had a feeling that was going to pay off, and deep down she knew she was on to something. At least, though, the matter with Mazzi Hegan was now cleared up, unless, of course, Dan had stirred up more trouble than the small infrared electronic device he'd made her was worth.

She now had the names of the girl in the hospital and her husband, and she had seen the way the girl's eyes had shifted slightly when she'd mentioned the body burned to death out on the creek, even if it wasn't Mazzi Hegan. Arriving back at her office, she sat down at her desk and typed in Dennis Willis's name, then Alla Bragin's. Nothing came through that she didn't already know. She typed in burn victims, and the page flooded with results—people burned accidentally, others due to arson, accidental kitchen fires, one man burned to death in an alley in Vancouver's Eastside, another young male burned to death and his fiancée badly injured after a fire at an address in West Vancouver, and a family home destroyed by faulty wiring in Delta.

Daltrey sat back, trying to remember them all. The guy in the alley was definitely murdered. There had been a friend of a friend whose daughter babysat the same guy when he was just a kid, years before he went bad and ended up getting himself killed. Almost a year ago, she'd seen a picture of the other guy, the student, on the front page of *The Province* the day after he'd died.

She closed the computer and sat back in her chair. Somehow the body in the boat was linked to Alla Bragin, now Alla Willis, the Russian whore who liked to spend the realtor's money now all her husband's was gone. The connection had to be there. But she had also been certain of a connection with Mazzi Hegan, and look what had happened with him and then Dan—the fucking prick.

Enough was enough. It was time to call it a day. Daltrey got up, walked down to the car park, and got in her car. She was going to go home, take a bath, then maybe go out and have a night on the town for once. Get herself a little drunk and try to find the butch lesbian she'd met once before to see if she could try to relive the memories the pictures she'd found of Patrick had stirred up in her.

The woman was wild, and she'd liked that. She rode a motorbike all year when most of the pussy men put theirs to bed as soon as the rains started. She'd been sitting alone on a wall by the art gallery when the woman had approached, and Daltrey could smell her leather jacket as she moved in closer, staring and smiling in a teasing way, telling Daltrey straight up she was cute and should try it with a girl. Then they were off for a beer and, after that, back to the woman's place where the woman had fucked her hard, grinding her pussy against Daltrey's and sucking her breasts until she came. Then she'd brought out the toys.

Within twenty minutes, Daltrey was back standing on the seawall below Alla's apartment block, staring out across the creek where the mysterious body had been burned only three nights prior. She looked up at the window where Alla must have been watching the rowboat on fire and wondered how many times Patrick had allowed himself to be hammered away on, up there in Alla's love den.

She looked toward Patrick's place and counted the floors until she found his apartment. He was in, the kinky bastard, and probably up to no good right now, no doubt looking into some other pussy parlor willing to give him what he needed. At least he had a sex life, which was more than she had, she thought, even if his was a perversely strange one.

Daltrey turned back around to Alla's place and noticed the curtains had changed. She stared for a moment, trying to remember if she'd seen it when she'd arrived. For a moment, she wondered if she'd been looking at the wrong place altogether, but no, she hadn't. Quickly, she walked along the seawall, trying to get a better look inside. No good—all she could see was the ceiling and the top of a chair by the window.

The first thing Patrick thought when he got the call was that the hot cop had fallen for him and wanted to have sex. Maybe, though, he thought, as he whipped himself in and out the shower and wacked on a touch of cologne, she'd found a place she wanted to buy and needed him to broker the deal. Either one was fine with him.

As soon as he opened the door, the first thing she said to him as she smelled the Clive Christian which still hadn't dried was, "You got a telescope?" And then, marching uninvited along the corridor until she reached the living room window, she followed it up with "And don't get any kinky ideas!"

Patrick looked confused. Following her in, he said, "May I ask why you need a telescope?"

Daltrey turned to him and glanced around. He had a nice place. Really nice. She said, "Because I want to look into your girlfriend's apartment."

Saying it to him just like that, as if it was her God-given right to be wherever she wanted to be.

Patrick was quiet for a second and then said, "I've got people coming over."

Daltrey looked at him and tilted her head slightly. Patrick got her meaning.

"No, my mother," he said. "But I do have one in the

bedroom that I use to look at the boats."

Of course you do, Patrick, Daltrey thought as she now walked uninvited toward his bedroom.

She entered the room and saw the high-powered telescope sitting next to Patrick's bed, pointing toward the condo building opposite. Quickly, she turned to him and asked, "Can you line it up on your girlfriend's place?"

Patrick walked over and fiddled with the telescope. "I had it in here because I was cleaning it."

Daltrey took over and a second later had a crystal clear view right into Alla's apartment and bedroom. Taking her eye away from the scope, she looked at Patrick. "This thing is good."

"You should see the moon."

"Yeah right, like you've been looking for cheese, Patrick."

He moved in nearer and sat on the bed, a little too close.

She took her eye away from the scope and looked at him. "Fuck off, Patrick," she said.

Patrick stood again and said, "I think she's still in the hospital."

"You call her?" Daltrey asked, remembering the curt nurse telling her there was a man who kept calling. "Did you go see her?"

He hadn't. "I was going to go in the morning. I've been very busy. You know how it gets. I've ordered flowers, though."

Good, maybe her husband Dennis can help you arrange them, Daltrey thought as she looked through the telescope. A shadow passed along the wall in the hallway in Alla's apartment, and a man appeared from what could only be the bathroom. He was young, maybe in his thirties, and was wearing track pants and a top. Daltrey asked, "Who's this guy?"

And without even looking through the scope, Patrick answered, "Her brother. She hates him."

Chapter Ten

It was the third time Dan had been to the washroom, and they had only been at the Slave offices for just over twenty minutes. He sat back down in the boardroom and apologized. "Sorry, I've been eating a lot of cakes lately, and they're not agreeing with me."

Mazzi Hegan closed his eyes. That was one piece of information he really did not need to know. Taking a deep breath, he said, "Listen, I'm willing to forget about the damage you've caused to my bathroom, my sheets, my shoes, my clothes, the interior of my Ferrari, and my favorite pure seaweed loofah I had imported from Tahiti that you'd been eating. I'll forget about everything including the money because that's the kind of guy I am."

Dan looked at Mazzi Hegan, then at his partner Sebastian sitting there with a fluffy dog on his lap, then at their lawyer with his beady little eyes, then at the private investigator who didn't like McDonald's. He said, "I thought that green thing was some sort of special food."

Sebastian smiled and leaned forward, lifting up his little dog so as not to squash him. "Dan, it wasn't food, you don't eat those things. Honestly, you don't. Now listen, I really don't know what you were up to that night in Mazzi's place, but the photos Mazzi took of you when you were trying to escape are just sensationally sexy."

Dan frowned. What the fuck was this guy with the dog talking about? He'd never considered himself sexy at all, far from it, but he had noticed since his nose was broken, women were now looking at him. "Can I see the photos?" he asked.

Sebastian shook his head. That was a no-no. Taking a deep breath, he said,

"I'm sorry, company policy is that models don't see their work, and besides, they're being rendered."

What the fuck was he going on about? Dan thought as he looked at the dog. "When did I become a model?" he asked.

Sebastian shrugged. "A couple of nights ago, we hope."

Dan looked at Chendrill, who stared back and raised one eyebrow.

Sebastian lifted his dog off of some papers sitting at the side of his chair and slid them across the desk toward Dan, saying with a smile, "What we want to do, Daniel, is use the photos Mazzi took of you in an advertising campaign we've been working on for a client. They absolutely love you. They think you're a sensation. If you accept and sign today, we'll draft you an advance of fifteen thousand dollars, which is about twelve percent of what you will get as a minimum when we run the campaign."

Dan felt faint. Fifteen thousand dollars is twelve percent of more money than he could imagine.

"But," Sebastian continued, "all being well, we still need you to do some more photo work at the studio and on the yacht, and then maybe a commercial or two, which could add another twenty percent on top of the initial contract."

More photographic work? He couldn't remember doing any in the first place, unless you called getting the fuck out of there "photographic work," he thought. Fuck, he wished he'd listened in math class at school instead of having sexual fantasies about the teacher. His head was spinning. He looked to the floor, wracked his brain, and did the math as the guy with the dog spoke.

Then, as cool as a cucumber, Chendrill leaned forward

and put it all into perspective. "Dan, it comes down to being able to walk into McDonald's and order thousands and thousands of Big Macs, all at once."

And without missing a beat, it all came together as it always did and Dan replied, "Yeah, forty-seven thousand three hundred and sixty-eight, to be precise."

******

Illya stood in the fancy apartment that looked out over the creek, admiring the way his new gray Adidas tracksuit hung on his frame in his reflection in the plate-glass window. The way the pants just clipped the top of his runners enough to put a little crease at their bottom was perfect.

Fuck, he looked good.

Twisting, he turned and stared at his reflection from another angle in the hall mirror. He'd seen this new tracksuit on a mannequin in a shop window across the road while getting a haircut and just knew it was going to be styling. Now he had one tracksuit for almost every day of the week. When he'd been in prison, one suit would have to last for months, and they were almost always counterfeit.

He sat down on the sofa, stared out the window, and lit up another cigarette. Alla had been gone now for almost four days, and there was no sign of her coming back. He'd resigned himself to that, but if she did return, he would make her pay back tenfold.

Illya looked at himself one last time in the lobby mirror as he left the apartment building, walking out and along the seawall toward the casino. It was hot out this late afternoon. He looked to the yachts below, moored with their flags flying proudly, looking good and going nowhere. Stopping, he looked back along the seawall, his eyes following two guys in shorts as they raced along on rollerblades, weaving through the runners and cyclists too scared to go fast, whipping past him, then the girl sitting on a bench along the way watching them also, catching her long hair tied up tight in a ponytail in the breeze as they flew past.

He looked back again at the crystal clear water. It would be cold, but never as cold as it had been the morning he'd jumped from the ship where he'd lain hidden, stowed away over a year before, lying cramped and sweaty as it headed west across seas and oceans. Weak and hungry, he'd leaped off the ship's side before first light as it waited for clearance on the edge of English Bay. His heart momentarily stopping as he hit the water, swimming for land through the cold with the early morning tide and arriving exhausted and frozen on the beach. He'd wrung out his clothes and left them to dry on a huge abandoned log in the sand and thought about how close his sister might be now as he warmed himself in the early morning sun.

The night his temper broke, he'd spat at his mother as they sat eating his celebratory homecoming dinner. Illya there holding his father's hand, breaking his father's fingers one by one as he waited, watching his mother as she ran to the bedroom to find the address she'd hidden so well, the one she'd sworn to her daughter she would never let her son see.

With all the money he could steal and as much canned food as he could carry, Illya had left his parents as they cried in the ransacked house he'd once called home. Heading out into the night, toward the huge cranes and ships he'd seen years before through the wide, innocent eyes of the young boy he'd once been, when his father had taken him there for the very first time, wanting Illya to see the docks he had worked since his late teens. Young Illya, happy back then, looking to the cranes towering high above the water like giant monsters with huge necks moving slowly along the dock, plucking supplies from the insides of ships. Where his father had kept his head down and his nose clean, providing for his family, working the ships and oil tankers that moored in the dark, dirty water alongside the naval submarines that sat waiting for repair like sleeping behemoths.

Within the day, Illya had found the ship that would take him to the new life his sister had set up for him. In the dead of night, with his bag full of canned goods and water, he sneaked up the gangplank and down into a corner section of the large engine room. Climbing up a bulkhead, hidden by tarpaulins, he lay quietly by day and by night, unseen and unheard, pissing and defecating in a tin as he fended off rats, his ears stuffed with rags to lessen the noise of the huge diesel engines that thundered away, powering him across the ocean through the Panama Canal and up the west coast of North America to his new home.

Illya reached the casino by the water at the end of the seawall and walked inside. He scoured the area around the roulette tables by the door, searching as he had each day for his sister and her lover, glimpsing the faces of the men and women throwing away their money in search of the thrill of winning what they would someday in the future give back.

He moved on, making his way back and forth through the maze of slots, passing lonely people whiling their day away, staring at lights and spinning characters drawn in a far-off land they would never see. He took the escalator up to a level where others were throwing their money away on high-stake card games they didn't understand, yet thought they could play. They weren't there, either, his sister and her lover, hanging at the bar, Alla with a margarita and Sergei with his expensive vodka drowned in fresh orange and full of ice.

It was just as he headed back downstairs that he saw Daltrey for the second time that day. The first, he remembered, had been as he'd turned to watch the guys on their rollerblades. She had been there sitting on a bench some eighty feet behind him, doing the same. Now she was in the casino, playing slots ten minutes after she'd been relaxing in the sun.

A cop? Maybe, but she was too good-looking for a cop, more like one of those greeters in a restaurant chain. He reached the bottom of the escalator and walked toward the roulette tables. He'd heard of pretty cops posing as hookers in the hotels in Moscow, but over here, pretty women had better options. Even so, in this day and age you could never tell, and if she was a cop, why was he now suddenly on the radar?

He walked to the other side of the casino and sat down next to a Chinese man on a blackjack table and laid down a hundred dollars he knew he would never see again on chips. Through the crowd, Daltrey was still visible and showing absolutely no interest in him. *Maybe I'm crazy,* he thought. *Maybe she's an addict.* But addicts didn't relax in the sun when there was a casino up the road, and they almost always had a boyfriend with them or were texting one. This girl was doing nothing but feeding the machine.

An hour passed, and nothing had changed. Illya sat on his seat and threw more money away, the woman with the ponytail still sitting there playing the machine, now texting and not even looking at him once. Fuck it, he was crazy, seeing things, cops in tight-fitting blouses with nice legs.

Maybe he should go over and give it a go, see if she wanted to earn real money, not the pennies dribbling from the machine she was on.

He looked at the dealer and asked for one last hand and lost. Shit. Getting up quickly, he headed for the door and left without looking back. Alla was not there, and neither was her flashy photographer boyfriend whom he should've told to fuck off as soon as she'd had her husband pay for his flight over and he'd never returned home.

His lucky card dealer who'd just taken him for five hundred hadn't seen either of them since the weekend. Maybe they'd run off together. Maybe, but to where? Maybe the States, both of them crossing the border on some remote farm or some mountain pass like he heard you could do. Maybe the two were now sitting at a bar in San Francisco or New York, laughing at him. Illya sat down on a wall just out of sight of the entrance and waited. If the girl came out, then she was a cop, and he had problems.

******

Daltrey was doing well. Surprisingly well, in fact. Six-hundred-dollars-in-pocket well, which was good for a girl who had only sat down because Illya had taken her by surprise by coming toward her down the escalator. It was a five-dollar-a-hit game, and with such a fantastic view of the table Illya was on, it seemed crazy not to stay.

Carefully, she looked toward the door through which Illya had just left and simultaneously hit the play button with her right hand, winning another two hundred dollars. *Wow.* She hit the button again, lost five bucks. Hit again, lost another five. Hit again, and went back up by another sixty.

In less than an hour, she was up two days' wages and had the new leather jacket she'd had her eye on coming her way.

Half an hour later, Daltrey was sitting in the casino's office with the security chief, talking to the dealer and reviewing the security footage of Illya throwing his money away.

"So how long has he been coming here?" Daltrey asked the dealer, who took in tens of thousands a day from customers with his smiles, but needed new shoes.

The dealer looked up from the floor and stared Daltrey straight in the eye.

"A year maybe, I'd say."

Daltrey nodded, thinking. It made sense. The timing was right. The guy had come here on the dentist's coin, no doubt.

"And he sits with you?"

The dealer smiled, then twisting his head with a frown, he said, "When I'm here."

"Does he win?"

The dealer shook his head, and smiling again said, "Most of the people who come here think they do. He's no different."

Daltrey looked at the monitor, at Illya looking straight at her as she sat at the slot machine across the floor, and wanted to say, *Well, I'm just about to leave with over six hundred bucks, so fuck off.* But instead, she asked, "Who does he come here with?"

The dealer shrugged, happy for this interlude in his otherwise predictable day. "He has a couple of friends—a girl and a blond guy of about the same age."

"Alla?"

The dealer nodded. "Something like that. She's really pretty. They're both Russian as well."

Daltrey stood from her chair and rubbed her hand across her face. Then she pulled the picture she'd taken of Alla in the hospital when she'd been pretending to sleep.

The dealer smiled and nodded, saying, "Yep, that's the girl. She lives close by."

"How do you know?"

"I listen."

Daltrey looked away from the monitors and smiled, weighing the information. "They take you for a fool, speaking Russian, and you understand everything they say?"

The dealer laughed. "My grandparents were from the Crimea."

Daltrey stared at the dealer, who was obviously no fool. "And they never knew?"

He smiled, almost laughing. "I got a kick out of their scheming, you know? The way they would always be trying to beat me."

"And they never did?"

"Sometimes, but not often."

Taking a moment, Daltrey stood and watched the monitors again. Then she asked, "And the casino just happened to match you with them every time they came in?"

Smiling, the dealer nodded. It was the way it was.

"Were they all here Saturday night?"

The dealer thought back. He didn't know what day it was today, Saturday having come and gone in a blur of video games, work, pizza, and masturbation.

"Maybe?"

Without being asked, the security chief moved to his computer and seconds later was scrolling through footage of Saturday evening until Illya came into view walking across the center of the casino, staring at the tables as he passed.

Reaching his dealer's table, he sat down at a table next to a couple.

Daltrey stared at the girl and said out loud, "Alla." Pointing to the blond guy next to her, Daltrey asked the dealer, "Is he the boyfriend?"

The dealer nodded.

Daltrey stared at the face of the good-looking young Russian man with his beautiful girlfriend who was lying in a hospital bed a few miles away, unable to feel her feet. She looked over to the security chief. "I need to see the boyfriend's shoes."

Three hours later, Daltrey had put together her version of Alla's evening at the casino before she'd been crippled and her boyfriend in his fancy shoes had burned to death in a small boat outside her apartment.

She watched them and then scanned the image of the casino on the screen to see who else might have been watching them play. Alla with her beauty and long, wavy hair naturally drew a lot of attention, her boyfriend some, and Illya very little. Among them, never looking at them once and timing his exit perfectly to follow Alla and her boyfriend out the door, was Padum Bahadur.

******

Williams was waiting, standing on the road in the distance as Illya exited the casino and began to quietly follow him back along the seawall. He'd received Daltrey's call an hour before and was there with a picture taken of the Russian already sitting on the screen of his phone along with a text telling him the man was about to come out the door.

This was it, he thought. He was doing the surveillance

work he craved, even if it was on his own time and it had to compete with his girlfriend's incessant texting. Williams stared at his phone. What the hell was the big deal anyway? He hadn't gone to her mother's birthday celebration, but he was working after all.

Illya stopped, looked around, and sat on a bench as Williams crossed the road behind in the distance and, stopping to watch him in the reflection of a shop window, answered another text.

What the hell was so interesting about this guy? he thought. He was foreign—that was certain—and looked like some kind of athlete. He hit send, and his girl responded in what seemed like only a second. How could she do it that fast? he wondered. It was impossible to write that quick, let alone read it. She must have already figured out what he was going to say and preloaded her response. He wrote back slowly, asking, How do you manage to text so fast?

As he watched, from the corner of his eye, Illya looking out across the marina, the phone buzzed in his hand with not one reply but two. Williams looked down at the phone in astonishment and read, You should care more about us than the speed of my response. The second text was simple and straight to the point. I'm done with texting, and I'm done with you!

Williams stared at the phone. She'd dumped him by text. They'd been together just over a year now, and fuck it just seemed wrong. Then Williams looked up to see Illya staring straight back at him.

The guy was on to him. He'd fucked it up, Williams thought, as his stomach tightened and a wave of sweat and sickness ran through him. Goddamn it. Quickly, he punched a response into his phone, trying to keep an eye on Illya at the same time. Come on, love, I'm working. He hit send and waited. Nothing. He tried again. Come on, love—I'll make it up to you. Nothing. He wrote, I'll come over right now! Still nothing.

Williams waited. The seconds passed as he stared at his phone, then suddenly in panic he looked up to discover that Illya, along with his girl, was gone.

Chapter Eleven

It was a quick double back, up and around the stadiums, to reach the Balmoral Hotel on Hastings Street on Vancouver's east side. Sitting at the bar, Illya ordered a beer and stared at the row of optics lined up in front of him.

The girl on the slots, however pretty, had picked him up outside on the seawall. Then there was the kid waiting outside way over by the road who had followed him, but seemed to be more interested in his phone. Cops? They certainly didn't look the part, but he definitely couldn't write it off.

As soon as he'd gone back to her apartment, he'd gotten that paranoid feeling that someone was on to him, following him. If it was real, then his sister had to be involved somehow, the fucking whore. Where the fuck was she? Taking a deep breath, he shook it off. Fuck her, he'd start from scratch. Keep the contacts open and find a new girl.

He looked around. The guy in the long coat with matted hair and dirty nails wasn't there. If he got some of that Rohypnol roofie shit they sold around here and some heroin, then maybe he could get started within a week and be back in business.

He looked through the window to the street. No one following him now that he could see. No pretty little thing or her boyfriend who was addicted to his phone. Just a sidewalk covered with the homeless and losers strung out on crack. Fuck, it was pitiful here. You didn't have this in Russia, he thought. What the police didn't sort out, the winters did.

It had been a long time since his first day here when he'd wandered around the area after waking up on the beach and putting his almost dry clothes back on. He'd walked through the park, not knowing where to go. He'd found the edge of town, lifted some food and a lighter and a couple of long, slim cans of hairspray from a store, and after an hour spreading the nozzles, he'd set off, drifting east until he found the cash he needed sitting in the pockets of a drug dealer working an alley two blocks from the police station on Main Street.

The guy had stood there with an attitude, dirt on his hands, hunched up under his hoodie, speaking to him in a language Illya could barely comprehend. His spotter across the road watching, smoking a cigarette and looking down at the ground, his eyes glancing up toward them as Illya had simply said, "Give."

The dealer was unsure for a moment, trying to be cool. Then he'd answered, "Give what?"

"Money!" Illya had answered, and before the guy could tell him to fuck off and pull whatever he was holding out of his pocket, Illya had blasted him in the face, blinding him with an explosion of flame that seemed to come from nowhere.

The dealer had gone down, screaming the way Illya's victims always did, his hands clasping at eyes that could no longer see. Illya bending down, pulling the dealer's wad of money from his pocket, putting it into his own without a care. Discarding the man's heroin with his foot, he'd fired up again, holding up the can with a beautiful girl on its side that spat death, showing the man more mercy than he had ever shown the addicts he supplied on the street or the ones he'd befriended at the rehabilitation centers he hung around in, quietly enticing and tempting the weak trying to go clean with his poisoned nectar.

******

Illya looked up as the guy in the long coat came in, his hair as matted and dirty as the last time he'd seen him, staring into nowhere through bloodshot eyes, passing his venom and disappearing again into the sea of desperation Hasting Street had become. An hour later, Illya was back at his new apartment that looked over the small city park, with enough heroin and Rohypnol to fell an elephant.

He sat down, put his brand new Nikes up on the leather sofa that wasn't his, lit up another cigarette, and looked around at the latest furnished rental apartment he'd found on the Internet and paid three months' rent for in advance. This time, telling the agent with the tight dress suit and fancy hair that because he was an actor working on a TV series shooting in town, he needed a furnished place to call his own for a while.

"The place is expensive, yes," the agent had said, "but the furniture is Italian leather, and all the linens in the bedrooms are of the finest Egyptian cotton."

Illya could've cared less. All he needed was a place to stay for a month to six weeks, and with the money he earned, it didn't need to be a shithole. The more expensive the place, the less info they needed. All he had to do was guarantee he wouldn't smoke, which was easy. He needed no references, just a lot of cash and bullshit, a production company address in town and another in Moscow along with a bank he'd found, and that was that.

It was the way he operated, moving all the time and never

settling down long enough for people to notice. His only failing was the casino, but the people who went there only paid attention to their wallets. With Alla and her boyfriend now suddenly missing, and the kid on the phone possibly following him in the afternoon, he was glad he'd switched to the new place the same morning of the day he'd last seen Alla and her poncing blond boyfriend. The problem was he hadn't told them, which in a way was better as now he was safe here in this expensive new apartment that was putting a dent in his cash reserves, with its view across the park and its Egyptian cotton sheets. A couple of whores was all he needed, he thought. New ones with long legs like his sister, girls who liked to be looked after properly and get fucked a lot. That was all he needed, Illya thought as he took another long pull on his cigarette and blew out the smoke across the room. Just another one or two new girls, and he'd be back on track.

******

The evening was still warm as Illya left his fancy new pad, took a right up toward Granville, and crossed the road at the lights to avoid the cops chatting on the corner like fishermen's wives. He carried along, the road loud now and busy, kids fresh out of school trying to look mature, walking to and fro as they moved from bars to clubs, high on dope, vodka spritzers, and whatever other shit was cheap enough to get them merry.

Four hours later, Illya was home again, leaning back on the off-white Italian leather sofa with his new Nikes up on the table and watching how the smoke from his cigarette dissipated along the ceiling as he blew another deep lungful up into the air. He was relaxed, the emergency over—for now anyway. He stared at the ceiling, the smoke like an art form, arriving at each corner of the room at exactly the same time.

Maybe he should get the girl he'd brought back to clean up the puke in the hallway when she came around. It was hers after all. Either that or he'd take his shoes off and do it himself later in his socks. She'd probably be too out of it to do anything for a while after having ingested such a huge hit of Rohypnol and the first taste of heroin he'd injected into her veins before popping out to pick up some milk and eggs from the all-night store on Davie.

He looked down at his new white Nike runners and twisted his left foot at the ankle so he could get a better look. They were cool—'styling,' as they liked to say here in this part of the world. Smiling, he spoke out loud the words the salesman had said to him in a language that still felt foreign. "Styling, man! Those are rad, dude."

And they were rad, really rad—even if they did have the girl's puke on them.

******

Dan walked the long way back to his home, keeping an eye out for the crazy taxi driver with the turban, he turned into the alley at the back of his mother's house. His nose was still sore, and he was having difficulty breathing out of his left nostril. It wasn't good, but hey, he had money coming because of it, so what the fuck!

He reached the gate at the back of the house and walked through it into the back garden. He'd promised his mother he'd cut it at the start of spring, but the lawn was now nearly two feet high. As soon as he opened the back door, she was on him.

"When are you going to cut the lawn like you promised? People are starting to sleep in it."

Dan looked back at the grass. It was so long now he didn't have a clue where to start. Seeing the flattened part his mum was talking about, he remembered lying naked in the grass the other night while the taxi driver patrolled the alley up and down looking for him.

His mother looked at him again and asked, "What have you done to your nose?"

Dan took a step back then went straight for the fridge, saying, "This gay guy hit me in the face with his man bag, and now he wants me to model for him."

Taken aback, Tricia stared at her son in disbelief. "What?"

"Yeah, he says I look good."

Tricia continued to stare a moment longer, then said, "And what else does he want?"

"He wants to give me a load of money."

"How much?"

Stuffing a half-eaten piece of pizza into his mouth, Dan closed the fridge door. "I'm not sure," he lied. "I've still got to do the math. It's a lot, though, and I know that you and I'll be eating out for a while."

"Where? McDonald's?"

Dan opened the fridge again, searching for more food and finding a Scotch egg. He closed the fridge and said, "What's wrong with that?"

Tricia walked away. She'd heard it all before. The next thing he'd be telling her would be that the deal had fallen through, asking if he could borrow some cash so he could get the bus into town to meet someone who was going to give him a job. Same old, same old. Turning, she looked out the window to the garden and asked again, "When are you going to do the lawn?"

Placing some more food into his mouth, Dan looked back to her and, in a flash of brilliance to get her off his back, said, "If you see an East Indian guy wandering around here, he's going to do it."

He walked back down to his basement room and sat on the bed. My God, what a bizarre few days it had been, he thought, and it had all started because Daltrey had found a shoe. The old gay guy with the dog had said he was in for some cash, and if that was the case, he was definitely going straight out and treating his mum to a bigger fridge.

Dan lay back on the small bed that didn't fit his feet when he stretched out and wished he was as good at math as he was at electronics. Somehow all the circuitry and diodes made perfect sense to him, and sometimes the math that went with it did also, but this was different. He was getting another twenty-five percent if he went on a boat. What boat? he thought. Fifty thousand Big Macs was a lot, though, so maybe he'd not only get his mum a bigger fridge, but get himself a bigger bed—and his mother a quieter one so he wouldn't be awakened every other morning when the baker came over to unload his buns.

Chapter Twelve

It was nearly a quarter to eleven that night when Daltrey finally left Patrick's apartment and walked out to the road. He was alright, she thought. A bit kinky, yeah, but beyond that, he was okay. She had called and asked quite frankly if she could hang out in his bedroom again and had, of course, met no resistance. The four hours had passed quickly—four hours of listening to his incessant teasing and jokes as he plied her with food and drink while she waited, watching the road and the apartment opposite for something or someone—but no one had shown. Williams, the little prick, had lost him, told her he was a slippery one and had just vanished. That could happen, but the biggest problem was that Williams had told her the brother had stared right at him.

She walked along the road, the night air cooler now, and reached her car. Maybe, she thought, just maybe, if she went around to the biker woman's house, she could just go up to the door and say, "I was passing by and thought it would be cool if you could show me how to do that thing you did to me the last time we were alone." Or maybe she should just say nothing. But the woman was probably out of town or with another girl, tight like she was, someone she could grind and play with, making her come over and over just the way Daltrey had that night.

Daltrey unlocked the car and got in and was about to drive away when, in the distance, she saw the lights to Alla's apartment come on. A minute later, having used her infrared key, she was banging on Patrick's door. Another minute later, he answered in nothing but a robe. Without a word, Daltrey brushed past him and turned into the bedroom. Patrick, following, stood watching as she took hold of his telescope and sat on the edge of his bed.

Then, without shifting her eyes for a moment away from the apartment, Daltrey asked, "Why are you naked, Patrick?"

"I do live here. you know. I can wear what I like. Besides, I thought you were done."

Not responding, Daltrey stared through the telescope at Illya as he began pulling a suitcase from the bedroom closet and filling it with Alla's lingerie and clothes.

"I thought you were going to call when he showed up."

"You think I've got nothing better to do all night than spy on other people's apartments?"

Daltrey shot him a look. "Yeah, I've seen the photos."

For a moment Patrick began to blush, but in a flash said, "Well, we've all done things, haven't we?"

Daltrey turned to him for a second and smiled. He wasn't wrong, and if the light hadn't come on, maybe she would have plucked up enough courage to go knock on the biker woman's door and do exactly the same thing. Looking at Patrick, she answered, "You think so?"

Nodding to her, Patrick moved across the room and stood at the bottom of the bed. "Don't tell me it hasn't crossed your mind. I've seen the way you look at me."

Daltrey laughed and looked back into the high-powered telescope that Patrick used to watch the boats. He was right, and my God, if he only knew he had her pegged. It had been stuck in her mind, and she'd felt this aching in her groin from the moment she'd seen the photos of him taking it. After all, she hadn't taken anything in a while from anyone. Lately, the only person brave enough to give her a shot was Dan, and that was never going to happen. But turning the tables and giving it to Patrick instead of it being the other way around with whomever she let pick her up could be fun.

Maybe, she thought, as she watched Illya wander about the apartment and pose in a full-length mirror. Why not? She may never even find the big biker woman, after all, and she liked Patrick, there was no doubt about that. He was a nice guy, not slimy like you'd first expect after seeing his face smiling back at you from the rear of every other bus that ran around Vancouver.

Daltrey looked over at him and, with a smirk, she said, "Because you've been so good to me, maybe I'll come back later and bring my nightstick." Raising her eyebrows, she stood and began to walk toward him. Stopping at his side, she whispered, "I bet you'd like that, wouldn't you?"

Three minutes later, she was back outside, watching the lights in Alla's apartment go off. Slowly sinking back along the road, she opened the front foyer door of the high-end condo across the street and sank down, tucking herself in behind one of the lobby chairs, hiding in the semi-darkness. From her position, she had him in her sights from either direction. No matter if he came out on foot or in a vehicle, it was an easy tail. Minutes later, he was there, popping out of the elevator, trailing a large suitcase behind him. He opened the door and stepped outside.

******

Patrick sat on the edge of his bed and watched as Illya reached the sidewalk and began slowly making his way along the street, pulling a suitcase behind him. From a distance away, Daltrey appeared out of the darkness and began to follow.

He pulled his eye away from the telescope and rubbed it for a second. He couldn't believe his luck—this was more fun than researching a wealthy Asian businessman, stalking him for a week, then accidentally bumping into him in a coffee shop and talking him into buying a penthouse. Daltrey was sexy—goddamn it, she was—and a real life hot cop to boot. She'd sat in his bedroom all evening flirting with him, and then told him she was going to do him with her nightstick. Wow—Christmas had just come early! That would be hard to beat if it actually happened, and from the feeling he got and the look in her eyes when she'd offered it up as a joke, it quite easily could.

Grabbing his telescope and tripod, Patrick moved out of the bedroom, along the hall, and into his living room just in time to catch Illya moving along the darkness of the road and stopping to fiddle with one wheel of the suitcase at the top of the sloping entranceway to an underground car park.

Where the fuck was Daltrey? he wondered as he lifted his eye from the scope and scanned the darkness of the road. He looked back toward Illya as he reappeared without the suitcase from the car park's entrance and walked quickly away up toward the main road, disappearing around the corner.

He worked the telescope back along the road, scanning the sidewalk, cars, and hedgerows. Then, as if by chance, he spotted Daltrey as she appeared from behind the rear of a van and began to move quickly along the other side of the street toward the main road, only briefly pausing to look at what Patrick could only presume was the suitcase Alla's brother had left behind, out of sight, at the bottom of the gated entrance to the car park.

Pushing his eye to the scope, Patrick watched as Daltrey

moved on. He adjusted the scope, focusing it in on her ass, then her feet, and then back to her waist. God, she was sexy. If she had a gun, he couldn't see it, not in this dim light, and he certainly didn't see one on her when she was sitting on the side of his bed.

He continued to watch as she reached the end of the road, then stopped and waited, hiding in a corner. Alla's brother was out there somewhere—that was a certainty. She was looking for him without giving herself up, but by the looks of her body language, he was gone.

Patrick waited as a young girl passed and then watched as Daltrey turned and began to make her way back along the road, following the girl, and then vanished down the slope of the car park entranceway. Out of nowhere, from the darkness, Illya appeared, zipping across the top of the entranceway. He began to creep along the wall, disappearing into the shadows. Suddenly, a ball of flame washed a golden light across the dark walls of the entrance, and Daltrey ran out into the open, her hands desperately trying to extinguish the flames engulfing her face and body as Illya moved in fast from behind, lashing out with his feet, kicking her legs out from beneath her and sending Daltrey's flaming body crashing to the concrete floor. Then he was on her like a flash, standing above her, squirting fire from both hands as Daltrey writhed in unbelievable agony below him until she went still.

Chapter Thirteen

Illya walked quietly along the side street, listening to the noise of the sirens in the distance drifting off into the night air. He was pissed—a wheel on the bottom of his sister's suitcase had come loose and fallen off and holding it now at an angle to keep it moving straight was irritating his already aching wrist.

He reached the doorway to his new place and took the elevator up to the executive suite apartment where he had the girl, loaded with heroin, tied to the bed and held captive in the spare bedroom.

Illya looked at the spot where the wheel of the suitcase should be. What a waste of money, and it wasn't even a knockoff. He was sure the dentist had probably forked out a good few hundred for it. There were two other matching suitcases—each with good wheels—in the wardrobe back at the apartment with the view of the creek. But how the fuck could he go back there now after leaving a body on the doorstep?

He reached into his pocket and pulled out the nearly empty can of compressed oil he'd used to kill the girl and gave the suitcase wheel a little squirt. He was lucky the wheel had broken as it had at the top of the ramp, because if it hadn't, he wouldn't have seen that woman again. Digging deeper into his pocket, he found the pin that linked the wheel and its casing all together and bent down to look at the problem. It was fixable, but he'd definitely need another pair of hands to get the pin to line up properly through the center of the wheel.

Dragging the case down the hallway of the apartment, Illya sat back down on the sofa and lit a cigarette. Fuck, what an evening it had been. That woman with the ponytail, whoever she was, not that it mattered, and then worst of all, the wheel of his sister's suitcase coming right off and straining his right wrist, hurting it again.

Holding it with his left hand, he squeezed it tightly, digging the tips of his fingers deep into the joint. He felt a sensation of warm, soothing pain begin to spread down the length of his forearm like an old friend visiting and reminiscing, reminding him about the time a prick of a guard tried to remove his hand with a door.

It was bullshit, that woman following him and making him do that. If she hadn't been snooping in the background, he could have just grabbed a taxi after the wheel broke and saved his wrist, but taxis kept records of fares picked up here and dropped off there, and that was no good. Walking quietly through the night with the suitcase had been definitely the best way to go; it had been a good way to relax, breathe the still night air in, and stop here and there for a break to watch and cover his ears as the police, fire trucks, and ambulances screamed by.

Still holding his wrist, Illya leaned back and took another drag from his cigarette. So who was that woman? he thought. First, he saw her relaxing on the seawall, then she was at the casino, and then he saw her sneaking around behind the cars back at the old place where Alla used to have guys fuck her. Coincidence? Maybe at first. She could have been a local, but a local wouldn't have been following him along the road. No way. She had to be a cop or something, maybe immigration. She was one or the other, no doubt about it.

He pulled another can of pressurized lubricating oil from

his pocket and gave it a shake. Holding his cigarette in front, he sent out a quick burst of flame and stared at it. The woman had taken the bait and gone down the car ramp too easily, like a mouse going for the cheese sitting on a spring-loaded trap, except Illya was the deathblow. He had appeared out of the darkness, hitting her with a vial of fuel and squirting burning oil all over her face and body.

Reaching down, he gave a tiny squirt of oil into the suitcase's good wheel and gave it a spin. He looked at the broken one, then got up and walked to the spare bedroom and opened the door. The girl was there and still alive, albeit a little paler. She was pretty, Illya thought. Nice skin and lovely hair, even if it did have dried puke in it. Lifting her gently from the bed, Illya cut the cable ties from her wrists and sat her upright, the girl's eyes rolling in her head as her mind struggled to regain consciousness.

"Hey beautiful, you need to wake up."

The girl looked around the room, her pupils large like islands of black slate set in the blue of a crystalline lake.

"You need to wake up. Wake up! I need you to help me fix something."

******

It was six in the morning when Belinda Johal, owner and operator of Belinda's Limo Services, arrived proudly outside Dan's house and began his usual wait for this week's hot model to appear. It was an easy gig for an East Indian guy fresh in from New Delhi whose backward English logo and slogan, Letting Belinda take you there, had caught Sebastian's eye and thinking how novel it would be to have a female limo driver, Sebastian without the slightest idea

Belinda was really a man from New Delhi with actual and not manufactured bad English had immediately signed him up for the executive limo service contract with Slave.

Now, though, Belinda was getting tired of the late night calls from Mazzi to take weird people home from his apartment or to simply park his car in a tight spot.

At six thirty, Belinda was out again and knocking at Dan's door. A few minutes later, it opened, and a sleepy and confused Tricia stood looking out at the East Indian man.

"Hello?" she said.

Belinda stared at her, his grasp of the English language still so tenuous it was hard for him to get maybe fifty percent of what was being said at the best of times. "Dan is here for my pickup?" he asked.

Tricia looked at Belinda, wondering both why the lawn guy was here so early and why he was driving a shiny Mercedes. "Did Dan book you to do the lawn?"

"Yes."

Tricia looked at the time. She had only gotten up because she thought it was the baker at the door. "Isn't it a little early?"

Belinda nodded and smiled. He liked this woman. In fact, he liked all white-skinned Western women, except the ones around this city who dressed like men and seemed to hate him. This one was nice, and she was so beautiful. As he glanced at her hands, he noticed she had no wedding band and then imagined her on his arm, wearing a big white wedding dress, and all of his family around him, smiling and happy.

He looked around the house and then at the lawn that had not been cut for months and thought it would take him about a half hour to whip around with a pair of shears, and it would be done. It would be a good gesture, and from this, love would somehow blossom between them both. Looking up, Belinda smiled, revealing his huge white teeth, and asked, "I am able to come here later as gesture and cut your grass. Would you like this, madam?"

Tricia nodded. "Yes, please come back later."

Tricia smiled politely and began to turn. It was so early, and the baker had not shown as she'd hoped. All she wanted to do now was sleep. As she was about to close the door, Belinda called out to her as he looked again at the travel memo and searched for Dan's name.

"Please and thank you, I am needing Dan now. Can he come with me to Slave for the studio, please?

Then Tricia got it, all the cogs lining up at once in her tired brain. Turning around, she walked back in, along the corridor, then down the steep staircase that led to the door where her son lived and spent almost all his life, calling out as she drew closer, "Dan, get up! The guy's here to do the lawn, but he has to drop you at the studio first."

******

Dan sat in the back of the limousine, looking forward in a dazed state as Belinda watched him warily in the rear-view mirror.

"Are you on drugs?" he asked.

Dan looked back at him, bemused as to why he would be asked such a question.

"Why?"

"Because you are not wearing a shirt, my friend, and your nose, it is having bleeding."

Dan reached up and dabbed his nose. The guy was

right—it was. He looked at the man with his smiling white teeth, still trying to figure out why this East Indian guy had come around to do the lawn when he'd only mentioned it as a way of getting his mother off his back. He said, "I walked into a wall."

By five after seven, they had arrived. Dan stepped out into the dark car park that lay to the side of the freshly built studio, hastily constructed from the remnants of a corrugated iron fencing company that had recently gone under. Wary, he looked back toward Belinda and asked, "What am I supposed to do now?"

Leaning forward, Belinda said, "Go inside through the door."

Dan looked around. It was so dark he couldn't see anything, let alone a door. Turning back toward the car, he asked, "Where is it? I can't see it."

Belinda stared at the kid, thinking that if he was going to be his stepson, he would have to deal with his drug addiction before he introduced him to his family. "You are wearing sunglasses for your eyes. This is why you are not seeing," he said, his voice a mixture of bewilderment and sorrow.

Realizing he was still wearing the sunglasses he'd been wearing the night before, Dan reached up and pulled them off. He felt his nose, and fuck, it was still sore. No wonder he'd walked into the wall in a panic when his mother had woken him, screaming that the guy he'd told her was going to do the lawn was standing outside the door.

Squinting and wearing unlaced shoes with no socks, a baggy pair of jeans, no shirt, and with his sunglasses back on, Dan stepped inside the newly converted studio and took in all the activity. Why the hell were so many people working so fucking early in the morning? he thought. My God, it was just crazy. Couldn't they have started at eleven instead? Then he heard his name. It was the voice he remembered from the night his nose had been broken.

"Dan, Dan! I love it! You're late, but oh my God, wow! What a look!" Mazzi Hegan said as he marched over and grasped Dan's hand. Looking him up and down, his eyes wide open, he said, "No need for wardrobe! No need for makeup! No need for catering!"

Having no clue as to what this gay guy was talking about, Dan said, "The guy said he was going to do the lawn."

Mazzi stared at him for a moment, not quite understanding, then shook it off. He was too excited to worry about the small details, so all he said was, "Good, and remember—no food. It'll make your stomach bulge."

Seconds later, Dan was standing in front of a sofa full of people he had no clue about. The most important of them all stood and, holding out his hand, introduced himself.

"Dan, Malcolm Shart, chief vice President of advertising, BlueBoy—love your work."

Dan smirked. If there was one thing he did know about, it was condoms. He'd used enough—on his own, that is, except for that time in the park, but the guide dog had fucked that up. Lifting up his sunglasses so he could see the man's face properly, he said, "I love your work as well. You ever need a tester, I'm your man."

Interrupting, Mazzi stepped in.

"Doesn't he look sensational? Dan, today Malcolm has requested you double up and do a photo shoot with Marsha."

"Love it," Dan replied quickly, even though he had absolutely no clue who Marsha was or what they were talking about.

After two hours of waiting and no food or drink, Dan was

on the stage surrounded by more green cloth than he had ever seen in life. The lights all around him were so unbelievably bright and fucking hot that it felt like summer. Looking over to Mazzi Hegan, who was now sitting on a chair, he called out, "Am I supposed to be in a field or something?"

Then he saw her staring at him. He knew her face from somewhere. She was the most beautiful girl he'd ever seen in his life. Her hair was long and wavy, and it looked as though all the beauty in this world had been condensed into her face to form perfection. She walked slowly toward him, her long legs seemingly flowing away from her incredible figure. Never taking her eyes from Dan's, she held her assistant's hand as she made her way up the short steps to the stage.

Breathing in her perfume as she reached him, Dan stared into her beautiful eyes and heard her whisper, "God, you're hot!"

Dan answered, "Yeah I am." And he was—he was so hot his balls were starting to itch.

"Hi," she said, leaning in some two inches from his face, her voice like velvet, and her aroma enveloping Dan's every bodily sense. "I'm Marsha."

Dan stared at her, for a moment unsure if he'd met her before, and then remembering he hadn't had a bath or anything since blasting himself at Mazzi Hegan's place. Beginning to worry if he was starting to smell, he said, "I'm Dan."

Marsha leaned in again. "I know who you are, Dan. I've seen the photos."

Then suddenly her robe was off, and except for the craziest pair of underwear he'd ever seen, she was naked next to him. Grabbing his head, Marsha puckered up her bright red lips and swiftly forced a kiss hard on Dan's open mouth, as her hands simultaneously groped and stroked his sweaty body.

Pulling herself away, she stared into Dan's eyes and gently licked the sweat from her fingers.

"God you're hot," she whispered. "I want you. God, I want you. Fuck me, Dan. I want you to fuck me."

Dan's nose hurt from the way this bombshell kept kissing it and wondered if it was beginning to bleed again in all the heat. He brought his hand up to it, checking, and then looked down at his crotch to see an erection so big that he thought if he didn't blow any second, he'd pop the buttons off the front of his jeans.

Marsha moved in again, this time briefly kissing his neck before moving down to lick the sweat from Dan's chest. Then in one long, swift movement, she drew herself back up from his chest, moved along his neck, and launched her tongue off his chin with the ferocity of a ski jumper.

"Oh my God —yes, yes!" Mazzi Hegan screamed as Dan looked down and noticed for the first time that there was actually a camera. "That was just fantastic!"

Dan looked to Marsha, her eyes still smoldering, and asked, "Are they filming us?"

But Marsha wasn't listening and came at him again with torturous whispers, kisses, eye stares, and chest, leg, back, and stomach fondling which assailed Dan's virgin senses. Then Marsha's long, silky tongue probed deep within his left ear and he couldn't take anymore, as all his resistance melted away and unloaded itself into Mazzi Hegan's silver silk underpants which he'd been wearing since the weekend. With his right leg shaking Dan stood there with his eyes closed, as Marsha right on cue pulled her tongue from his ear and left the stage. Fuck, he thought as he opened his eyes again and looked discreetly at his crotch and then out to the crowd of technicians and production people to see if anyone had noticed.

Now that his body had let go after Marsha had oozed sex all over him, he was starving. He looked around the stage. Everyone here was eating—except him. This was bullshit. He called out to Mazzi or anyone that would listen, "Hey, can I get some food?"

Hearing this, Mazzi turned. "Oh, you can't eat, Dan. We've got to keep your stomach flat. Two hours, and then you can eat."

Dan looked around again at everyone eating sandwiches. Why the fuck not? he wondered. His stomach never got fat, even after he'd missed a meal and then eaten at Burger King right after slamming home two Big Macs and two large fries.

He called back to Mazzi as he delicately popped one of the pastries he'd had delivered earlier from his favorite bakery into his mouth. "What about Marsha?"

Mazzi wiped his mouth with a napkin and gently folded it into a tiny little square. Then he said, "Marsha doesn't eat, darling. She's a model. Now stick with it. We'll get you some water, and Marsha'll be back soon. In the meantime, we're going to get a few close-ups."

Fuck me! Dan thought. He'd had enough of standing up on this stupid platform, sandwiched in green like a hot dog in a lettuce sandwich. He wanted to go. He was hot and sticky, he'd come in his pants, and all he wanted to do now was tell them all to fuck off and get the fuck out of there and head straight to Mickey D's for an Egg McMuffin.

Mazzi Hegan sat on his chair, watching and waiting. He had Dan up there now, and he'd gotten the beauty shots—the sexy stuff from that overpaid slut who barely had a nicer ass than him. The guys who liked that sort of thing would be happy. What he needed now, though, was a studio version of what he'd seen that night in his apartment block's elevator. He needed Dan raw and desperate, like the caged animal he knew he could be. Starving him and cooking him up there in the lights on the stage for hours with just enough water to stop him from dying seemed to be working.

Standing, he walked over to the stage and called up to Dan. "Dan, you're doing fantastic, baby, just fantastic. Now we're going to bring in another model, and we're going to do exactly the same action we did earlier."

Dan reached down and picked up another bottle of water from the edge of the stage and poured it over his head. He was awake now. Marsha had certainly seen to that. Another model, he thought. Bring her on, but this time, he'd show her some moves, and it would be him doing the groping, kissing, and licking up of all the sweat. Then he saw the next model—and it was a guy.

Phillipe Tu La Monde strutted his stuff through the newly converted corrugated iron factory as though he were the top billing in Milan and made his way to the green screen stage. He felt good and sexy, and at the last moment, he'd decided he couldn't come out of his trailer without covering his chest in glitter.

He reached the stage, blew Mazzi Hegan and Sebastian a kiss, draped his arms around Dan, kissed him on the lips and received a fist to his jaw so hard that when he hit the floor, he thought he'd lost every porcelain crown on his perfect white teeth.

Mazzi Hegan jumped straight off his chair, and the first words out of his mouth as he looked at his camera guy were,

"Keep shooting!" This was perfect. He was almost there— Dan was about to break. The sheer volume of tension and confusion emanating from his whole being was incredible.

Phillipe Tu La Monde sat up and looked around, dazed and confused. Then he heard Dan talking to him from above and saw him pointing toward Mazzi Hegan. "If you want to kiss a guy," he said, "go talk to him."

Phillipe Tu La Monde looked over toward Mazzi Hegan, unable to believe what had just happened. He knew of Slave's reputation and its ability to produce incredible photo campaigns, but my God, was this what it took? Confused and holding his jaw, he stood back up. "He just hit me!" he shouted to Mazzi Hegan.

Mazzi moved closer and called back to him in French. "Faites-le vous aimer!" Then in English. "Make him love you."

Holding his jaw, Phillipe Tu La Monde looked back toward Dan. Dan's body language said, Come near me, and I'll kill you. Mazzi Hegan screamed out again, "Make him love you! Make him love you!"

Phillipe Tu La Monde stepped forward, giving Dan the look that had worked so often in all the gay clubs he'd ever been to. Dan stepped back, and Phillipe Tu La Monde moved forward. Dan stepped back again, closer to the edge of the small stage, and looked behind him to the string of glaring lights below. Phillipe Tu La Monde came closer, his soft, pampered, manicured hands scratching out like a tiger in the hot studio air. Snarling, his top lip now bigger from the punch than any amount of collagen injected into them could ever make it, he said to Dan, "I know you want me."

Dan looked behind him. With all the lighting gear below, there was no room for him to jump.

Phillipe Tu La Monde continued to scratch the air. "You want to fuck me, don't you, Dan?"

Dan answered as honestly as he ever had. "No—I want you to fuck off."

"No, you don't. I know you want me. You're hard, Dan, you're hard. I know you're hard. Come to me, feel me, fuck me, Dan. Fuck me."

That was it—he'd had enough. He could take no more. In an explosion of temper, Dan moved fast, collecting half the glitter from Phillipe Tu La Monde's sweaty chest on his arm as he pushed past and headed toward the steps.

"Enough!" he screamed. "Enough of this fucking gay shit!"

Like lightning, Mazzi Hegan grabbed his camera and leaped onto the stage as Dan, angry and crazed stood trapped between him and Phillipe Tu La Monde at the edge of the stage.

Chapter Fourteen

It was around midday when Charles Chuck Chendrill got a hysterical call from Sebastian that there was an emergency. Dan had lost it during a photo shoot.

He pulled his car out onto the road and headed down Hastings toward the old corrugated steel factory. What on earth were these guys doing there anyway? And what could Dan have done to warrant bringing him in again at a thousand bucks a day?

Parking his car outside, he slammed the door, glancing at Mazzi Hegan's red Ferrari as he headed past the trucks toward the factory's entranceway. Opening it, he felt the heat from the lights inside hit him as he stepped in and walked half-blinded along the old concrete factory floor. Stopping to grab a piece of ham and cheese pizza from a box on the service table, he headed in the direction of the green screen and spotted Mazzi Hegan at the front by the stage and Sebastian sitting quietly with his dog, watching.

The place had changed, he thought. What had once been a busy hub of activity was now nearly empty. He stopped by Sebastian and, still looking around, said, "I didn't know this place had gone bust."

The last time he'd been here was to arrest a Polish guy for the attempted murder of his mother-in-law, and when he'd met the woman after she'd gotten out of the hospital, he'd understood why.

Sebastian looked up at Chendrill and smiled. "Thank God you're here, Chuck. The place just went crazy."

Chendrill looked around. Crazy how? No one was doing

anything. In fact, from what he could see, some of the technicians seemed to actually be asleep. He looked back down at Sebastian and said, "How?"

Sebastian moved his dog into a better position on his lap. "Mazzi's guy totally lost it and punched out this model from Paris. I'm worried he's going to come down here and attack me."

"Why would he want to come at you?"

"I don't know...people just do that sometimes. They go crazy. You were a cop...you should know."

"Sounds like you need a bodyguard, not a private investigator."

Sebastian scoffed. Waving his right arm in the air before putting it back on top of his dog, he said, "I'm not the bodyguard type, darling."

Chendrill stared up at the stage with its walls of green. Mazzi Hegan was snapping away at a guy covered in oil and wearing a pair of bright silver underpants. "Is that Dan?" he asked.

Sebastian nodded as Dan turned and stared at a fat guy by the stage double-fisting a huge slice of pizza.

Chendrill laughed. "I didn't recognize him."

Sebastian nodded and smiled. "It's Daniel. Bless him, I don't think he knows what to think of it all. I'd like to say it's been fun for him, but Mazzi's been tormenting him all day."

Chendrill smiled. When Sebastian had called and said it was an emergency, this was the last thing he'd expected.

"Mazzi brought in a slut to get him all worked up," Sebastian continued, "and then sent in this gorgeous guy to mess with his head."

Chendrill looked from Sebastian to Dan, who was still

staring at the fat guy with the pizza.

"Now he's starving him and using that fat guy actor he hired to torment him, and from the looks of things, he's even got you involved."

Chendrill looked down to the pizza in his hand, back to Sebastian, and then to the service table loaded with more boxes of pizza. "Why doesn't he just walk over there and get a piece?"

"He can't," Sebastian answered, placing his hand on his chest. "Mazzi's screwed his shoes to the floor."

Smiling, Chendrill looked up and watched the frustration ooze out of Dan as the fat guy moved in closer and placed the pizza box just out of reach on the edge of the stage.

Sebastian lifted a bottle of water to his lips and took a drink. "We're onto a good thing with this kid, Chuck, but I think he's going to need looking after."

Chendrill knew exactly what was coming, and he had no interest. "I'm not a babysitter, Sebastian," he said, cutting him short. "It's not what I do."

Sebastian looked out across the stage at Mazzi Hegan snapping away, oblivious to the fact that Chendrill was even there. Smiling, he turned back to Chendrill and said, "You'll be at full rate, and I'll let you use Mazzi's Ferrari."

******

By eight in the evening, Chendrill was back sitting at Dan's favorite table in McDonald's, watching him as he slammed home a triple double-decker with fries.

"How come you get to use the Ferrari?" Dan asked.

Chendrill shrugged. "They like me."

Dan lifted his burger to his lips, but before eating it, he

looked at his feet and said, "You know he's ruined my shoes!"

Chendrill laughed and stared back without speaking. Then he said, "Sebastian said you punched the guy out?"

Dan stuck the burger into his mouth and took a chunk, saying straight back with his mouth full, "Well, he shouldn't have kissed me."

"He was only acting—that's what they do."

Dan shook his head. "Let me tell you, he wasn't acting, and neither was the first chick."

"Really."

Dan waited a second and then stuffed some more burger into his chops, followed by some fries. "Yeah, really."

"You can tell?"

Dan nodded and stared at Chendrill. He could, there was no doubt about it.

"How? I'm telling you they're acting."

Dan shook his head. "She wasn't acting."

"How do you know?"

Dan smirked. "Because she asked me to come back to her hotel and fuck her."

Chendrill stared at him and began to laugh. "Marsha? I-just-got-voted-the-sexiest-woman-in-the-world   Marsha? She asked you back?"

Grinning, Dan nodded.

"When did she do that? When you were up on that stage?"

Dan nodded and raised his eyebrows again. "Up on the stage…and again at the end before she left, but there's only one problem."

Chendrill waited, then asked, "Which is?"

"She wants me to wear the silver underpants I stole from

Mazzi Hegan while I'm doing it."

******

Chendrill drove Mazzi Hegan's red Ferrari along Burrard Street and swung a left into the Sutton Place Hotel.

"If you whip the clutch on a tight turn like that, you can get smoke off the back tires," Dan said to him from the passenger seat as he pulled up. A doorman opened the car door, and Dan got out. Turning back to Chendrill, he said, "You going to wait? If she's anything like she was on the stage, I could be back here in about two minutes."

Chendrill nodded. He didn't doubt it—he'd seen Marsha in magazines before. She was hot—not just hot hot, but real smoking hot—and if he was Dan, he would never have stopped off for a Big Mac and fries with a cheeseburger chaser before whipping over to her swanky hotel to do the deed.

He looked back up at Dan, now in a plain T-shirt and the same jeans and his shoes with screw holes in the heels that he'd been wearing when he'd been dragged out of his bed by his mum in the morning, and asked, "What about the silver underpants?"

Dan grinned. "I've still got them on."

Chendrill laughed then said, "I've got things to do, so think of Margaret Thatcher and tell her she's beautiful so I don't have to come back and pick you up in ten minutes."

******

Marsha was waiting in the bar with her assistant when he got there, and as soon as she saw him, she said, "You know

125

you've got ketchup on your shirt?"

Dan looked down. She was right, and suddenly he was pissed at Chendrill because he was supposed to be looking after him. He said, "Be thankful I've got one on. I wasn't wearing one this morning when they picked me up."

Marsha looked at him, then back around the room. She was the center of attention and knew it. Now this hot guy with the broken nose was here with her, and everything about him said he couldn't give a shit. Truth was, she'd been beginning to wonder if he was ever going to show at all. "You got lost, right?" she asked.

"No, I was hungry, so I went to a restaurant," Dan answered as he took a seat at the bar right next to hers.

Marsha raised her eyes. "Really, you ate? Wow, what did you have?"

"Beef."

"Really? That's from a cow, right?" she asked and looked around the bar to see who was looking at her. It had been a while since she'd eaten beef, and when she had, she remembered wondering how the people who killed the things managed to get the cheese out. Then, remembering something a girl who'd wanted to wear her tight leggings to a club one night had said to her, she said, "What about that sickness you can get?"

Dan looked back at her and laughed. He knew exactly what she was talking about—he'd seen a documentary about mad cow disease while waiting at the vet's with his mum after almost killing the neighbor's cat while he was supposed to be looking after it.

He shook his head. Beef was not a problem for him. "I'm not concerned about it," he replied.

Marsha looked around again and then at Dan's broken

nose, his chest, and his tight jeans. Staring Dan straight in the eyes, she asked, "So have you got them?"

And smiling back, Dan answered, "I'm wearing them."

******

The penthouse suite at the Sutton was nice, Dan thought, nicer than his basement suite at his mum's, but not as nice as Mazzi Hegan's suite in Yaletown a few blocks to the east. Dan walked around the place, looking at the paintings on the wall.

"Nice place," he said.

"For today. I'll be in London tomorrow, and there's another fantastic place I stay when I'm there, right by the palace." Then she said, "That's a Money copy. A clothes designer I know in Milan has the original."

Dan turned and said, "You mean Monet? My Mum's got one just like it."

"Yeah, Money, that's what I said."

Marsha smiled and moved herself closer, then closer still, saying, "You like to tease, don't you?" Her lips touched his neck gently as she spoke. "Why don't we go to my bedroom?"

She stood at the bottom of her bed and began to slowly take off her clothes. Dan watched as she seductively dropped each item, one by one, to the floor until there was nothing left to the imagination. Leaning back, Marsha sat down, then pulled herself up the bed and lay there, her breasts slightly hidden in the soft silk sheets. Looking back at Dan, she said, "Come to me."

This was what she wanted—and seeing Dan in Mazzi Hegan's photo pitch material for the shoot was the only real reason she'd taken the condom job in the first place.

He leaned forward and climbed up along the bed that was bigger than his room. Kneeling at her feet, he stretched upward and began to take off his T-shirt.

Marsha stared at him and said, "Take off your jeans."

He took them off and, now only in Mazzi Hegan's silver underpants, climbed on top of Marsha's naked body. She pulled his head down and began to kiss him hard, her tongue probing deep into his mouth and Dan's into hers.

Gasping for air and breathing deeply, Marsha pulled away. "Have you been eating gherkins?" she asked.

He had, in fact. The triple-pounder with cheese had had a particularly large one, and it was beginning to repeat so much Dan could still taste it himself. He moved toward Marsha, slowly kissing her neck and licking her ears. He could feel himself growing even bigger now, stretching Mazzi Hegan's underpants to the limit.

Marsha called out to him and, grabbing his hand, moved it down to her crotch. "Touch me there."

Dan moved his fingers, feeling the softness between her legs. As he kissed her neck, he could hear her breath drawing in and out as she became more and more excited.

Then she said, "No, there."

Dan moved his hand.

Marsha spoke gently into his ear. "No, not there—there."

Dan continued feeling her below.

She whispered to him again. "No...move it up a bit."

Dan responded.

"No, not like that. Yes...no...no. Yes, move it like that— no, move it a bit over. No, not there, up a bit. No, down. There, yes! No, to the side. There, yes, there...like that, like that."

Moving Dan's head down, she guided his mouth gently to her soft breasts.

"Lick my nipple, my nipple, yes. Now the other one, yes. Now keep your hand moving down there—not there, not there, no…back where you were. Yes, now bite my other nipple and move your other hand a bit up to the other side."

After twenty minutes had passed, and Dan's hand, arm, mouth, neck, and tongue were about to have a seizure, Marsha pushed him away and said the words he'd been waiting to hear from a woman since he'd first seen a picture of her in one of his mother's lingerie magazines and knocked one out to it when he was thirteen.

"Fuck me, Dan, fuck me."

Dan pulled back as Marsha reached out, grabbed a complimentary BlueBoy from her bag, and stared up at him.

Dan hadn't a clue, but whatever he'd been doing must have been working because this was it. He was in. He was there, and he was going to get it at last—and with the girl who'd just been voted the most beautiful woman on this planet.

Marsha leaned back and opened her legs. Dan climbed on top of her, trying his hardest to stop his body from shaking and having what had happened to him on stage happen again. He began to panic, but then he remembered the calm words of counsel Chendrill had passed on as he'd sat there in his blue Hawaiian shirt at the wheel of Mazzi Hegan's Ferrari, and in his mind, he began the only chant that could save him. Margaret Thatcher, Margaret Thatcher, Margaret Thatcher.

Dan let her image take over his subconscious and his mind. He repeated it over and over—Margaret Thatcher, Margaret Thatcher, Margaret Thatcher. Seeing her there before him with her bouffant hair and pokey face. Then out of the blue, just as he felt himself growing large enough to rupture the BlueBoy and felt Marsha guiding him into her, he said Chendrill's mantra out loud.

"Margaret Thatcher, you're so beautiful."

Marsha froze and stopped what she was doing. "I'm sorry?"

Dan looked down at her as he hovered there above her, propped up on his elbows, his whole body shaking, Mazzi Hegan's underpants halfway down his legs.

"Did you just call me Margaret Thatcher?"

Dan shook his head. "No."

Moving away, Marsha began to push Dan off. "Yes, you did." She moved, kicking Dan right off and spat out, "My name's Marsha, okay? Marsh-aaaa. Not fucking Margaret, okay? No one calls me Margaret. I'm Marsha, Marrrrshaaa!"

And that was that.

Chapter Fifteen

About two minutes after Chendrill had left the hotel, news of Daltrey filtered its way far enough through the grapevine to reach him, and the news of her passing hit him hard.

Burned to death in an alley in the posh part of town. Fuck, what a way to go, but why? What was going on? The word was an accelerant had been used, and they'd found traces of oil on her body and in the alley, along with her gun and ID where her body was found. Why? he thought as he turned the corner and headed down toward the bridge across the creek coming back from Kitsilano.

Daltrey was dead. What harm had she ever done to anyone? She was a cop, yes, and she sometimes caused trouble, upset people, sent them to a holiday camp called prison for a bit, but to be burned to death? That was just wrong. He pulled Mazzi Hegan's car up to the side of the road and just stared as people passed by, looking at him and the car. It felt good to be driving the Ferrari—real good—but he'd have been happier to ride a bicycle for the rest of his days if it meant Daltrey could have still been around.

He pushed down the clutch with his left foot and slapped the car into first, then spun the wheels and hit it. Dan was right—the tires smoked if you wanted them to, no problem, but from the looks he got from everyone around, he knew it would be the last time he did that.

The alley was short and tight with barely enough space for two cars. Chendrill got out of the Ferrari and walked to the end. The electric gate was now open for the day, but he was sure it would have been closed when Daltrey had burned to death here. He looked to the floor, the concrete still charred where they must have found her body.

It was the third murder by burning he could remember in the last year—the first a drug dealer in the alley and the other the guy on the creek a few days back. Daltrey had been looking into that one and must have gotten close to the suspect to have been torched herself.

Who had she been after? He thought back to all the conversations they'd had the last time they'd met, but came up with nothing. She played her cards close to her chest. But she had dated Dan—how crazy was that? Dan the man, up there now in a swanky hotel getting it on with Miss Long Legs of the Year, Marsha.

Chendrill looked to the ground and then around to the sea of condos behind him. Maybe two hundred of them looked down over the alley. Daltrey had died at around eleven. Someone somewhere up there must have been looking out their window and seen something. He'd been told the call to 911 had come from a motorist coming in from a night on the town. Despite the smoldering, the driver had still nearly run over her lifeless body.

When he was a cop, he'd have knocked on every one of those apartment and condo doors. He walked back out of the alley and looked up to the main street at the top of the road. Up there somewhere, there'd be a camera, he thought. He walked up to the road and looked at the shops that spread out in both directions—a dentist showing off a set of huge, perfect white teeth in its window, a nail salon, another dentist with more teeth than his neighbor and showing before and after photos, then a financial advisory service bordering on a Ponzi scheme. He stopped to check his own teeth in the reflection of the plate-glass window, then moved on and found another nail salon and a convenience store.

Chendrill entered the store and smiled at the elderly Japanese guy behind the counter. He picked up some gum and floss, glanced at the cheap CCTV camera aimed at the doorway, and asked, "What's the chance of me having a look at your footage from that camera for yesterday evening?"

"You police?" asked the store owner.

Chendrill shook his head. "Once upon a time, I was. Now I'm a private investigator."

"This not cinema," said the store owner. "Very busy."

Chendrill looked around the shop. It was empty and had little chance of being any different any time in the near future. Looking back to the owner, he held up some mints, adding them to the gum and floss, and said, "Okay, how much do all these cost? Fifty bucks?"

Sitting on a swivel chair with a broken backrest, Chendrill watched the footage from the night before on the black and white six-inch screen of a monitor that should have been thrown away in the eighties. Over a hundred people had come into the store. Barely visible through the door, five had passed the shop in the period from nine onward, and around eleven, four had passed by—that was about five minutes before the fire trucks and cops had started to move past.

There was a woman, a couple, and a guy in track pants just back from holiday who was having trouble with his suitcase. Chendrill stared at the pictures and snapped a still shot with his phone of each person who headed away from the alley. He thanked the owner who'd just hit him for fifty and quickly headed back along the road toward the alley, only to discover Mazzi Hegan's Ferrari was gone.

******

Patrick sat on a chair and lifted his head from the eyepiece of his telescope. He could not remember ever being this upset, having puked continually throughout the night as he'd sat and watched the events unfold as the fire brigade and ambulance service and finally the police had sealed off the alley as a crime scene. Now this guy who drove a red Ferrari and looked like Thomas Magnum was sniffing around and staring up at him in his window.

Fuck, Patrick thought, he should just go to the police and tell them everything that had happened. But then what? All the questions would start. Why do you have a telescope in your room? Why was Daltrey in your room? Why was she talking to you? Where were the photos the prostitute had taken that Daltrey had found? Why hadn't he called it in when he saw Daltrey burning to death?

Why hadn't he? It was a good question.

Patrick looked at his hands, and he could see they were shaking. It must have been instinct, intelligence overriding natural human response. A car had come, and he could see the driver calling it in, and minutes later he'd heard the sirens screaming out in the distance, growing closer by the second. He didn't need to get involved. The guy would be caught— there was a system in place for that. But deep down, he knew he was dirty. And the more he looked at it, the worse it became.

After all, he knew the answer this guy down below was searching for, along with the name of the people who'd towed his car. He knew who had killed this girl who had only minutes before whispered in his ear. He'd watched her stalking the man and then watched him stalk her and stand above her, pouring flames down upon her long, brown hair and her beautiful, smooth skin. Then he'd watched him calmly walk away, trundling his suitcase behind him.

Patrick put his hands on his face. He stood then sat and then stood again, watching Chendrill standing in the alley, staring at the floor where Daltrey had died. Patrick knew he was in deep, so deep, and every minute he waited before calling the police got him in deeper. He and his celebrity status as a realtor was sinking. Slowly, he moved to the window and stood there with the curtains pulled back, looking out, before turning and heading to the door.

Chendrill stood and waited in the alley. He'd seen the man standing there in the window watching. Going with his gut, he knew he would be coming down, and as soon as he saw Patrick appear from around the corner, he knew who he was.

"They towed your Ferrari" were Patrick's first words as he drew closer.

Chendrill smiled and said, "You've come all the way from up there to tell me that?"

Patrick nodded, his face smiling.

"That's nice of you. You saw them pull it?"

Patrick nodded again. Chendrill dug deeper. "Tell me, what else have you seen from up there?"

Patrick hesitated for a moment and then asked, "Are you a cop?"

Chendrill shook his head. "How many cops drive a Ferrari? I'm a private investigator."

Patrick stared at him for a moment, working him out, this guy with long hair and a moustache dressed in a Hawaiian shirt. "Well, then it must pay well," he said.

"Not as much as selling houses. A client of mine lets me use the car."

Patrick stared at him, liking him instantly. Obviously, the three hundred thousand he was spending on advertising every year was paying off.

"Same as the guy in the '70s TV series. You kind of look like him."

Chendrill liked that one and wished he had the car here now so he could get in and come back with a quick one-liner like, "Yeah, but he was an actor!" But he didn't. The car was gone, so instead he said, "Why don't you hire me? Then I can help you sort out this problem that's troubling you."

******

They sat in the corner of a small bar, thanked the waitress, and both stared discreetly at her backside as she walked away. Then Chendrill came straight out with it.

"So you saw something going on that night, and you think you may know the person who did it, but if you let it out that you know him, it could have bad repercussions for you?"

Patrick couldn't believe it. How the fuck could this guy know that just like that?

And the strange thing was that Chendrill didn't. It was a wild guess based on the guy's nervousness yet his willingness to come down and speak to a stranger.

"If I did, could I be in trouble?" Patrick asked.

Chendrill shrugged. "If you had a reason for wanting the girl dead, you could be. Have you spoken to the police?"

Patrick shook his head. This guy, this PI had a way about him. He asked the right questions, but didn't give a shit about the answers. "They rang my door buzzer," he said.

"But you didn't answer."

Patrick shook his head.

"No? Why?"

Patrick paused, his mind whirring, then took a deep breath. "The girl who died, I'm sure you know, was a cop. Her name is Daltrey. She was in my bedroom just before she was murdered."

Fuck me, Chendrill thought, not another one. First Dan, and now this guy. Daltrey did get around. He took a deep breath and asked, "You were lovers?"

Patrick shook his head again, then said, "I wish! She was using my place to watch an apartment opposite. I was in a café, and she approached me. Next thing I knew, she was in my bedroom, but not for sex. She just wanted to keep an eye on some apartment."

Chendrill smiled. That was Daltrey, moving outside the system, thinking outside the box. "Do you know the apartment she was watching?" he asked.

Patrick nodded again then paused for a moment before saying, "And I think I saw the guy who set her on fire. It was the same guy she was watching."

Chendrill sat there for a moment, taking it all in, remembering Daltrey and the way she could smile and get you to do things you wouldn't usually do for other people. Then he asked, "What was the last thing she said to you before she left?"

And with those words, Patrick's walls came tumbling down.

******

Chendrill took a cab down to the towing company and walked through the security gate and past the cabin with its line of people waiting to pay money to the pricks who'd managed to ruin their evening. He spotted Mazzi Hegan's red Ferrari at the back of the lot and moved toward it. Opening the door with his key, he sat inside and waited, watching the wannabe Hells Angel with an attitude at the gate showing off his fat gut and tattoos to the drivers as he checked their release papers before setting them free.

He shouldn't have gotten himself into this situation with a client's car, but had he not, he would never have met Patrick, Vancouver's Premier Realtor, as he liked to call himself. This man had his own kinky secret, a secret which had come spilling out along with everything else that had gone down that evening Daltrey died and in the months before. Patrick was now a terrified man who told lies for a living, spitting out half-truths as he tried to maneuver his way around questions delivered to him by a man trained to spot just that.

There was more to it, though—a lot more. More than blackmail in the making from the beautiful whore who was now lying in a hospital. Daltrey had been, after all, using the same tactic to get use of Patrick's apartment so she could watch the same place he'd been visiting and getting off to every evening through his telescope. She hadn't given Patrick back the photos but had instead left it open, making it a game. It was the way she operated.

Chendrill waited, watching as the tow truck driver with the fat gut lifted the gate for the second time and left it open while he checked the next car's papers. Chendrill quickly started the engine and crept Mazzi Hegan's Ferrari forward. As soon as the time was right, he hit the gas and gunned it at an angle, straight under the open gate, out of the yard, and across the sidewalk, sending the Ferrari sideways as he hit the road out front.

Fuck 'em, he thought as he reached the end of the road and saw the tow truck driver standing in the middle of the road in his rearview mirror. Pulling out onto the main causeway, Chendrill laughed and said out loud, "You steal my car, I steal it back."

Chapter Sixteen

Ralph "The Thief" Ditcon knew he had a nickname, but had no idea why. In his eyes, his exemplary career as a detective was what any police officer in the world would be proud of. Truth was, on paper it was nothing less than an incredible record of thirty murder convictions. He had what was seen as an uncanny ability to step in and solve the crime of any investigation that other not-so-special policemen were stalled on.

As the news of Daltrey's terrible death rippled through the ranks of the Vancouver police force, Ralph Ditcon—now in his fifty-second year—had a crime to solve, and his incredible record and the powers that be deemed him the one man capable of getting to the bottom of it all and bringing the persons involved to justice.

Daltrey's apartment was clean and tidy, Ditcon thought as he wandered about the place, lifting her clothes. The curtains in the rooms were all pulled back to precisely the same width at either end of every window. All of her towels hung equally spaced, centered on each rail. There was not a speck of dirt anywhere in the place. He remembered her and the fantastic work she'd done putting together her first murder case against a suspect whose wife had disappeared while swimming off the beach at the Spanish Banks. After five weeks of sniffing and digging, Daltrey had found the woman in a shallow grave in the woods close to a cottage the couple had rented the year before, a hundred miles away. That's when Ralph Ditcon had stepped in. Using his criminal judicial expertise and Daltrey's notes, he'd brought the case to a successful conclusion.

The next time Ralph "The Thief" Ditcon had stepped in to help wrap up a case involving the suspicious suicide of a young man in his early twenties, Daltrey had no notes.

"They're up here," she'd said, tapping the side of her head, and as she walked away, she'd smiled and called out, "Go ahead, finish. Once you've worked it all out, give me a call, and I'll come in and help you with the arrest."

Six months later, when Ralph "The Thief" Ditcon had gotten nowhere and taken some time off to sit with his toes in the sand on the beach of Salt Spring Island, Daltrey had stepped in and arrested the young man's best friend. And from then on, that had been exactly how she'd rolled—on her own and with the jigsaw left undone till the last second.

It was late in the evening when Ditcon got his first lead. A call had come in from a local tow truck company that a car towed from the alley where Daltrey had been murdered had been stolen from their compound under suspicious circumstances. Obviously, something in the car had been important. Whoever it was had something to hide, and within two hours after a very upset and irate Mazzi Hegan had been pulled from his silk sheets, Ditcon had Chendrill sitting behind a desk, answering questions in an interrogation room and Chendrill wasn't holding back.

"You are so far off base you may as well be in China."

Ditcon stared at him, trying his hardest to look as though he was in control of the situation. "So why were you there?" he asked.

Chendrill smiled. God, this guy was stupid, he thought. If he didn't have a case handed to him on a plate, he didn't have a clue. "Why do you think I was there?"

"You were involved."

141

Chendrill shook his head, laughed, and said, "I'm more involved than you are right now."

"You're telling me you're investigating Daltrey's death?"

"No, I'm telling you I'm not investigating her death, but from spending just ten minutes at the crime scene, I already know because you've got me here that I'm further down the road than the detective in charge of the case."

Ralph stared at him, this smug prick who had left the force because he couldn't handle it. "What makes you think that?" he asked.

"Because you've got me sitting here in this chair."

"So why did you steal the car?"

"You can't steal your own vehicle. They stole the car from me. I went and reclaimed it."

Ralph "The Thief" Ditcon waited, wanting to pull a cigarette from his pocket and light one up, but remembering he'd quit smoking, then he said, "You need to start thinking about what trouble you could be in here,"

Chendrill sat back in the chair and stared back at this detective who did not have a clue. "The only person around here who's in trouble is you, and that's because you and I both know you don't have a clue as to what you're doing."

******

It was five in the morning when Chendrill stepped out of the police station on Main Street on Vancouver's east side and heard the man's voice as he passed by, asking him in a whisper if he wanted hash. The man's face was tight and as wrinkled from the crack and crystal meth he'd forced through his system. God damn it, Chendrill thought. It was shameless, selling drugs right outside the police station. He looked along the street toward the homeless, lost souls on Hastings and began to walk. The man's voice whispered still, trying to earn what he needed to get his next hit.

Only in Vancouver would you get that, Chendrill thought. He hated it. In fact, he hated the whole situation so much it had caused him to resign. How could you be a policeman and drive right past pimps, underage whores, and drug dealers spewing heroin and shit onto the streets from their alleys not more than a block from the police station where you worked? It was a hypocrisy he could no longer live with, but the moment he had walked, a sinking feeling had set in, a feeling he'd turned his back on the people who paid his wage to make what little difference he could with the means given.

He reached the end of the road and hailed a cab that smelled sweet from the sweat of the driver. Tired, he closed his eyes in the backseat. Another night wasted, just because he'd parked on a corner. Fuck me, what would they do in Italy? It would be big business for those guys. He looked over at a tow truck driver sitting opposite him at the light, his arm hanging from the window, huge rings pushing the fat away from his porky fingers. He laughed as he remembered the guy's face as he'd whipped past him and spun the Ferrari out onto the road, just like Thomas Magnum would have done.

Fuck him. Fuck that guy who made a living stealing cars from hardworking people with real jobs—if you could call babysitting up-and-coming fashion models for a hundred an hour a real job.

Chendrill laughed quietly to himself as he sat in the back of the taxi and headed home. He wondered how Dan had got on with the supermodel and if he'd taken one for all the boys in the world who lived in their mum's basement.

But all that was just nonsense, because his old friend and ex-lover whom he'd admired from afar was lying in the morgue, burned like a cure for a Sunday morning hangover, and the man assigned the task of finding out why couldn't find a lost sock in the dryer, let alone a girl who was hiding a secret bigger than the private room Patrick was paying for at the Vancouver General Hospital. And with that thought, Chendrill, the ex-police detective who hated the police system and did his best to look like Magnum PI, knew that if he did not get to the bottom of it, no one would, and if that happened, it would follow him to the grave.

Chapter Seventeen

Illya stood next the girl and tried to wake her up. It had been almost forty-eight hours since he'd slipped the date rape drug into her drink in the busy bar and walked her back to his new place through the early evening crowds.

She wasn't doing well. By now she should have been a little more responsive. He had been hoping to start selling her off within the week, but it wasn't looking good. How could he sell her? Who would pay for a girl who just lay there with her eyes rolled back in her head and drooled? Some would, he knew, but those kind of perverted people weren't welcome, and chances are he'd end up killing one of them anyway.

Gently, Illya picked the girl up by her arms and tried to walk her around the room. What the fuck was with the heroin he'd given her? he wondered. She should never have been this out of it. Illya reclined her in a chair, walked out to the kitchen, filled a glass of water, came back in, lifted her to a sitting position, and put the glass to her mouth.

"Come on, beautiful, have a drink."

Working on instinct, the girl half-drank the water, her body taking what it could, the rest running down her cheeks and her front. Gently, Illya lay her back in the chair. He looked at her long legs and her destroyed party dress and knew he had work to do. Maybe it was a lost cause. Maybe her body was too innocent and fragile to take what he had coming for her. Maybe she would not make it at all and end up dying after being fucked too many times by one too many of the town's businessmen sent his way by a concierge he kept happy in one of the hotels in town.

He walked out to the living room and through it to the balcony. Leaning on it, he looked at the park across the road—all sectioned out, its grass neatly cut, rubber on the ground beneath the swings to save the kids' lives when they fell two feet, the dog park positioned to one side, fenced in and full of gravel to save the city workers from getting dog shit in the mower. You didn't get that in Russia, Illya thought. All you had there was concrete, and you had to be quick and climb fast when a pack of stray dogs came running through.

It was good here. They had a good system, Illya thought as he finished his cigarette, flicked it out onto the pathway below, and made a decision. The girl thing was not working. It wasn't worth the effort, and he should have learned that from the past. He needed a real whore, one he didn't have to teach how to fuck. After all, he wasn't offering a training program. He'd get a whore who was already set up, like he used to do back home, and he'd hit her until she submitted to his demands. Terrorize her until she gave him what he needed and make her work for a living like his father had at the docks—all day and night instead of just getting fucked once or twice a day in the afternoon or late in the evening after the bars closed.

He went back into the bedroom and picked up the girl from the chair. He walked her around the room three times, picked up her handbag, then walked her out the door into the elevator and down to the foyer. Holding her as he had the night he kidnapped her, he crossed the road to the park and placed her down on the newly cut grass, fifty feet from the playground. It was a good place for her to wake up, he thought. She'd come around, open her eyes, and the first thing she'd see was all the kids playing on the swings.

******

Dan woke up in the morning in his own bed in the basement to the sound of the East Indian taxi driver pacing up and down outside his window and the faint muffled noise of his mother having sex with the guy with the bread van who smelled of too much aftershave.

Fuck, Dan thought, how had the taxi driver found him? He thought he'd given up. Now he was outside pacing around like a Tamil tiger, carrying a pair of garden shears and waiting to strike.

Dan let out a deep breath and reached around along the side of his bed for some food, pushing aside the broomstick he'd been using to bang on the ceiling earlier when his mother's lovemaking got too loud. He found an empty packet of chips, peeled the bag open, and began to drag out with his tongue what crumbs he could find at the bottom.

Above him, his mother was about to orgasm, and she was definitely acting. He'd been living below her for nearly two years and was beginning to be able to tell the difference. Soon there would be silence, then mumbling, and then movement. After a quick visit to the shitter, the guy would be out the front door, down the path, and straight into his van.

Dan threw the cleaned chip packet onto the floor and stared at the ceiling above him. How the hell had he blown it the night before with the girl who'd just been voted the sexiest woman in the world? How was he now laying here instead, listening to his mother being fucked by a baker who wore his trousers too tight? It was disgusting, his mother going at it and the strange way she always groaned. Reaching to the side of the bed, he grabbed the broomstick and, in frustration and protest, thumped its end over and over into the ceiling above.

What a waste of time yesterday had been, all that nonsense with Marsha and the gay guy. Then having his feet screwed to the floor—what the hell was that all about? Throwing the broomstick down, he stared at the ceiling and let out a long breath. So that was that. His modeling career had come and gone in one day. He'd arrived in a limo and gone home on the bus.

Dan listened to the noise of the footsteps upstairs passing over him. The toilet flushed, and on cue, the front door opened. Mr. Tight Pants appeared outside the basement window and passed by the taxi driver, who was now cutting the lawn.

Everything was getting so confusing. He had chicks throwing themselves at him, but his mum was getting more action than he was. Now the guy who had been trying to kill him only a couple of nights ago had found him and was cutting his lawn. He could have sworn he'd only told his mum about the taxi driver doing that in case she saw him and wondered why he was hanging around.

Turning back toward the ceiling, he called out to his mother above. "Did you arrange with that taxi driver to do the lawn?" He waited in silence for the reply, and when it didn't come, he picked up the broom again and whaled on the ceiling. "Why do you keep seeing that baker guy?" he shouted. "If you need free bread and cakes, I'll buy 'em for you. After all, I'm working now. Anyway, what's the point in being with him if the first thing he does after he's shot his bolt is look for his car keys?"

For a moment, there was silence upstairs, then movement, heavy and frenzied. Dan sat up and swung his legs off the bed, staring out the window at the morning sun hitting the long grass as Belinda cut away at it the way Dan was supposed to have done.

For the life of him, Dan just didn't get it. Maybe his mum had seen him and had struck up a deal? Nonetheless, he certainly wasn't going to complain. He stared out at Belinda, who was bent down and giving Dan the thumbs up through the sunken basement window.

It was confusing. Perhaps Chendrill had seen the taxi driver wandering about outside the house with his hockey stick. Maybe he'd spoken to him, and it was all good now? After all, that was Chendrill's job.

He turned to stare at himself in the mirror leaning against the wall, its top cracked from a year before when he'd tried to walk to the bathroom with a garbage bin on his head. He looked at himself from the side, tensing his stomach. He looked good—had muscle in all the right places just like the guys he'd seen posing in ads.

Suddenly, his mother came rushing down the stairs and was in the hall on the other side of his basement bedroom door. "What are you doing home?" she shouted.

Releasing his pose, Dan stared at the door and watched his mother's shadow moving as she paced back and forth. "I live here?" he answered.

"Not anymore you don't. Didn't I ask you to leave over a year ago?"

It was true. Dan remembered her telling him to get out the day she'd discovered him cleaning his toenails with her toothbrush.

He shrugged and thought about opening the door, but she had been known to attack. Instead, he said, "If you're embarrassed about me hearing you with that loser, then don't be with the man. You can do better."

"I don't see you dating any princesses," his mother

snapped back.

Dan laughed to himself, thinking about Marsha, and said, "If I told you, you wouldn't believe me anyway."

"You're right there," she said from behind the door, and then he heard her begin to walk away.

It was the way she had always been—the flare of a temper that was red hot, but cooled as quickly as Dan as a child could make it to his room and throw himself under the bed or into the wardrobe to hide.

Then, as she reached the top of the stairs, she said, "The only thing you've ever had a relationship with is your sock."

Dan looked down at his feet as a surge of embarrassment swept over his body. She was right—using a sock had become a habit for him since he'd discovered that it felt good when the white stuff came out the end of his dick, thinking as kids often do, the secret was just his.

He took in a deep breath and then blew it out, looking up at the bang marks, old and new, on the ceiling as he heard his mother enter her room above. Fucking cow, he thought, being a bitch just because she couldn't keep a man longer than it took him to blow his wad and run. Then looking down again, he said to himself quietly, "At least my socks stay with me."

He looked back to the mirror again and felt his stomach begin to rumble. Daltrey was about the longest girlfriend he'd managed to keep so far, and that was only because she wanted the infrared door entry system he'd bragged about being able to make.

Had he fucked her? No. Had he even done anything sexual with her? No. Was she even a real girlfriend? Probably not, he thought. She had a nice ass, though. Yeah, she had a real nice ass, real nice. Soon the infrared system would falter, and she'd be back, saying, "Hey, Dan, how's it going? What're you up to?" the way she did. Then she'd meet him, and they'd have coffee or something, and she'd be all chummy, and then somewhere in among it all, she'd say, "Hey, you know that thing you made? Well, it doesn't work anymore!"

And he'd say, "Well, go find some geek who's just out of tech college and see if he has the chops to figure it out. Because I'm a male model now with Slave—you ever heard of them? They've got a contract with BlueBoy."

She did have a nice ass, though, real nice. Oh yeah, it was nice. Real peachy, the way it stayed tight as she walked and stood out just the right amount. She looked so sexy in those jeans she wore that bunched up at the top of her boots and her nice pert little titties under her T-shirt.

******

An hour later, the garden was all done, and Belinda, turning down all offers of money from Tricia, had smiled, holding his hands together in a praying motion. With a shake of his head that could only mean he had done the chore out of the kindness of his heart, he smiled at her. Through teeth so brilliantly white from years of scrubbing them with fish oil and baking soda back in New Delhi, he said, "No, Miss Dan's mother, it is an honor for me to take such a small part of my day to come here to be helping of you."

Dan was standing in front of the mirror, looking at himself and tensing his stomach muscles when Charles Chuck Chendrill pulled up outside in Mazzi Hegan's Ferrari. They sat in the kitchen as Chendrill sipped a cup of tea that had been made for him by Dan's mum. He looked down the hall over the cup's rim, hoping she'd come back.

"You liked that, did you?"

Chendrill looked across to Dan, who sat there with a smirk, and said, "Liked what?"

"My mum."

Chendrill smiled. Shit, was he that obvious? "Maybe," he answered.

"I don't see what guys see in her. There was an East Indian around here earlier cutting the lawn for free trying to get in her pants."

Chendrill put his cup down on the table, careful not to leave a rim mark, and said, "That's because she's your mother."

Dan stared at him for a moment, then laughed. "Wow, thanks. They teach you that at cop school?"

Chendrill nodded. The funny thing was that they did. It was all part of the human psychology course.

"I thought this East Indian was the same one who'd been looking for me since I did a runner from his cab the night I got into trouble with the gay guy at the camera place," Dan said. "But then I realized it was the guy who picked me up yesterday at the crack of dawn and dragged me to that green warehouse."

The whole revelation had come to him as he was pulling his sock off in the bedroom and he'd looked out the window again to see Belinda—and recognized him.

Chendrill stared at him, grinning. "And you couldn't tell the difference between the two?"

Dan shook his head. "Didn't help that I was wearing sunglasses. Besides, I only saw the backs of their heads."

"How do you know they're not the same then?"

Dan stood and walked to the window. "Because I'm

intelligent." He looked outside at Mazzi Hegan's car then turned back to Chendrill and asked him again, "How'd you scam that?"

"All part of the incentive package offered by your two new friends."

Dan nodded. "My mum's looking at it now," he said.

Chendrill frowned. "She likes cars, does she?"

Dan nodded and walked back over to sit down opposite Chendrill. "She likes Ferraris."

Chendrill smiled. "Has she got a boyfriend?"

"There's a guy comes sniffing around, and there's the Indian guy who did the lawn who's also sniffing, but he'll not get anywhere."

"I take it she doesn't like Indian food then?" asked Chendrill as he took another sip of his drink.

Dan shook his head. "No. He's fighting a lost cause. Hot and spicy is not her thing—it gives her the runs."

Chendrill looked at the table a moment before saying, "You knew Daltrey?"

"Yeah, but you knew that." Dan watched as Chendrill took a deep breath.

"I'm sorry to tell you," Chendrill continued, "but she's dead, Dan. She was murdered yesterday."

Fuck me, Dan thought as a strange feeling of emptiness hit his body. He'd been thinking of her only an hour ago and had put one of the new fluffy socks he'd received for Christmas to use in the process. He looked up from the floor and over to Chendrill. "Murdered?"

Chendrill nodded. "It happens. Rarely, but it does happen. She was found burned to death two nights ago in the entranceway to a parking garage in Yaletown."

Jesus, Dan thought, that had to be painful. A couple of

years before, he'd decided to try and shave with a lighter rather than a razor, and his face had taken weeks to heal.

"Why?" Chendrill asked for him, and then said, "I don't know, but I'll find out and take it from there. She was watching someone in an apartment, one block down from where her body was found."

Dan took a deep breath. Daltrey was the first person he'd known who had actually died, not counting the woman along the road whose budgie he'd killed through an open window with his pellet gun years ago.

"Last time I was with her, she was carrying around some guy's shoe that was all burned."

"At Mazzi Hegan's place?"

"Yeah, she thought it belonged to him." Dan shook his head.

A door opened along the hallway, and Dan's mum appeared and walked back into the kitchen. "I'm going downtown," she said to Dan.

Chendrill looked to Dan's mother, her hair combed back tight to her head and her eyes all made up.

Fixing some things on the counter, she looked to Chendrill and smiled.

"Is that your car?"

"It's not mine," Chendrill said and smiled back. "I get to drive it as a bonus for keeping your son out of trouble, and he's in that now because he was supposed to be downtown first thing this morning."

She looked at her son, ashen and sitting barefoot at the kitchen table. "What's wrong with you? Is your nose still hurting?"

Charles Chuck Chendrill answered for Dan. "I can't speak for your son's nose, but I'm afraid I've just delivered some bad news about one of his girlfriends who was killed recently."

Unsure whether she was more shocked that Dan had a girlfriend or that the one he'd had was now dead, Tricia walked over to the table and placed her hand upon her son's shoulder. "Oh my God, that's awful. I didn't know you were seeing anyone, Daniel."

"Well, there you go. I'm full of surprises," Dan answered without looking up. "Don't worry—it's not like we were about to be getting married or anything," he added.

Tricia took a deep breath, then looked at Chendrill and asked, "Is he involved in this?"

******

Still in shock, Dan sat at the back of the bus and watched his mother chatting and flirting with Chendrill in the front seat of Mazzi Hegan's red Ferrari as they followed behind. How had she swung that? he thought. The guy had been sent over to pick him up, and somehow he'd ended up on the bus.

He closed his eyes and thought of Daltrey. Fuck, she was dead—here one minute, gone the next. He looked away and stared into nothingness. Fuck. Jesus, he'd been about to call her to tell her to look out for his pictures, tell her all about how interesting this big thing—this campaign thing, whatever this thing the faggot with the dog had been going on about—was.

And what about the infrared door-opening device he'd made—and she likely still had—probably all twisted and melted if she'd left it in her pocket?

He took a deep breath and let it go. The poor girl. Dead, fucking dead. Never coming back. Never going to flirt and

prick-tease him the way she'd liked to do. He'd never see
her again. Never smell her hair, hear her laugh, catch her
smile, stare at her ass. A surge of sorrow built and grew,
slowly flooding his system from the pit of his stomach, rising
and choking him as visions of Daltrey played over and over
in his mind. The emotion inside welled up to the point where
all that kept him from tears was the intense itching that was
beginning to grow all around his balls.

******

The first thing Mazzi Hegan said when Dan came into the
office of Slave was, "You didn't wear those trousers in my
car, did you?"

Dan looked at him, his hair perfectly combed to one side
so you could see the roots all stretched out with gel.

"Why, what's wrong with them?"

"They've got jam on them, that's what."

Dan looked down and around the back of his trousers.
He hadn't had any jam since the day before yesterday and
had only put these trousers on in a hurry when he'd seen the
Ferrari pull up outside.

"Well, where's Magnum PI?"

Dan laughed.

"We sent a car for you this morning. Where were you?"

Dan thought back to the East Indian guy, waiting for him
outside and doing the lawn. "The guy in the turban? He was
doing the lawn."

Mazzi Hegan looked at him. What the fuck was he
talking about, a guy in a turban doing the lawn? "Belinda?"
he asked.

Dan didn't have a clue what Hegan was talking about,

but he said, "Yeah."

"Belinda's a woman. She doesn't do landscaping, Dan. She does our pickups." Frustrated, Mazzi Hegan took a deep breath. "Listen, kiddo, you could be the goddamn hottest guy in the world, but if you're a no-show and a letdown, you'll be going nowhere."

Dan looked at a sexy girl who was staring at him with her ass parked behind the reception desk. Smiling, he raised one of his eyebrows. What the fuck was this gay guy going on about? Where was he supposed to be going? He couldn't remember being told he was supposed to be anywhere this morning. "Where am I supposed to have been?" he asked.

Mazzi Hegan answered quickly, half turning and rolling his eyes to no one in particular. "The boat—on the boat! We had a whole crew there this morning at seven, and now they're just sitting around. You're costing us thousands of dollars! Where the fuck were you last night?"

"With Marsha," Dan answered.

Mazzi stared at him in disbelief. There wasn't much he could stand about that little slut except that straight guys seemed to adore her, and that made them pay attention to his work, but if she was the reason his day's shooting was all fucked up, then the next time he talked to her, she'd be feeling his wrath.

Then Dan said, "And my girlfriend was murdered."

Mazzi looked at Dan, startled. "I'm sorry…your girlfriend was murdered?"

"Yes, and I had to get the bus."

Mazzi raised his hand in the air and then brought it down gently upon his head so as not to mess with the lines in his hair. "Oh, and which one of these two events was the primary reason for you fucking up our whole day?"

"The bus."

"I thought Charles Chendrill was sent to pick you up."

Dan nodded. "He did show up, but he's taking my mum shopping."

"In my car?" Mazzi Hegan spat back.

Dan nodded again.

"He's got your mother in my car?"

"What's wrong with that?"

Mazzi Hegan held back, the words white trash circling in his mind. "Nothing...there's nothing wrong with your mother, okay?" He was tired from the shoot yesterday and then partying all night with Phillipe Tu La Monde after. Then there was the visit from the police, and going in again in the morning to finish on the boat with Dan, who'd not shown up because his girlfriend had just been murdered. Unbelievable nonsense. He took a deep breath and then said, "You need to concentrate more on being professional if you want to be a professional."

Concentrate on what? Dan thought. Concentrate on getting licked by a guy who should have been born a girl? Concentrate on being starved and having your feet screwed to the floor with a drill? If that's what being professional is, then he was doing just great.

Two minutes later, they were heading out to the marina in Coal Harbor in the back of Belinda's Mercedes, listening to Mazzi talking to Belinda. "Will you please check with your boss, Belinda, and find out why she didn't pick up Dan this morning?"

Belinda Johal listened, then looked back and said, "Belinda is a he and not a she, sir. She is not the boss. I am a he, Belinda is the boss. I wait for him, and I cut the lawn, sir."

Mazzi Hegan sat there in the car, not quite knowing what to think. He looked over at Dan, who was shifting in his seat. His bollocks were itching, and he was unable to keep still. After staring for the longest time, Mazzi said, "What is it with you? You do the most peculiar things."

Dan, desperate and dying to get his hand down his trousers to give himself a scratch, took his eyes off the road. He looked around to the man who thought he was peculiar, but had a painting of a guy taking one in the ass above his bed. "What?"

"You can't keep still."

"I'm excited. I can't wait to get there and be professional."

"Shame you didn't feel that way this morning at six when your ride arrived. Then we wouldn't have had a whole crew sitting around doing nothing all morning."

Dan stared out the window, thinking. If you called eating and doing nothing working, then that just about summed up what he'd seen the crew doing yesterday. "Well," he said, "from what I saw yesterday, I'm sure nothing has changed then."

The car moved on through downtown—Mazzi Hegan in silence, Dan wondering why his balls itched so bad, and Belinda happy to be there and in love with Dan's mum.

Pissed, Mazzi watched Dan out of the corner of his eye. God, this guy was such a prick, this fucking guy with his broken nose who was so fucking sexy and couldn't keep still. He was right—the crew on his shoots did nothing more than eat, and it drove him crazy, but what could he do? He couldn't do what they did, and he needed them there, but fuck, it drove him mad. Even an imbecilic prick like Dan could see he was being ripped off.

159

The car pulled up outside the gangplank to the marina, and in a flash, Mazzi Hegan was out the door. They reached the yacht and hurried up and along the gangplank onto its mahogany deck. The first thing Dan said as he saw everyone come to life around the staged area that had been set out for him to stand on—or be screwed down to—was, "I need to use the toilet."

Dan sat down on the toilet of the massive yacht that had been rented for the sole purpose of making him look sexy and stared down at his pubic hair. Fuck, he was itching. He parted the hair just above his penis and looked at the skin. It was red, but no redder—and no more unwashed—than usual. Pulling up his scrotum, he leaned down and looked below.

Caught in the beam of a stage light blasting through the small porthole, he saw it. It was small, tiny in fact, and clinging to a solitary hair. Then, next to it, what could only be another louse moved down toward the warm darkness of the underside of his sweaty and rancid testicles.

"Hello? Dan, we're ready for you!" said the sweet voice of a young girl from the other side of the lightweight door.

What the fuck was this? Dan thought. A bunch of insects had invaded his nuts, and they'd started eating him for lunch.

The girl called again, "Mr. Dan, we need you outside."

Dan stood and bent down. Trying to see under his crotch, he lifted his leg, placing his foot up onto the sink.

The girl called again. "Mr. Hegan's waiting for you outside."

Dan looked to the door and said, "One second."

Then he heard Mazzi Hegan's voice. "Dan! What the fuck are you doing now?"

Dan stayed silent for a moment, then replied, "Hang on a minute—I think I've got crabs."

"What!"

"I think I've got crabs."

"Why do you think that?"

"Because they're crawling all over my testicles."

"Open the door!" Mazzi Hegan cried.

"I can't. I need to go to the doctor," Dan replied quickly.

"What about the photo shoot?"

"I can't do it. I'm being eaten."

"Open the door, Dan!"

"I can't work today. I've got to go to the doctors."

"Open the door, Dan," Mazzi Hegan said again through the door.

"I can't."

"You can't get to the doctors if you don't open the door. Open it just a touch so I can see your face and let me talk to you. It's important."

Half pulling up his trousers and underpants, Dan unlatched the door, slid it back a bit, and looked outside as the enormous flash from Mazzi Hegan's camera hit him square in the eyes, blinding him.

Like lightning, a big ugly grip leaned forward, stuck his arm in, and ripped the door open. Mazzi Hegan lifted his camera, and as Dan tried desperately to see and pull his trousers all the way up, Mazzi began bombarding him with a flashing strobe light, taking picture after picture.

Chapter Eighteen

Charles Chuck Chendrill dropped Dan's mother off at the shopping mall and watched her wiggle her little ass through the main doors and disappear inside. She was sexy, he thought, real sexy, and from what he could tell, she liked him.

He put the Ferrari into first gear and pulled away slowly—without screeching like Magnum PI used to in the series—and thought back to the way she'd laughed at his jokes, played with her hair, and smiled while he talked with her over coffee and dodged the questions she'd quizzed him with about Dan's girlfriend who'd just been killed.

She'd been a good mother as far as he could tell—good in the sense that her crazy son wasn't into drugs and hadn't been arrested, even though he didn't have a job, until now that is.

"So you're saying Dan's a model?" she'd asked.

"Yep."

"What does he model?"

Chendrill laughed, then said, "Underwear!"

"You're joking, aren't you?"

Chendrill shook his head and smiled. "Nope, I was there at the studio, and he looked styling."

Tricia picked up her cup of coffee, took a sip, and stared at him, holding his gaze. "Well, I suppose he could get away with it. He's pretty ripped. I always told him he should go out there and get going as a dancer."

"Dancer?"

Tricia had put her cup down, answering with her eyes

before saying, "You'd better believe it. He gets it from me. The next time Dan and I go out, maybe you should come. I'll show you what I'm talking about."

******

It was just about an hour later when the nurse came into Alla's room and told her that the policewoman who'd been in to see her had been found burned to death in an alley. Alla's stomach knotted up. It had to be Illya, she thought. She wished she'd pushed him in front of one of those huge trucks that came thundering along the road that led to Moscow when he'd first made her go up there as a teen. All she would have had to do was creep up behind him and give him one firm shove, and it would have been done. But she hadn't.

She let out a huge breath and closed her eyes. God help her, she should have gotten away from Vancouver the moment she'd arrived, gone anywhere, just disappeared, but she hadn't done that either, and now she couldn't feel her legs.

******

She'd had trouble from men all her life, and the only one who had ever been kind and showed her true love was the one she had shit on the most. Sergei loved her, yes, but he had been happy to send her off to have sex with strangers and then continue to freeload the way he did. Dennis, though, poor old Dennis, was still there for her, still the pillar of strength she needed, even though she'd destroyed him, bled him dry, then sat back to let her brother finish him off.

The door clicked as the nurse left, plunging the room into a silence of deep, faraway murmurs that filtered through just enough to let Alla know where she was and that she was still injured.

Reaching out, Alla lifted the bedside phone and made a call. Seconds later, Dennis answered.

"Dennis, it's Alla," she said, then got straight to the point, her voice now almost childlike. "Do you still love me?"

Dennis stayed quiet on the end of the phone for a moment before answering. It had been a hard run for him, a fairy tale turned nightmare, and deep down in her heart, Alla knew that he knew the woman he loved was not altogether innocent in the making of it all. He took a deep breath, and through the earpiece, she heard the sadness in his voice.

"Alla, you could have done more."

Alla began to cry again. "It was my brother, Dennis, destroying everything as he always has."

Yes, she did exhaust his money bringing her blond photographer boyfriend over and buying him fifteen-hundred-dollar shoes and going to spas and partying, but she still loved him. She heard the door open and the nurse reenter, and she said quietly into the phone, "You know I still love you, Dennis."

For a moment, she lay still, listening to her husband's silence. Then she heard Chendrill's voice say, "So who's Dennis?"

******

Charles Chuck Chendrill picked up a small chair from the corner of the room, set it next to the phone, and sat down. He asked again, "So who's Dennis?"

Alla remained silent and looked to the door as Chendrill continued to make his huge presence felt, letting her know he was there and not going away.

"He's not out there, and neither is Patrick. I'd say you have about a minute to start talking, or I'll speak to someone and get you moved out of this fancy room and onto a secure ward."

Alla asked quietly, "Who are you?" Her voice was soft and warm, but on the inside, she was terrified.

"A friend of Patrick's," Chendrill answered.

Alla smiled. "You're here to help?"

He nodded. "Yes."

Then Alla asked, "Are you a policeman?" Chendrill shook his head, and Alla asked again, "You're not a police officer?"

"No."

"But you are with Patrick?"

"Yes."

"So you're here to help?"

Chendrill nodded.

"Then why did you tell me you'd have me taken out of here?"

"Because you're frustrating me, and I'm a busy man."

This girl was already getting on his nerves, trying to appear all soft and gentle like a little newborn bunny. He took a deep breath and said, "The police officer who was working to find whoever assaulted you was killed a couple of nights ago."

Alla stayed silent, staring up into Chendrill's eyes, then said, "I'm sorry to hear that."

"So am I," replied Chendrill. "Do you have any idea who

may have done this to you or to my friend?"

Alla shook her head. "A man came to my apartment and hit me."

"You're saying one of the men who came to your apartment for sex hit you?"

Alla looked away from his face and down to the patterns on his shirt. She knew this guy with the moustache and hair and the loud Hawaiian shirt from somewhere. She'd seen him before, but not as a client. Those she always remembered. She looked back up to his face and said, "Think of it whichever way you would like to. He hit me, and now I'm here. Not all people out there are good."

"And what did he look like?"

"I don't know."

"You don't know?"

"Correct."

"Was he a white guy, a black guy, a Latino guy, or maybe Asian? A mix, perhaps?" Chendrill persisted. He took a deep breath. "So what you're saying is that you don't want to tell me. Was it this Dennis then?"

Alla shook her head. "The man who hit me was Asian-looking."

Chendrill stared at her, thinking. "What do you mean? He was half-European?"

Alla shook her head again. "No, he was Asian, but not from the Far East."

"So who's Dennis then? Your boyfriend?"

"Husband."

Chendrill smiled, glad to be getting somewhere. "And does he know you're here?"

"He's been to visit me, yes."

"And does he know what you've been doing for a

166

living?"

Alla lay quiet, and her silence said it all.

Answering for her, Chendrill said, "I'll take that as a no then. Patrick told me you had certain pictures of him that my friend found. Did you have any other pictures of him?"

Alla stared up at the man and wished for the life of her she could sit up. "I don't know what pictures your friend found. I had some of us playing around together. They were going to be a surprise."

"What, like a birthday surprise?"

Alla looked away. "Kind of."

"And did you keep birthday surprises for any of your other clients?"

"There were no clients. Patrick and I, we were in love."

"In love?"

"Yes—in love," Alla snapped, wishing she could get up, stand by the bed, and tell this fuckhead where to go.

Chendrill leaned forward and whispered quietly into Alla's ear. "Remember, I'm not a policeman—all I need to know is that you don't have any other photos of Patrick."

She claimed she didn't and the only photos would have been the ones Daltrey found. But where were they now? Chendrill wondered as he pulled Mazzi Hegan's Ferrari into the fast lane of the highway and gunned it. And were there any more? he thought as he slipped the car down a gear and whipped past on the inside of a guy doing a hundred in the fast lane. Dan's mum had liked it this morning when he'd done the same, and he'd liked the way her legs had squeezed together in the process, her jeans clinging tightly to her calves all the way down to her little shoes.

Daltrey had to have hidden the photos somewhere, if indeed she had them at all. Knowing her, they'd be in a safe deposit box, and the key would be hidden a long way away from her desk on Main Street.

Three people had been intentionally burned to death over the last couple of years, two within the last few days, Daltrey included. And she was linked somehow to the guy with the fancy shoes she'd found floating out on False Creek like an overdone piece of chicken.

He shifted gears again and moved Mazzi Hegan's Ferrari back into the fast lane, accelerating into the long, smooth bend that took him high up and onto the Port Mann Bridge. Ripping along under its long wires stretching hundreds of feet above him and reaching its crest, he hit the floor and gunned it down the other side, crossing the deep brown water of the Fraser River two hundred feet below in a matter of seconds.

Still going, Chendrill kept his foot to the floor and flew off the bridge and onto the clear, straight stretch of highway on the opposite side. This car was fine, he thought, as he passed all the seemingly stationary cars to his right. In a flash, he passed the next junction and then another, then some small road repair stations, and then a policeman standing on the shoulder holding a speed gun in his hand.

Chendrill glanced into the rear-view mirror at the policeman, now just a tiny blur behind. He looked back at the road ahead and then quickly at the speedometer, which read just under 300 kph. Shit!

Keeping his foot to the floor, he glanced in the mirror again. Nothing happening. No cars chasing him or lights flashing in the distance. He took the next exit and headed south toward the U.S. border, and then took a sharp right back toward Vancouver. He knew the procedure—by the time they'd reacted to the report that would come in, put their coffees down, and checked the cameras, they'd first estimate he'd be heading east and would be by now another ten miles or so in that direction. It was possible they'd start looking at cameras and data tapes—if they could be bothered—and if they did, there was a chance Mazzi Hegan was going to have a whole lot of talking to do.

The basement where Dennis Willis now lived looked decent enough and pretty much the sort of place in which Chendrill had found many a divorced man living, except Dennis Willis wasn't divorced. He walked up the graveled drive, looking at the windows that needed painting, knocked on the door, and waited for Dennis to get off the sofa.

Chendrill liked Dennis from the moment they met. Maybe it was because his teeth were the shiniest things in the room or just the fact that he was one of a rare breed of person who were simply decent. The first thing he said to Chendrill as they sat at a table on old, ill-matched chairs by the window was, "If you think the chairs are bad, then you should see what's under the tablecloth."

Chendrill smiled and said, "The chairs are fine." They were. In Chendrill's mind, he could see nothing wrong with them, but he knew most women would moan.

Dennis said, "I think that almost everything in here is pulled together from someone else's vision. I don't think there's a single piece of cutlery in the kitchen that matches." He smiled and stared at the table. Then, looking up, he said, "Are you here about my wife?"

Chendrill nodded.

"Is she in trouble?"

Chendrill paused for a moment then said, "I'm not sure. Health-wise, yes, I don't doubt it. Elsewhere, I can't answer. I'm not the police—I work privately."

Dennis smiled. "So how's business in the world of private investigation?"

"Good, for now. I've got a couple of clients."

Without hesitation, Dennis asked, "And they're interested in me?"

Chendrill shook his head. "No one's asking about you, and that goes for the people I'm working for. I'm here for myself and for an old friend who was talking to your wife the day before she died."

Dennis closed his eyes and said, "I'm sorry for your friend."

Chendrill nodded his thanks. "We weren't close. In truth, I can't really say she was a friend, but I liked her and respected her."

"Her?"

"Yes. She was a cop. I knew her when I used to be one."

"I used to be a dentist," Dennis said. "You know what a dentist and a cop have in common?"

"What?" Chendrill asked.

"Everyone hates you until you get your teeth smashed in, and then they love you."

Chendrill smiled. "Until they get the bill."

Dennis nodded. "And I don't get to send them out anymore. That's one of the reasons I'm living down here."

Chendrill looked around the basement suite. It was tidy enough, but there wasn't a thing in there that didn't look worn and tired, and Dennis fit right in. "I'm sure you've got your reasons," he said.

Dennis stayed quiet for a moment, then said, "Yeah. But for the moment, though, till I get my license back, I'm a movie man. And when I get work, I sit most of the day on an apple box, then move stuff for other people who are making

170

the kind of money I used to make."

"I take it you and the wife are no longer living together?" Chendrill asked, stating the obvious.

Dennis took a deep breath. "Sadly, no. I lost my dental practice, and I became a different person, you know. I think I just wasn't good to be around."

Chendrill nodded. He could relate to that. He'd been a complete pig just after he'd quit the force, and it had taken him a while to settle down into a new life. He looked up and asked, "So she left?"

Dennis nodded. "She moved in with a friend."

"Does she work?" Chendrill asked, already knowing the truth.

"Yes, she's a hostess. You know…she's pretty. She works at trade shows, that kind of thing."

That kind of thing, Chendrill thought.

"But soon I'll be staring into people's mouths again for a living, and maybe she'll come home."

Fuck me, Chendrill thought and took a deep breath. If you only knew. Then he asked, "When did you last see her?"

Dennis smiled. "Recently…at the hospital."

"Do you know who hurt her?"

Dennis shook his head. "Maybe a boyfriend I suppose, or maybe her brother."

"She has a brother here?"

Without looking up, Dennis nodded. "Yes—but I didn't tell the policewoman that when she came to tell me about Alla."

"Why not?" Chendrill asked.

"Because I don't think he's supposed to be here, and I don't want anything coming back on Alla."

******

Charles Chuck Chendrill drove along the outskirts of Surrey until he reached the highway and then headed back toward Vancouver. So Dennis, the nicest dentist in town, had been played. If he hadn't known it before, then he certainly did now; after all, sometimes it's not only pythons who wrap themselves around their prey before they eat them. But for some reason from what Chendrill could tell, Dennis still didn't seem to care. They say love is blind, but who was he to talk? Where was the woman in his life? Who did he love, and most of all, who loved him as much as Dennis loved his beautiful wife, a whore lying in the hospital? The answer was obvious—no one.

Looking down, he checked his speed. Again, he was way over. Slowing down, he brought the car back to ninety, and it felt as though it was not moving at all. He checked his mirror and remembered himself gunning it earlier on the way out of town when he saw a police car way in the distance. He thought he'd leave the car parked in town tonight and maybe report it stolen. Say he'd left it in the morning, and now it was gone, taken on a 300 kph joyride on the highway by some crazy nut. That would nip that little problem in the bud.

He shifted the Ferrari down a gear and slipped in between two trucks as the police cruiser passed by. Just as it did, his phone rang. Slowing down further, Chendrill answered. It was a very irate Sebastian with another emergency.

"Chuck, your man's been taken to the hospital. You'll need to go pick him up."

"Who's my man?" Chendrill asked.

"Dan, of course. He's at the hospital."

Chapter Nineteen

Dan sat in the waiting room of the STD clinic, an offshoot to the Vancouver General Hospital, and wondered what problems below the belt everyone else in the waiting area had going on. One thing was for certain—none of them were itching like he was. In his mind, some were so ugly he couldn't imagine how they even managed to contract a disease in the first place.

Then he heard his name. "Dan Treedle?"

The nurse directed him along a short, sterile corridor to a little room. She was wondering what could possibly be wrong with the first person she'd ever seen brought into a sexually transmitted disease clinic by ambulance. Opening the door, she introduced him to a doctor with lenses in his glasses so thick Dan had no idea how the man could see at all.

"Hello, my name's Dr. Samuelson. How can we help?"

Dan stood, then sat, then stood again and said, "I think I've got crabs."

Dr. Samuelson stared at Dan's face and said, "You look like you've been hit in the face."

"Yeah, I was in this guy's place the other day, and he hit me with his man bag and broke my nose."

"Okay," the doctor continued, "you need to get that looked at or you may develop serious respiratory problems. Now, you say you feel you've got some kind of lice?"

"Yeah, there's definitely something running about down there."

The doctor stepped back, pulled a pair of surgical gloves

from the drawer, and put them on. "Well let's take a look," he said. "Please pull down your trousers and lie down on the bed."

Embarrassed, Dan undid the tops of his jeans and pulled them down. He lay back, Mazzi Hegan's underpants glistening in the bright, high-powered inspection light.

The doctor turned quickly, shielding his eyes from the glare. "My goodness! You'll have to lose those, son, or I may never see again."

Dan slipped the underpants down and away from the bright light, and the doctor leaned in and began carefully inspecting Dan's pubic region. Digging down to the roots of his pubes, he pulled out a piece of breakfast cereal and held it up to the light.

"Oh, what do we have here?"

Dan looked at it closely and said, "It looks like a Cheerio."

The doctor carefully placed the Cheerio in a metal bowl and went back in.

A thirty-year veteran of sexual health medicine, Dr. Samuelson had seen it all—until now. Reaching over to the counter, he grabbed a magnifying glass and looked closer.

Straining to look himself, Dan raised his head. "Can you see them?" he asked.

Without looking up, Dr. Samuel replied, "I see what looks like the residue from the bottom of a packet of Corn Flakes."

Dan looked surprised. "I don't like Corn Flakes."

The doctor lifted Dan's testicles and moved them to the side, looking more intently. "Seems to me you've got yourself a yeast infection mixed in with what looks to me like breakfast cereal. Could be the remnants of Corn Flakes.

Maybe Frosties."

That was it, Dan thought. The way his mother had been carrying on with this guy from the bakery every other day, it was no wonder he'd picked up something from her in the bathroom. That and the fact he'd had a huge pig-out on a couple of packets of breakfast cereal earlier then fell asleep with the bowl on his face.

Dr. Samuelson stepped back, turned off the light, and asked, "Have you been somewhere hot and sweaty?"

Dan nodded, remembering the heat from the lights in the stuffy studio the day before. "Yeah, they had me on this stage yesterday with my feet screwed to the floor."

"Really? When did you last have a bath?"

Dan couldn't remember at first, then he said, "I had one last Sunday at the guy's place who hit me with the bag, except it was a shower if that counts."

Dr. Samuelson lifted a clipboard. "When did you last have sex?"

Dan thought about it. That was a tough one. Shrugging his shoulders, he answered, "Last night."

"Full penetrative sex?"

Dan sat up and began to pull up his trousers. "Not really," he said.

Dr. Samuelson waited then asked, "That's a no then?"

"Yes."

"Did you have oral sex?"

"We were kissing."

Dr. Samuelson ticked another box. "No again. Are you sexually active at the moment?"

"I've been with a few girls lately, but we didn't go all the way, because with the first one, her guide dog bit me, and then the second one thought I was gay. The one last night didn't like it when I called her Margaret Thatcher."

Lowering his clipboard, Dr. Samuelson stared at him for a moment, then said, "Really? May I ask if you are gay?"

Dan shook his head. "No, I'm not. Actually, you might know the girl I was with last night—she's that supermodel, Marsha."

Dr. Samuelson stared at Dan a moment longer. This guy was priceless. He couldn't wait to get back to the nurses' station to tell them what he'd heard. Lowering his bottle glasses, he looked at Dan, his eyes sunken and red. "You were with some girl who looked like Marsha last night?"

"Yeah, I was with some girl who looked like Marsha last night, because she was Marsha. You can't get much closer than that."

"And you say you didn't have full penetrative sex with this girl, but there could be a chance that your pubic area etcetera rubbed against hers?"

Dan nodded. "It did, but she doesn't have a jungle down there like me. Hers is more like one of those landing strips the girls you seeon the telly late at night have."

Dr. Samuelson nodded, not quite understanding. "But not full of food?"

Dan shook his head and said, "No, she's a supermodel. She doesn't eat."

******

Mazzi Hegan sat in the boardroom and flipped through the stills he'd gotten of Dan in the toilet. Pissed off, Sebastian paced up and down behind him. He didn't know what on earth was going on. No one had gotten back to him to tell him anything. The only information he'd received was secondhand from the girl in reception saying that Dan was seriously ill and being taken by ambulance to the hospital. Luckily, he'd managed to pass that on to Chendrill as soon as he'd answered his ruddy phone, and then, all worried, he'd walked into the boardroom and found Mazzi in there, his feet propped up on a table, eating cheese and drinking wine while looking at the stills of Dan struggling in the toilet of the yacht he'd just spent five thousand dollars to hire for the day.

Mazzi Hegan listened to his partner—who knew more about advertising and design than anyone he'd ever known—unload and waited until he'd finished. Then, looking up at him, he said, "Yeah, but have you seen these shots? They're bloody good, though."

They were. Sebastian couldn't deny it. This guy was good. Nothing he produced ever looked staged. It always had such a raw element to it, something he'd only seen coming from frontline war photographers.

Mazzi Hegan looked at Sebastian with a smile and said, "Who needs a yacht when you can get shots like this?"

Sebastian leaned in to look at the crystal clear shot of Dan struggling in the toilet with his pants around his knees. The look of terror on his face was accentuated by the sharp movie light crashing through the window and exploding in his hair.

"You don't get gold like that up on deck."

"Why's he look so worried?" Sebastian asked.

"He's got crabs."

Sebastian screwed up his face and said, "Eh?"

Mazzi looked up and said, "It's okay—I called an ambulance."

And he had—he had as soon as he had heard the stress

in Dan's voice, but not before he'd acted on instinct, getting the door open and aggressively shooting until he'd gotten what he needed. That's what this advertising campaign was all about. It was about fear and desperation, not yachts and backgrounds and wind in your hair. It was about being raw and scared and frustrated and dirty.

Sebastian took a seat and called for his dog, who was rummaging around the floor looking for scraps. "Don't you think an ambulance was a little overboard?" he asked.

Mazzi looked up from his computer. "He said he had crabs. What was I supposed to do?"

Sebastian closed his eyes and frowned. He'd caught them when he was a student working on a farm in Bavaria after a lederhosen night in the small town at the bottom of the mountain—and all he'd done was take himself through the sheep dip. "Come on, it's hardly an emergency," he said.

"For you, sitting here, it's not! I mean, what did you expect me to do? I haven't got a car, you know. You've commandeered it. How was I to know how infested he was?"

Sebastian looked at him. "You could have had Belinda take him. She's always very helpful."

"Belinda's not here," Mazzi snapped. "She's got some dark guy with nice teeth driving for her."

Sebastian smiled and said, "Well, good for her." Then he asked, "Just how infested was he?"

"Well, he was very distressed."

Sebastian got up again and walked to back to the computer. The reality of it was that as over the top as it was, it was a good thing what Mazzi had done, calling an ambulance and all. He was going out tonight and using Belinda, and he could do without any of Dan's friends crawling all over the dog.

"There's only one problem," Mazzi said. "I may have mentioned in the heat of things that it was probably Marsha who gave them to him."

Chapter Twenty

Still pissed about the evening before and suffering from the rigors of a first-class flight all the way to London, Marsha arrived through the airport gate to screams from the paparazzi asking her if she had crabs.

Within an hour, she arrived exhausted in her suite at the Ritz and heard it again, this time from Gill Banton, her agent, who asked her straight out, "Word on the street is that you were rushed to the hospital in an ambulance with pubic lice?"

"What the fuck is going on?" Marsha said, suffering from dehydration and jet lag and not quite able to take it all in. "Well, there was this guy from Papua, New Guinea on a shoot the other day who left me a little sore, but he was so big, I couldn't resist."

Gill Banton was silent on the other end of the line.

Marsha flopped herself down on an enormous luxury sofa that looked out across Green Park toward Buckingham Palace and said, "I don't even like crab. It's really messy."

"You need to be taking this a little more seriously."

Marsha laughed. She spun herself around and stretched her legs into the air. Dropping her head, she looked at the view outside, upside down, and asked, "Does the Queen know I'm here?"

Gill waited, not bothering to even acknowledge such stupidity.

"Please let me know, has anyone told the Queen I'm here?" Marsha asked.

Realizing the question was never going to go away, her

agent continued, "Yes, we informed the palace, and the Queen's coming right over." Then she asked Marsha again, "So you're okay down there? You haven't got anything?"

"No! But there's still a problem, isn't there?"

"Why?"

"Because I don't like people thinking I've picked up a bunch of creepy crawlies that have found a new home around my crotch. It's hardly good for my reputation. Are you going to sort this out?"

Gill took a deep breath. Sorting out this particular supermodel's problems was her daily life—if it wasn't crabs today, it would be that she thought she was pregnant tomorrow. "It's being done as we speak," she said.

******

Dan left the hospital and headed home on the bus, feeling relief in the knowledge that he had no pubic lice crawling around his groin, and it was only a yeast infection, which in his mind was crazy because he didn't have a clue how to make a loaf of bread. He reached his mum's house and walked in through the back door to find Chendrill standing in the kitchen talking to his mother. As he brushed past him and opened the fridge, he said, "I thought you were supposed to be looking after me, not my mum."

"I am," Chendrill said. "As soon as I found out you were in the hospital, I came straight here to see if she was okay and wanted to join me for dinner."

Lifting a milk carton from the fridge, Dan poured a mouthful, swallowed, then said, "Well, I had to get the bus back from the hospital."

"So what's wrong with that?"

Wiping the milk from his chin, Dan stared at Chendrill. "I thought you were supposed to be looking after me?"

"I am. I'm keeping you grounded. The last thing Sebastian needs is for you to go getting yourself an ego."

Confused, Tricia looked from Chendrill to her son and asked, "Dan, what's wrong? Why were you at the hospital?"

Closing the fridge, Dan stared at his mother, then moved off, saying, "Because I've got a yeast infection."

"How the hell did you get that?" his mother asked as she watched him walk away down the hallway toward the staircase that led to his room.

Dan disappeared down the staircase toward his room in the basement. Hitting the bottom step, he called up, "You tell me!"

******

Chendrill parked the Ferrari and then held Dan's mother's arm as he guided her down the steps to his favorite Italian restaurant in Gastown. Picking a table close to the window, they sat down.

"Well, this is a nice surprise," Tricia said with a smile.

Chendrill nodded, smiling back. It had been a while since he'd been on a date, at least one with a woman worth pursuing. "It's a nice surprise for me also," he said. "It's very good of your son's new employer to give me an excuse to come over to make sure he's okay."

"Were you really supposed to pick him up?"

Chendrill smiled and nodded.

"Won't you get in trouble?"

"I think they like rebels. That's why they've hired Dan."

They ordered their food, both having pasta and sharing a

two-hundred-dollar bottle of Bordeaux.

Taking a sip, Tricia said, "This is lovely."

Chendrill smiled again. "And so are you."

Tricia blushed at this big guy with the fancy car coming on to her like this, making her feel special. "Thank you."

Chendrill watched the way she played with her hair. Her eyes glanced up for just a moment as she gently brushed her tongue slightly against her front teeth and lips.

"This is the last thing I expected to be doing this evening," she said.

"Same here, but I thought, you know, it would be nice to go out and meet the mother of the next big shot in electronic research and development."

Tricia began to laugh, holding her hand gently across her mouth. "He told you that, did he?"

Chendrill nodded.

"Did he also tell you he was a genius?"

Chendrill nodded again and smiled. "Yep, said he was going to be big one day. And you never know—he could be."

"You think so?"

"Maybe."

Tricia stared into space for a moment and then, beginning to laugh, shook her head and said, "I don't think that's going to happen—unless they pay a lot for food tasters, and then he could work twenty-four seven."

Chendrill reached over and pulled a breadstick from its glass holder. "I know…I've seen him eat." Then he said, "You never know," and took a bite of the bread.

"It's true, you don't. One of his teachers at school used to tell me he was a genius."

"And was he hitting on you?"

Dropping her hand to the table, Tricia thought that one

over for a moment. "No, I don't think I was his type, if you know what I mean."

Chendrill did, but looking at her sitting there before him with the soft light from behind catching her hair from the side, he couldn't see how this woman could not be anyone's type. Unless, of course, as she was hinting at, they played for the other team. He said, "May I ask about Dan's father?"

Closing her eyes, Tricia nodded, then she looked at Chendrill and said, "To be honest, he was only in my life for a short time and then disappeared, like some people do. So I'd be lying if I said I knew him well. He was Croatian. I was young, and so was he. We were together, and then one day he was gone, and as a going away present, he left me with Daniel."

Chendrill nodded, happy just listening to this attractive woman's pureness and honesty.

"Funny thing is, though," said Tricia, "I do remember him telling me about his crazy grandfather who was a known genius at a big university there. He used to say the man was nuts—couldn't get himself dressed properly in the morning or have a serious conversation, but would go off in the morning and start working on a four-hundred-page math problem."

Chapter Twenty-One

Frustrated, Illya paced the living room of his new apartment and pulled another drag from his cigarette, blowing the smoke down over the leather sofa. Why he was so frustrated, he could not even figure out himself. After all, where was he now? Stuck in a seventeen-man cell in a shithole of a prison just outside Moscow? No! He was living in a luxury apartment in one of the most beautiful cities in the world and had thirty thousand dollars in cash sitting in his jacket pocket.

Illya took another drag on his cigarette and stared out the window, watching the smoke dissipate in a circular cloud as it hit the double-glazed glass sitting inches from his face. You need to have some fun, he told himself. Get out and stop worrying about this shit.

He left the apartment and walked out past the cultural center. Turning right onto Granville Street, he entered the first bar he came to, sat down, and ordered a beer. The place was busy and loud. A hockey game blasted out from the TVs above his head. He looked around and saw plenty of girls in the bar, some who were quality enough to turn into the kind of whore he could make decent money off of.

His beer came and, knocking it back, Illya immediately ordered another along with a whiskey—and then another. It was a good feeling—the way he'd felt in prison when he'd managed to extort vodka from a weaker inmate or a friend. He'd sit back on his bunk at night, slipping the bottle between his lips and thinking back to his mother and father. Thinking about his sister and how he'd terrorized any boyfriend who'd come to see her, all so he could stop her from getting loved up before it was time for her to go and work for him up on the road. After she'd done that for a while, boyfriends wouldn't matter.

He ordered his fifth drink along with another chaser and looked around. Same people there—loud, smiling girls and some nice boys. He looked at one, picking him out of the crowd, his blond hair, long and unkempt, almost like a surfer but without the tan. Illya caught his eye then stared at him hard as the kid looked back, unsure what to do.

Illya looked back away from the kid, catching a glimpse of himself in a small, stained mirror above the till. He was there now, drinks on the table, big money sitting on the bar and bigger sitting in his pocket. He was the man, and as far as he was concerned, everyone around here knew it.

Slowly and with purpose, Illya pulled off his muscle shirt, exposing arms and shoulder blades covered in tattoos. The tats all beautifully drawn with purpose and skill in pen ink and ash, the blood rinsed away with rain water collected in a small, rusted tin that sat by the window of a damp cell inhabited by an artist with nothing but time on his hands and enough connected insanity to depict Illya's life in pictures. Communist-built tower blocks and burning dogs, cats, and rats that ran up his arms. A gun inked across a shoulder blade. A man dead on a road that stretched across his shoulders, his body smoking as the rain fell around him. Beautiful women stood with his sister on his back, along with the prison, with bars and cells and alleys, and bodies that lay burning on a washroom floor.

He could feel them now, these Canadians with their bright smiles and perfect teeth all looking at him, their eyes burning into his flesh one moment, but averted when he looked their way. Illya, the gangster, sitting right there among these people who'd only ever shouted at someone when driving. He was the man.

Honing in, he stared at the kid again. His eyes burned a hole in the young man's soul, intimidating him and letting him know he was his mark, and there was nothing he could do to get away from him, so he'd better submit.

Illya knew the feeling from his first year in the Vladimir Central Prison. Everyone there knew that as a teenager he had killed a gangster without pulling a gun, and no one gave a shit. The stares came daily. Every time he sat alone or lifted his head, someone would be there looking, wanting his youth. Until one day it came, fast and furious, from out of nowhere. Men holding him, beating him, and using him as a woman. And then it was their turn to pay and die, and they did, in a way most men fear to go—execution by fire.

The kid looked up and stared back at Illya. What the fuck was this loser with the shitty tats staring at him for? Who the fuck was he? Did he know him? He got up and walked over to Illya. "Sorry, do I know you?" he asked, smiling.

Illya stared hard at the kid with the neatly shaved goatee. "You don't know me."

Shrugging, the kid smiled and said, "No worries. I'm sorry…it's just that you kept looking over, and I thought we knew each other, that's all."

"We don't know each other," Illya replied, "so fuck off."

Surprised, the kid stared at him, and as he began to turn, Illya spoke again.

"You think you can come over and scare me? You think I am pussy? Hey, I'm not a Canadian piece of pussy meat like you, so fuck you, and fuck your friends who you sitting with right now. Except girls. They can come here join me, I will entertain them like you can't if they want."

The kid turned away, ignoring Illya and his badly spoken English as Illya ordered another drink. Fuck, he was loving it now. The guy would go over and tell his friends he'd just met this fucking tough motherfucker from Russia, and then if they were brave, they'd take him on. Go outside and party as they liked to say here. He watched them now, all at the table, listening and laughing at what the kid was saying, looking over, their sly glances passing him by as they pretended to look at the door or the hockey game on the TV.

Illya continued to stare, holding onto the kid's every move. Fuck, he was fearless, staring down these guys and their girls, them all there not knowing what to do or how to handle him, this tough fucking gangster with his tattoos.

Then the kid got up again, came back over, and said, "The girls want to know why you've got two guns tattooed on your chest and why you've got pictures of burning animals all over your arms."

Illya laughed, then smiled. "Why don't you ask them to come over here and ask me themselves?"

"Because you frighten them."

Illya loved that one. "Tell them I not Russian bear, I Russian sable, and treat them fine." Then as he took a swig of his drink and pointed right at the girls, he said, "Tell your girls they want work for me, they have apartment, clothes by designer, and earn thousand dollar every day."

"How?"

"Bring girls over to me, and I tell them. They work for me, in less than year, they buy condo for cash. All day at spa make themselves look beautiful."

The kid looked at him again, smiling. "Really?"

Illya flicked his head. "Tell them."

Then the kid asked another question. "That road on your shoulders, the girls want to know where it goes."

"Straight to place where dream come true," Illya answered. "Now go, ask girls, come see me."

The kid smiled and looked toward his friends, who were signaling him to come back.

Illya watched as the kid walked back and spoke to the girls at his table. He was feeling good now. The beer and the whiskey and the rum he'd now switched to were kicking in. These fucking pussies here couldn't drink. When they did, they just got loud and started whooping it up, screaming like cats. They never sat quietly like they did in Moscow.

The kid came back to the bar and said the words that would cause him to regret for the rest of his days ever getting into a conversation with the Russian. "The girls said if you want to pimp out anyone, why don't you go ask your sister?"

At first, through the noise of the bar, Illya didn't think he'd heard it right, but then he realized he had. He called back to the kid as he walked back to the girls at the table. "You know Alla?"

The kid sat down and stared back at him, smiling.

Illya looked at the girls and said, "You know my sister, Alla?"

The group looking back at him began to laugh. Illya looked at the kid, who stared right back and said, "We don't know your sister."

They did. He knew it. Why else would they ask? How would they know he had a sister? How would they know she was a whore who had worked the side of the road that he ran before the police came making a fuss about him burning that prick who drove the Mercedes?

Illya looked back to the bar and his drink, dismissing the

kid with his impoliteness. Peering up, he watched the kid at the table, slapping his hand down, high fiving the others, laughing. Fucking sons of bitches, he thought. If they were in Russia, they'd read these tattoos and know what they meant. There would be no laughter then, just respect. He looked at the barman, staring him down until he dropped what he was doing and came right over, handing him another beer and chaser without being asked.

The night passed, and the drinks kept coming. Illya watched the hockey game and the table with the kid, his and his friends' attention long ago shifted away from the crazy tattooed Russian at the bar. But the kid was pissing Illya off now. The fuck? Coming over for no reason, opening the conversation with strange questions, then moving straight to the subject of his sister. He knew something—there was no doubt about it. What did he know? How did he know Alla? Was he fucking her?

Maybe. He was blond, and Alla liked blond men. The fucking prick. If he was fucking her, he should have been paying Illya. Maybe he knew her husband or was a nephew or something. He'd seen a picture of a kid on the guy's fridge when he'd gotten into town and started taking over. Could be. Probably was. That's where she was—back with the husband, the one he'd fucked who'd started crying. That's how he knew Alla. He was the kid on the fridge.

Then the kid got up slowly and, looking briefly toward Illya, passed him, heading toward the toilet. Illya stood as the kid entered the washroom. He traced his steps, opened the door to the restroom to check that it was empty, and then with a sharp, precise twist of his body, he slammed his fist hard into the kid's kidney as he stood minding his own business taking a leak.

The pain of the hit came fast and sharp, knocking the wind out of the kid's body as he felt an arm quickly wrap itself tight around his throat and begin to squeeze the life from him. Then the Russian spoke as the kid looked down in panic, realizing who it was as he stared in shock at the guy's tattooed arms.

"Where my sister?"

Desperate to breathe, the kid clasped Illya's arm with one hand and held onto his unfastened trousers with the other. He felt himself being pulled back away from the urinal and pushed through a door into one of the toilet stalls. His face slammed down, hitting hard and spurting blood onto the top of the white toilet tank.

The Russian asked again, "Where Alla? Tell—where?"

Struggling, the kid tried to speak, but could not, the pressure of the Russian's arm still crushing unrelentingly on his throat. He felt the man behind him, tugging his trousers further down his legs. The Russian released his throat and grabbed his hair, slamming his face down hard again into the top of the toilet tank and sticking both fingers into his eye sockets. Then as the man pulled his underpants down, he felt the Russian's hardness pushing against him, and heard the man say, "Move, and you'll never see again."

Then the pain came as the Russian's mouth pushed down, biting him hard on the shoulder. The smell of booze poured from the man's mouth as he bit down harder and harder with each breath. He felt a violent poking and prodding from behind as he struggled, then movement, and then a searing pain, worse than anything he had ever felt before, as the Russian pushed hard against him, ripping into him and fucking him violently, taking him as a woman.

Chapter Twenty-Two

Illya sat on his sofa and stared out of the large window to the city below. It was now two thirty in the morning, and it had been a good night. Good fun, actually. He took a cigarette from the pack, lit it, and opened another beer. He'd have liked to have stayed longer at the bar after he'd gone into the toilet and raped the kid who had long hair like a girl, but it was best to get out of there because he knew if he kept on drinking, he'd only start causing trouble.

That fucking pussy, he thought. He looked like a girl, fought like a girl, and had screamed like a girl as well, when he'd been fucked.

He took a large pull on his cigarette, blew it into the air, picked up the Georgia Straight paper. Opening it up at its rear, he looked for the ad he'd paid in cash to print week after week for the last six months. Finding it, he stared at the picture Alla's boyfriend had taken of her standing in a sexy negligee, her face obscured just enough, and her ass sticking out like a peach. Then he turned the page and stared at another.

******

It was just after four in the morning when Mary Sanc stepped out of the cab and rang the buzzer. Three minutes later, she was standing in a short skirt and high heels in the living room of Illya's new luxury apartment, listening as Illya said, "Go to bedroom, get undressed. I'll be there in minute." Apart from, "You look nice, young and fresh," that was all the small talk Illya had given her.

Mary turned and headed down the hall toward the bedroom to get laid for the thousand dollars she'd asked for coming out so late. It was the same foreign guy on the phone, she thought, and he hadn't flinched when she'd talked money. She called back to him along the mirror-lined hallway that seemed much longer and bigger than it should have been for the building.

"Don't be long out there."

She walked into the bedroom and looked around. It was a nice place—large and luxurious—and through an adjoining door, she could see a huge bathroom with a sunken shower big enough for them both.

Sitting herself down on the bed, she thought there was a time she'd have let him bring her here and do her for free. As Illya appeared through the bedroom door, she turned to him, smiled, and asked, "What's a good-looking man like yourself doing here with me when you could go out there and get it for nothing?"

Illya smiled. "I have it once for free already tonight, but what is that word you say here? Kinky?"

"Kinky."

"Yeah, I a kinky motherfucker with too much money."

Mary smiled. Good for her. If she did a good job and fucked him well, maybe he could become a repeat. She stared at Illya, then looked around the room and noticed the large phone book sitting on the chaise lounge that looked out to the window and the city lights beyond. This guy was from the Russian mob maybe, wanting a taste of Canadian pussy before he went home.

"Why are you here in Vancouver?" she asked.

"Actor, on TV series."

Could be, Mary thought. Actors paid for sex all the time.

Paid for the girls to leave was the saying, or the way their egos dealt with it. But now, looking at him closer, this guy was no actor, not with those tats. And he was too hard around the eyes.

Whatever he was, it didn't matter. In a couple of hours, she'd be out and away, back in her own bed after a quick bath, and a thousand dollars better off. There was a pair of Jimmy Choo's she'd had her eye on for the last week, and after wrapping her legs around this guy and pretending to come a couple of times, she was going to get them.

Then Illya walked over to the chaise lounge, closed the curtains, picked up the telephone directory, came back, and hit her with it hard across her back.

The pain was incredible as it ripped through her, knocking the wind from her lungs and what felt like the life from her small-framed body. Just as she managed to gasp air into her lungs, Illya hit her again with the telephone book, bringing it down hard onto her kidneys and sending a crippling pain she'd never thought possible through her body.

Desperately, Mary called out, but the more she did, the harder Illya hit, pulverizing her kidneys. Only when she'd stopped crying out and thought the only thing left to do was die did Illya stop. She smelled the beer and the cigarettes on his breath as he leaned down and quietly spoke Russian words she couldn't understand in her ear. Then he calmly moved back and from nowhere produced a flame that shot out from his right hand and was aimed so perfectly that the heat at the tip of its three-foot length pinned her face to the luxurious Egyptian cotton.

Terrified, Mary stared up at him through the heat of the flame, unable to move. The pain in her back was all but forgotten as the heat from the flame increased.

She heard Illya call out to her through the roar of the flame. "You work for me now, and you going to earn that thousand you ask for, and when you have, I tell you time to leave—if you not do as I say, I burn your face away. You run, I find you and burn you just same."

And as Mary looked up at him through the flame, she saw the evil in his eyes and knew his words were true.

Chapter Twenty-Three

Alla Bragin lay in her hospital bed listening to the night. In the distance, someone was crying, calling out for help—but it wasn't coming anytime soon, not for her or for anyone else.

Dennis—or her sick brother if he was still alive—was her only hope, but what good would he be? She imagined him coming into the room, seeing her unable to move from the waist down, and then turning around one hundred and eighty degrees and walking out again. Dennis was her best option. He still loved her despite everything. There was little she could do now that could be worse than what she'd done already to him, and nothing could change that.

She took a deep breath, listened to the women along the corridor screaming and crying, and then closed her eyes. It was odd—she could feel her feet, but couldn't move them. At least she thought she could feel them. Who the hell had it been? she wondered. It was hard to picture the man's face now in her head, but she knew he was Asian. Well, kind of.

And he'd killed Sergei. Burned him to death, so he'd said. But Sergei could just as easily be drunk somewhere with Illya. It had happened before, but somewhere inside, she knew that wasn't the case. She had sensed the truth in the man's words when he'd told her it was Sergei burning out there on the creek. Then he'd gotten up and hit her. She opened her eyes again and stared at the ceiling as the memory of the blow crashing into her lower back and the hot feeling inside that had enveloped her came flashing back. It had to have something to do with the girl, she thought. That girl—so warm, so giving, so incredibly kind to her boyfriend, their whole lives ahead of them.

That cunt, Illya, always fucking it up, always destroying everything and everyone in his wake. Taking, taking, taking. And now, because of him, she was stuck, an exotic fish in a tank with everyone coming by to stare. And she couldn't get out.

Slowly, Alla shuffled her way to the other side of the bed. Fighting her drips and monitors, she reached out and pulled the bedside phone onto her chest and began to dial the number she thought she had long forgotten. Thirty seconds passed before Dennis answered, and she lay silent for a moment listening to him.

Then she said, "Dennis. Please, Dennis."

"Alla?"

"Please help me, Dennis."

Dennis stayed quiet on the other end of the line. Then he said, "I don't know. A man was here Alla, and he said some things about you, and they made sense."

"But you still love me, though, don't you?"

"Not like before. Not after what you did."

Alla began to cry, her tears real, born of shame and the fear that she was now crippled and had no one left in the world to help except this glimmer of a man whose life she'd once been a part of, and had destroyed.

"I'm a human being, Alla. I have feelings. You forget that, I think."

"I'm sorry, love. It was my brother—he made me. I was terrified of him. I still want you."

There was silence on the line, then Dennis answered. "You say was? Are you saying he's not with you now?"

"No, but I'm still frightened of him. But I'm more

frightened that I cannot move my legs."

And she was terrified, more terrified than she had ever been. The faint hope that sat inside her was that she thought she'd been able to move a toe, just a toe, and as she lay watching the sheets at the end of the bed, she was certain she hadn't been dreaming.

"That's why you're calling me?"

"Yes."

"What happened to you?"

"A man hit me."

"Why?"

Good question, Alla thought. She took a deep breath, and letting it out, she answered truthfully. "I don't know."

"You don't know?"

"No."

"Where?"

"My back, at the bottom."

"No, I meant where were you?"

Then she did lie, the transition between the two answers so seamless it would be impossible for anyone other than herself to tell one from the other.

"I was in the hallway by my apartment, and he came out of nowhere. He hit me, and I made it back to the apartment and collapsed."

Dennis stayed silent for a while, then said, "A man attacked you for no reason? Was he a client?"

"Sorry?"

"Your brother used to say you used to be a prostitute, Alla. I didn't believe him, but now after what has happened between us, I don't know anymore."

There was silence then between them, and Alla knew how much it must have hurt Dennis to say those words.

"Illya's a bad man, Dennis. I'm not like him."

"You're not?"

"You know I'm not."

Alla stayed quiet for a moment, letting her husband listen to her breathing over the phone. Then she said, "I want to apologize to you, Dennis. That is why I called. I just wanted to say sorry and tell you that I've never not loved you."

******

Mary woke to see Illya standing next to her. She felt her right wrist being untied from the side of the bed, and then a few minutes later, a man in a business suit was standing in the room. How long she'd been out from the pain in her kidneys, she couldn't tell.

The man stared at her, not knowing quite what to do. "Good morning," he said.

Mary nodded. So it was morning, but which morning?

She heard the man say, "You're a very pretty girl."

Mary looked at him and wondered what the fuck he had seen in her to make him say that because she couldn't remember ever feeling worse than she did right at that moment.

So this was the start, this was the first of the men she'd now have to fuck before she'd somehow be able to get the fuck out of there and away from this Russian pimp. Then she'd have her revenge.

Still looking at the guy, she said, "Get it done, and don't expect me to pretend I'm enjoying it."

Illya stood on the other side of the door and listened. Not the best response he'd have liked from his newest employee, but she could be educated, and if this prick wasn't happy, then he could fuck off and put a complaint in with someone who gave a shit.

By the afternoon, Mary had had four showers and three lectures from the expert.

"You need to moan more, pretend to cum, tell them you love them and how they feel. Tell them they're good and say you want more."

Fucking bullshit, Mary thought.

Other men came passing through the apartment, and with each one she'd lay down for, her plan to mutilate this Russian prick had grown, taking her to places she'd never known possible. And with the one who was in her now, pounding and gasping away, it was no different.

She would pay all the money in the bank—and she meant all of it, every cent she'd saved for laying down and lying, just as Illya was trying to coach her how to do now. She'd hire her old flame in the Hells Angels, who used to brag to her after they'd fucked about the bad things he'd done with his friends, and they'd come up here to this fancy pad and cut off Illya's cock and balls and fingers and then after go to town on him with a teaspoon. And she'd watch and smile as he pleaded to her and said "we were partners" or some Russian shit like that.

She'd watch as he stumbled about, and say, "Find me and burn me now, you tattooed motherfucking cunt."

Then she'd leave him up there, bleeding and on his own, trying to find the door, and when he did, he wouldn't be able to open it because he'd have a broken arm and no fucking fingers.

Mary felt the guy on top of her push hard into her and stay, then moan and come. He lay still for a moment then pulled out.

How many was that? she wondered as she watched his fat ass walk away from her in just his socks and disappear into the bathroom. Six or seven?

"I'll bring the clients, and we'll split the money," the tattooed Russian cunt had said right after the first guy had come and gone. "I'm a businessman. You'll get the thousand dollars you asked for. Don't worry about that."

But at what rate? she thought. Back alley Moscow rates? Ten dollars a go? By now he must have pulled in almost three thousand, and the afternoon wasn't even over.

She looked at the guy's trousers. Sitting up, she put her hand into his pockets and began rifling around for a phone. She found it and turned it on then stopped. What would she do? Call the cops? Call a friend? Tell them she'd been abducted? Then it would all be out to her friends and family that she'd been whoring, even if it was only part time. And worse still, she'd have to look over her shoulder for this psycho for the rest of her life.

Mary stared at the door and listened as the man with a fat gut, who smelled and had bad breath and had just fucked her without saying a word, took a leak in the bathroom. No, she'd wait and ride it out. See how it went. Then if she wasn't getting out, or if he became violent again, she'd have a plan and maybe be able to kill him herself. She sat up and, still naked, stared out of the window at the rain outside and the mountains in the background covered in clouds.

Right now, she should be at home or out buying the pair of Jimmy Choo's she had her eye on, but she was stuck here with this fucking tattooed monster. He had said he'd let her go, and strangely, she believed him.

But when?

She looked back to the bathroom door and heard the

toilet flush. Illya was standing outside the bedroom door now, the flick of his lighter lighting another cigarette giving him away. She thought what she'd do was not wash anymore or anything like that. Eventually, she'd stink worse than a fish shop or this prick's mother or any other whore he'd beaten into submission and pimped out. Then that guy, that Russian fucking psycho could go muster up some other girl he could talk into coming over with the promise of big bucks and his bullshit about being an actor in a miniseries. He'd kick her out, and she'd make a call and then clean herself up and come straight back within the hour, looking like a million dollars, and sit and let her looking good be the last thing he saw as her ex-boyfriend and his friends dug his eyes out with a teaspoon.

Chapter Twenty-Four

Dan stood in the shower and looked down at his pubes as the water ran through them. He had the cream the doctor had given him, but couldn't remember if he'd said to put it on before or after having washed. After seemed logical, but none of what had been happening to him lately was logical. Fuck, it was sore down there, and it stung when he rubbed the soap in. So the answer was obvious, it was as he thought—tomorrow if he showered, he'd put the cream on before he got in.

As soon as Dan turned off the shower, he heard shouting outside. Getting out, he toweled off quickly and looked out the bathroom window to see a man in an apron looking up at him. Still with the towel wrapped around him, Dan came out of the bathroom to find his mother standing in the living room with tears in her eyes, holding her long blond hair in a bunch.

"What's going on?" he asked.

Tricia shook her head. Looking to the floor, she said, "It doesn't matter…it's that guy, you know, the baker. I told him to stop coming around now as I didn't feel good about it anymore."

Dan looked at his mother. She had to be kidding. "So what about all the pastries and shit?" he asked.

"I know you think free food means as much to me as it does you, Dan, but you'll be surprised to know that I didn't spend the last couple of months dating this guy just because he brought cakes around three times a week."

Dan could already feel his stomach beginning to rumble.

The thought of getting up and not being able to stuff his face with freshly baked goods was too much to bear. "Maybe you should think about this for a while," he said, "before you make any rash decisions. You know, think it through first."

Dan walked to the window and stared at the man and then his bread van, which was parked behind him.

"I thought he was taller," he said.

Tricia stared at her son for a moment and wiped her eyes. "What do you mean?"

"I've only ever seen his legs."

"You've met him with me at the patisserie loads of times, and you spoke to him."

Dan looked back at the window and said, "I've never seen him before in my life."

"I've been dating him for months, Dan!"

Dan turned away and looked back through the window, the short Italian baker still out there looking pissed, the guy's fat little legs kicking out at nothing as he paced up and down the curbside along the length of his van.

"Is that what you call it?"

Tricia took a deep breath and felt the frustration and embarrassment run through her. Her son was right. They'd been out a couple of times when he'd first chatted her up at the patisserie his family owned. She'd liked his smile and the way his dark hair was always neat and combed tightly to his head and the way he always made her feel special. But when had they been out since? The truth was they hadn't, even when she'd laid with him in bed after they'd made love and told him, "We need to go out more."

And as he'd rested there, doing his best to look sexy, and smelling of the cologne his wife had bought him for Christmas, he'd answered, "Baby, of course I'll take you.

204

There's a nice restaurant we can go to and then to a concert."

But as the time went on, and the kitchen filled with delicacies, she realized it was only Dan's stomach enjoying the relationship.

Tricia looked up and in a stern voice said, "Yeah, and that's why it's over."

Then, hitting the nail on the head, Dan simply said, "Yeah, well, I suppose it's hard to compete against a Ferrari when all you've got is a bread van."

******

By the time afternoon had come, the baker had left, and Dan had resorted back to masturbating after reading through a website showing bar code circuitry which enabled ticket guns at concerts to be circumnavigated by using binary code. Then he'd seen a picture of a pretty girl in the bikini at the bottom of the page, reached for his sock drawer, and was just about there when Mazzi Hegan's Ferrari pulled up outside.

They were chatting in the kitchen when Dan came upstairs, his mother glowing, wearing her tight jeans and a new top, and Chendrill still sporting his seventies' haircut and Hawaiian shirt.

"You ever going to go on holiday, or are you just wearing those shirts for a bet?" Dan asked.

"At least I've got a shirt," Chendrill replied.

Dan opened the fridge as his mother asked, "What are you doing down there?"

"Looking at stuff. Trying to find a way of getting into Dead Mau5."

"Who?" his mother asked.

"He's a DJ—Canadian," Chendrill said, trying to sound

cool. "You like him, do you?" he asked Dan.

Dan pulled a block of cheese from the fridge and broke off a chunk. "If I didn't, I wouldn't be looking. Why are you here anyway? Am I supposed to be somewhere again?"

Chendrill shook his head. "No, just doing what I'm being paid for and looking out for your safety."

"Really?"

Chendrill smiled. The kid was on to him. He wasn't as stupid as he made himself out to be. He nodded and said, "And that includes seeing if your mother wants to go to dinner again."

Tricia beamed. "That depends where," she said.

"I was thinking Italian."

"Yeah, she'd like that," Dan said. "She can't get enough of them."

******

They sat down at a corner table, each picking up a piece of bread and placing it on their side plate as the waiter poured some red wine.

"So you're the real deal, then? A real live private eye?" Tricia asked.

Chendrill smiled. "Yep—that's me." He was, but it was not the life he'd thought it would turn out to be.

"And you work for these guys who are paying Dan all this money?"

Chendrill nodded. "Yep, they think I'm incredible."

"Why?"

"Because a year ago, I found the CEO's little dog after he lost it in the park, and now he won't stop hiring me."

"Where was it?" Tricia asked, as she picked up her glass

of wine and took a sip.

"At the dog pound."

Tricia gave him a look, unsure as to whether he was joking. "You're kidding?"

Chendrill shook his head. "I'm not. The owner of the company, Sebastian, called me. He was hysterical. I told him, I'm sorry, but I don't do dogs. I only deal in serious matters. Then he started screaming into the phone, saying, 'I'll give you ten thousand dollars.' So I went to the office of Slave, the company Dan is contracted to, and I've never seen such a fuss made. Sebastian was, like I said, hysterical. The other guy who hates me, Hegan, especially now since Sebastian's given me his car, was being all huffy, and on top of it all, the girl at the reception desk was in tears."

Tricia sat back in her chair, smiling. "So what did you do?" she asked.

"I called the dog pound, and they said he was there, so I went over and picked him up."

"That was it?"

Chendrill nodded. "Yep."

"And you charged them ten thousand dollars for that?"

"No, they paid me ten thousand dollars for doing that. There's a difference. Like I said, I don't usually do dogs."

Tricia smiled again. "What about cats?"

"I'm too old to climb trees."

"And now they pay you to babysit my son and give you the company car to boot about in?"

"They like him. They say he has an air of rawness about him."

Tricia stared down at the table for a moment and fiddled with her fork. "There's definitely something about him," she said.

"Yeah, like we mentioned before, he's a genius and is going to be a famous name in the electronics industry."

Tricia looked up from her bread roll. "Well, he did fix the doorbell, so he must know a bit about how it all works. But when he was a young boy, I always thought he'd end up as a professional dancer."

Chendrell was enjoying himself—this was getting better. Dan, the electronic genius, slash ballroom dancer, slash catwalk model. It wasn't the first time she'd bought up Dan's dancing, so there had to be some truth to it and even if it was simply mother's pride, it was all good listening as he liked this woman. She had a naiveté about her and was as sweet as a freshly bloomed flower you'd find in a meadow on an early spring morning, not that he'd been to any meadows lately.

He said to her, "Anyway, I'm glad I'm looking out for him as it gives me the excuse to keep an eye on you and make sure you're okay instead."

She was, Tricia thought. She was more than okay. Sure, the man was stuck in the seventies, but there was really something sexy about him.

"So how did you get brought into looking after Dan?" she asked.

Chendrill picked up his glass and smiled. "I was not brought into looking after him. I was brought in to find him."

"And I'm guessing he wasn't at the pound."

Chendrill laughed. "No, not this time, but I did check. Dan, I must say—and please excuse me—had found himself in a peculiar situation."

"Like what?"

"Let's say he has a rare talent and was discovered."

"By who? Was he found in a shopping mall like that Marsha woman?"

Chendrill laughed to himself. Out loud, he said, "Similar. The head photographer of Slave snapped a candid photo of him, and they brought me in to track him down."

"What was he doing? Was he on the street?"

"No, in an elevator."

"And you found him? From a photo? How did you do that when there are a million kids living around here?"

Chendrill smiled and watched the waiter as he brought two salads to the table.

"I nearly steered clear of these guys altogether this time 'round. You see, I'd been working solid, and I was on my way back home, having just become free."

Tricia smiled politely and toyed with the top leaves of the romaine lettuce covered in dressing as Chendrill continued, "I'd been working for this English guy out at a farm in Aldergrove. He'd married a Canadian girl he met at the Ascot races—the place in the UK where they wear those fancy hats—and they settled out here. You see, he inherited a racehorse over there, and lucky for him, it was a big winner. Earned him a fair whack of money by the look of the place. Anyway, he met this girl half his age and followed her back here, and for the last five years, he's been putting the horse out to stud."

Tricia took a mouthful of salad, swallowed, and asked, "And you were there to check up on the young wife?"

Chendrill shook his head and frowned, "No."

"I thought that's what private eyes did?"

"Sometimes—but no, I'd been there for a while watching one of the stable guys. The owner was convinced he was stealing the horse's sperm."

Taking the fork from her mouth, Tricia looked at Chendrill in astonishment, then said, "Sorry?"

The case had been different for Chendrill, and it had all started when a friend put him forward as a recommendation to an Englishman he'd met on a golf course.

The Englishman explaining his problem about his suspected goings on as he cheated in the rough, and the friend having heard enough had simply told him, "Chendrill will sort it out. He's the best detective you'll ever find."

And the Englishman had said straight back, "Tell him he's hired."

Chendrill had entered the Englishman's property along a small road lined with old cedars dividing a series of paddocks with fences painted red, white, and blue, each with its own stallion or mare named after members of the British Royal Family who were still alive or long gone. Their brass nameplates, brightly polished, shone in the sun, sporting the names Queeny, Lady Di, Prince Philip, Charlie Boy, and George IV, all of them alongside another sign that read, *Horses bite and so do I—so do not touch.*

And reading it, Chendrill knew it was going to get interesting.

The mansion was new, but the wife was newer, a right little hot potato, who it turned out was local, from Kitsilano in Vancouver. While traveling around the UK looking for a rich husband, she had found one at the races.

The man from Ascot sat Chendrill down at a table on the veranda that looked out across a garden and further on toward more paddocks at the back of the property, and the first words he said as he handed Chendrill a thirty-year-old Macallan were, "Would you like a scotch?"

And the second thing he said after he'd stood silent, staring at his horses out in the paddocks, was, "Would you like another?"

His main concern was that the stable further along the road and nearer to the U.S. border had just had a foal, and in the opinion of the guy from Ascot, the foal came from his champion thoroughbred by the name of Prince Charles, but no one had given him the one hundred thousand he charged for putting his stallion out to stud.

"How can you tell?" Chendrill had asked.

"You've just got to look at it," the man from Ascot replied, his English accent tight with frustration. "Go see it. Thoroughbreds are the result of centuries of breeding. They're mixes of Arab and North African Barbary. Good God, man, they don't just appear on the farm next door where all they normally churn out are ponies!"

Chendrill finished his second scotch and then had a large Bushmills. He thought it rude not to have a taste of a 1964 Macallan and then a quick taste of a fifty-year-old pure malt Dalmore, followed by a Chivas Regal. By the time he'd gotten away, his head was spinning, and he had enough knowledge of horses to last a lifetime. He found his way to the paddock and the most comfortable-looking bale of hay he'd ever seen in his life, and slept.

******

Tricia sat there and smiled as she listened. Many years ago, she knew an English family, and the father had had a penchant for scotch, so she understood the feeling. After a while, she'd found it best to just say no or have only one at the start of the evening.

She took a sip of wine and asked, "So he knocked you out before you even started?"

Chendrill nodded and smiled. "Yeah, kind of, I suppose.

Anyway, about two hours later, I surfaced, and there was this Englishman out there riding around his paddock drunk on the back of this million-dollar thoroughbred that was strutting and twitching all over the place. And the guy calls me over and tries to get me to get up on the horse to take it for a ride."

"And did you?"

Chendrill shook his head. "Not a chance. Can you imagine if it took off at racing speed and cleared the fence and kept going with me on its back? If I even got that far! No, I went off and found the farm and the stall where the foal was kept, and I have to be honest, after seeing the little thing running about in the paddock, I couldn't see what this crazy Englishman had seen. But I crept into the stable in the dead of night and managed to grab a hair sample off the little thing."

Tricia laughed, watching Chendrill twirling a loop of spaghetti around his fork. "Do you have like a special nighttime Hawaiian shirt that you wear for such clandestine investigations?"

The sad thing was that Chendrill did—a black Hawaiian shirt with dark palm leaves. He'd picked it up while trying to look like he could surf on Waikiki Beach, and it served as a cool camo. He'd worn it that night as he'd snuck through the farm grounds and into the stable in the darkness, awkwardly reaching in and cutting some hair from the young foal's mane. Then he'd let science do the rest.

"And he was right?" Tricia asked as she watched Chendrill's moustache bobbling up and down as he delicately worked his way through a mixed mouthful of Italian sausage and tomato.

He shrugged, swallowed, and began to laugh. "How the

hell he could tell, God only knows. You know, the funny thing is that as I drove up the driveway to this guy's mansion with the results, he jumped out with binoculars from behind a tree and said to me, 'He's in there now, in there stealing my sperm!' So both me and this crazy Brit stinking of scotch sneaked up and into the thoroughbred's stall and caught one of the stable boys relieving the beast into a giant condom and pouring it into a coffee flask."

Tricia put her hand to her mouth and started to laugh. "No! Please, no!"

Chendrill began to laugh along with her.

"So what did you do?" she asked.

"Well, I confronted the kid. He denied it, of course. Said it was yogurt his mum had given him. And the drunk Brit screams out, 'Go on, then. Eat it. Drink the fucking stuff!' Then he grabs the huge condom the kid had hidden and slaps him around the head with it. Then he attacks him with his arms flailing out all over the place, and they start fighting. I tried to break it up—you know get in there between them— but then, the contents of the flask ended up all over me."

Tricia could not help herself and burst out laughing.

Chendrill continued, "And so, I ended up dragging the kid, who was no bigger than you, over to the mansion with this English guy from Ascot, all red in the face with his comb-over hair all over the place, in tow and carrying what's left of the flask as evidence. I thought the man was going to drop dead of a heart attack. When we got there, this stable boy slash, wannabe jockey confessed to stealing and selling the magic potion for five hundred dollars a pop, and it turned out loads of foals over the last couple of years in British Columbia had been seeded by this horse that won the Grand National. Anyway, I left stinking of horses and goodness knows what, and I got another call from Sebastian at Slave about another 'absolute emergency' that I had to attend to right there and then. I thought to myself, could what they have to offer be any worse than what's just happened to me? So I went straight over."

"Lucky for me you did," Tricia said, still smiling.

"No," Chendrill said straight back with a grin and the slightest glint in his eye. "I can honestly say, the luck was all mine!"

Chendrill pulled the Ferrari up outside Dan's home, got out, and walked around the other side to open Tricia's door. She was a good woman, Chendrill thought, and when she asked him in, it was hard to decline, but something inside him was not sitting right with everything he'd been told by the dentist. And if there was one thing he knew about himself, it was that when he felt this way, he was always right. So he said, "I'm sorry, but please tell Dan to stay in his room and not get into any trouble."

Then he leaned forward, pulled Tricia in to him, kissed her straight on the lips, and held her there.

Trisha loved it, this man in the red Ferrari holding her like he was and kissing her outside her small, old home on Vancouver's Eastside. Her there, surrendering to him, kissing him back as she pushed her breasts hard into his chest.

Chendrill held onto her for the longest time, enjoying the feel of her breasts against him. Eventually he let go, and with his eyes wide and clear, he looked into hers and said, "That felt nice."

Chapter Twenty-Five

Almost an hour later, Chendrill was sitting at Dennis's dining table with its new white cloth, sharing one of the beers he'd bought for him.

"Was the brother of your wife, who was here illegally, violent?" he asked Dennis straight out.

Dennis nodded and looked to the floor.

"Dennis," said Chendrill, "I'm a private eye. Whatever you tell me will go no further. I'm not here to cause you trouble. I'm just trying to discover what happened to my friend."

Dennis looked up at him, then said, "I was thinking after you left that your friend was possibly the pretty woman who came here, am I right?"

Chendrill nodded. "Daltrey was her name."

Dennis nodded and closed his eyes. "That's right, like the singer."

Chendrill took a deep breath and then another swig of his beer and thought back to his time with her. "Like the singer" was one of the first things he'd ever said to her when they'd met in the canteen, and she'd said, "Yeah, I'm glad my surname wasn't Tucker, because I've been hearing people say that my whole life." Looking back to Dennis, he heard him say, "Yeah, her brother was violent, very violent, he had this trick where he could suddenly produce fire out of nowhere. The man scared the shit out of me. Alla told me he'd been to prison in Russia for burning a pimp to death, and now he's doing the same here, no doubt."

"You told this to Daltrey?"

Dennis stared at his new tablecloth. "I wish I had because after you left, I did a bit of research and chances are my silence cost her her life."

Chendrill shook his head. "You don't know that it was him, Dennis. You've done nothing wrong."

But there was a lot more, Chendrill could tell, and fishing for it now was not the way to go—it could wait. It would come in its own time, and only when Dennis was ready. Changing the subject, he asked, "You said you were in the movies now?"

Dennis shrugged and said, "Yeah, still humping heavy sandbags around all day. If you call that being in the movies, then I'm in the movies. That's what I do."

"What are you working on?"

"TV—series, mostly. Just day calling and sitting around in the rain and being treated like an idiot by people who are just that, but it's work. Soon I'll be getting my dentist's license back, and I'm going to take a real job up in the northern territories where the money's good. They're screaming for dentists up there, and I can't see it being too taxing because when I was last up that way, most of the people I saw didn't have any teeth."

Chendrill laughed and said, "Yeah, you're right."

"So that's where I'll be soon, and if you need to see me there, you'll have to sell your rocket and buy a truck to get through the snow."

Chendrill smiled, and said, "It's not my car." Then he asked, "Can I ask what happened to your license?"

Dennis looked away and then to Mazzi Hegan's Ferrari sitting in the street outside. "It got pulled after I pulled one too many of the wrong teeth out. Before that, years ago, I used to own one of them," he said, nodding at the car, "but I married this woman I met on the Internet. It was great at first, then the brother turned up, and all hell broke loose."

"What kind of hell?"

Dennis stayed quiet, but after a moment he looked at Chendrill and said, "Hell as in hell. He said that I'd married a whore, and that before coming here, my wife had sold her ass up on this road that he's stupidly got tattooed on his back."

"He said it to you just like that?"

Dennis shook his head as he thought back to Illya screaming at him, drunk on the vodka Dennis had bought and throwing Dennis's personal belongings around the house while shouting, "Your wife, the cunting whore, she fuck many men every day and give me the money. One, two, three, twenty men every day. She is cunt whore, your wife."

Chendrill stared at him for a moment without speaking then said, "He spoke to you like that?"

"No, worse," Dennis replied, feeling the upset of the year before well up in him. "Alla screamed at me when I told her what he'd said. She said he was crazy, but her brother said to ask her how she got the scar on her leg. I did, but she said it was from horse-riding when she was young. She said there were wild ponies around that they would all ride. But he said all the whores who worked the road fucking guys in the cars had the same scar from where their legs got stuck between the seat and the door as they sat on their laps, riding their cocks."

Chendrill sat there listening. This was the way the brother spoke to Dennis while he was eating his food and drinking his beer? Fuck me, what a piece of work.

"And she does have a scar like that?" Chendrill asked.

Dennis nodded. "But the truth is, I don't know how it

could be from horse-riding because it's on the outside of her leg. I mentioned this to her, and she started to cry, as girls do, and I felt like a prick. But her brother kept at me, saying, 'You idiot, you idiot, you married a whore.' Then she turned on me. Said I was a bastard for not believing her, that I was the kind of guy who called his wife a prostitute. I asked her brother to leave, and then it got ugly. He attacked me, saying he was part of the package that came when you had to buy a wife over the Internet—'your fucking mail-order bride,' he'd say. After about six months, I was a mess. She was fucking with me and spending so much, and I wasn't sleeping because I thought he was going to come into the room and attack me. So I rented a place for myself."

"For yourself?"

Dennis nodded, and in complete embarrassment looked away to the floor.

"Yeah, for myself. A house a few miles from here, actually, and I happily went, for a bit. I went back when this other guy came on the scene—Sergei, his friend. A good-looking blond guy. He was around all the time, living in my house. He was always there when I'd come over to see Alla, you know, after work. Or they'd all be out late hitting my credit card hard. I couldn't concentrate at work or do anything right anymore, and that's when I started making mistakes—small at first, then big ones.

"Then Alla went out one night and never came home. That was the last time I saw her, but she was still using my credit card. And then it got worse. At first, I thought maybe she'd just needed a break and would be back, but then I said, as she's obviously gone, I wanted them both out, and they had till the end of the week to go or I'd call the cops. Anyway, there was a fire at the house—I don't know how it started, but I can imagine. A kid was killed, another kid was injured, and after that Illya and his friend disappeared off the face of the earth.

"I lost the plot, there was big trouble, there were lawsuits coming in at me from all angles, and I was answering questions from the police about the kid I'd never met who was illegal and had been in the house. I kept making more mistakes at work, and then one day I just couldn't take it anymore—my wife had left, my home was gone, and I was about to lose my business. I drove myself to a point I knew on this lake out beyond Mission. I was like a man possessed. I remember crying all the way, tears streaming down my face so that I could barely see. I got out of the car and ran down the slope like a blubbering mess and threw myself off this cliff about thirty feet high into the deep water below, and I hit the water and sank deeper and deeper."

Chendrill sat there and listened, waiting for more, and when it did not come, he said, "So what happened? Why are you still here?"

"Because the water was bloody freezing, that's why."

Chendrill laughed. There was more to this man than he let on. He was a character and a good soul, caught out by bad people it seemed. In life, some people just don't see it coming, and he was one of them.

"And you swam back out?" Chendrill asked.

"Like an Olympic champion. The water there's fresh off the glacier. If you want to drown yourself, go find a hot spring or one of those big communal hot tubs they have in the condo buildings downtown."

Chendrill laughed again and sat back in his chair. This guy, Dennis the dentist with the wife with the scar on her knee, was a funny guy. He wondered if he'd be able to stay in contact with him after all the shit had left the fan.

"Have you heard from your wife lately?"

Dennis nodded his head. "Yes, she called me."

"And did she know the guy who burned in the fire?"

Dennis shrugged. "I can't say for sure. Maybe. I'll never forget his name, though, or the pictures the police showed me. Bernado Gomez. He was twenty-three, from Mexico."

"And you told them about Illya?"

"I told them that Alla's brother and a friend of hers had been staying at my house while I wasn't living there, and I didn't know where they were."

"And what did they say?"

"What could they do? The guy and his friend just disappeared."

"Along with your wife."

Dennis nodded again and looked back out the window. "Along with my wife, along with my business, along with my home, and along with my life," he mumbled.

The clouds were low, and it looked like rain as Chendrill drove back into town. As he swished the first drops of rain from the windshield with the wipers, he felt the heavy sag in his stomach he had felt many times before. He was getting closer to the truth—there was little doubt about it.

Daltrey had found Alla's brother, and after that, the brother had more than likely found her. That was the most logical conclusion. And Dennis had done nothing but get himself into a situation that he wasn't capable of getting himself out of. He was guilty of nothing more than being lonely and falling in love. In fact, Chendrill doubted, give or take the odd root canal, if he'd ever hurt anyone in his life.

Illya Bragin, a guy who had a talent for producing fire without anyone seeing it coming, was the possible killer of the guy on the boat, along with his old friend Daltrey, and a young Mexican kid by the name of Bernado Gomez. And he was out there somewhere.

Chapter Twenty-Six

Marsha's agent Gill Banton sat back and let the guy from Venezuela who was half her age rub the oil into the inside of her big toe for what must have been the twentieth time that evening. It felt nice, the way he was hitting that spot right there at the joint, the way he held the ball of her foot and worked his way up from the heel and ended up right back there at the sweet spot. It was now almost one in the morning, and she was still working. Marsha was pissed— she'd been in London for just over a day, and no one had yet called to say hello or bothered to invite her over to the palace to meet the Queen. In fact, the only call she had gotten was the one she was on now from her agent, telling her that the problem with the crabs was getting a little out of hand.

"I haven't got crabs," Marsha said irritably into the phone as the young man who wanted so bad to hit the catwalks of Milan switched to Gill's other foot and wondered whether he should take his top off or not.

"I know you haven't," Gill said in frustration, closing her eyes and leaning her head back into the satin pillow of the huge cream-colored sofa she'd picked up in Barcelona. "But that isn't the issue, is it? The problem is that the media all over the world thinks you do. And please don't suggest for one moment that this is the reason the palace hasn't been in touch."

"Well, it might have something to do with it."

"It has nothing to do with it," said Gill as she lifted her other foot and slowly stroked it up and down the young man's chest. "And by the way, you managed to leave everything—and I mean everything—at the hotel in Vancouver again."

Marsha looked around at the suite full of cases and bags and said, "Well, it's all here."

"Yes, it is, but Buffy had to sort it out."

"Buffy?"

"Yes, Buffy. She works for you."

"She does?" Confused, Marsha stared at her cases that still hadn't been unpacked for her and tried to recall whether she'd ever met a Buffy in her life.

Hearing the slightest of groans, she then heard her agent Gill Barton say, "Buffy works very hard for you, Marsha. She's been with you for nearly two years. She packed your bags."

Marsha looked back again to her luggage for a moment and said, "I'm sure I checked in, though."

"You checked in, but your luggage didn't. Buffy had to stay behind and pack them for you, then fly with everything by private jet so you could have clean knickers to put on when you got there. Which, I might add, cost you a whole lot of extra money."

"The fucking bitch."

"Anyway, I've put out a press release saying you're in a very committed and loving relationship with this guy you slept with in Vancouver, and that the whole thing is nonsense."

"Why?"

"Because it's okay press for a male renegade actor or a reality TV personality to have crabs, darling, but bad press for a supermodel—even if you do support animal rights. I've built you up to be the figurehead for multinational corporations, Marsha. Forgetting to pack your clothes and leaving them all behind falls within supermodel territory and is okay, but having crabs, my dear, is nothing but bad press. You're there to advertise a product, darling, the people you're signed to could easily dump you and rehire some sexy new model who gives incredible foot massages—doing that gets them global attention for free. So keep that in mind."

Taking a deep breath, Marsha said, "You can't say I'm in a relationship with the guy. He's a jerk, and he insulted me. He called me Margaret Thatcher!"

In a huff, she stood and walked over to the window. She wasn't worried—she was the sexiest bitch this planet had ever seen and had the magazines to prove it. She looked out again across the park to Buckingham Palace in the distance, the morning sun now cutting through the dense trees and lighting Victoria's memorial at its center.

She waited, listening to the silence on the other end of the phone that seemed to last forever. Eventually giving up, Marsha took another deep breath and then said, "Hello?"

As the guy from Caracas worked his hand up past her knee, Gill said, "Well, I've done it now, so be prepared. I've arranged a couple of interviews with some magazines for you this morning at Langham's Brassiere. Buffy will fill you in, but don't eat or say anything negative about the guy, like you've split up or something, or they'll take it that there's a reason."

Marsha ran her hand through her hair and stared at herself in the ornate and enormous mirror hanging on the wall. She then turned her eyes to a portrait of King Charles I on the wall and asked, "Why do the guys here wear funny clothes and have such long hair?"

Gill was silent for a moment on the other end of the phone. This time, it had little to do with what was happening on the inside of her thighs. It was the years of babysitting these beautiful people who hadn't a clue about the real world. Ten percent of their pay or not, she was growing tired of it all, and as the young man's hand reached the top of her legs and gently stroked the underside of her little cotton panties, she released the tiniest gasp and then said, "It's called history, darling, and if you can't remember the name of the last guy you slept with, it's Dan, Dan Treedle. He's from Vancouver, he works out of Slave, you've been together a while now, and he's the greatest lover and sexiest man you've ever met."

******

Dan sat at the small desk in the corner of his basement room in just his socks and a T-shirt, vibrating in between his feet sat a fan on full blast blowing cold air straight into his crotch as he stared at an electronic wiring diagram that was open on his computer.

Just by looking at it for a few minutes, it was easy to see he could put together a card. Then by adding three diodes and an AA battery, he could defeat the alarm system on any Ferrari built since 2005. Not that he was going to do it, but Mazzi Hegan's Ferrari was pretty good fun to drive, and after all, truth was, why should his bodyguard get to ride around in it when he was the talent?

Reaching down into an old box, he pulled out a series of circuit boards, stared down at them, and then back to the screen. Daltrey's death was still playing on his mind and had left a lump in his stomach. Only a few days ago, he'd sat where he was now and put together all the components for the small door and elevator infrared system he'd made for her. Which was fine because from his antics, he now had a shitload of cash coming in, got to use one of those big showers and drive the sports car, and had even gotten a little tittie action with the chick from McDonald's and Marsha to boot.

******

He stared out the window and thought about Daltrey. She was a good girl really. Funny and full of herself, but they'd had fun, and she had laughed at him when he'd not been able to keep down those overpriced oysters. Perhaps they could have gone somewhere together as a couple, out to Whistler maybe, or he could have wowed her with some moves on the dance floor, and then she would have really fallen for him. Maybe they could have had kids or a dog. She was gone now, though, and even if it was written in the stars for them both, it was no longer and could never be again.

There had to be some kind of funeral coming up or a wake of some sort. Maybe Chendrill could find out, and they could go together. Maybe his mum would go as well, and maybe this time, those two could get the bus, and he could take the car. Then when they got there, he could turn up late at the graveyard in the Ferrari, like they do in the movies. He'd slam the door and stroll in with everyone looking at him, and they'd all wonder who he was and say, "Hey, who is this guy? Wow, that must be Daltrey's boyfriend."

And then Dan would stand there proudly while everyone else was crying, and he'd take his mum by the hand and lead her over to Daltrey's coffin and say, "Mum, I'd like to introduce you to my girlfriend."

******

Chendrill drove along the highway back into town and remembered that he was supposed to report Mazzi Hegan's car missing. He'd forgotten. Signaling, he slowed the car down, pulled off right, and then took a left onto Hastings. As he passed the fairgrounds, he thought about Tricia and maybe popping in to see if Dan was behaving himself. Either that or go back to the hospital and start asking Alla Bragin about her brother and how a young Mexican kid managed to burn to death in her husband's home.

******

Alla Bragin lay in her hospital bed, trying as hard as possible to concentrate on moving her toes. Just as she thought they had, the door opened, and the prick in the Hawaiian shirt stepped into her room. He walked across the room and sat down uninvited next to the bed.

"I think you better tell me about this boyfriend of yours, Alla,"

Alla closed her eyes. Fuck, could this get any worse? Everything she knew was unraveling, and if this prick knew about Sergei, then how long was it going to be before Dennis found out?

"Did Dennis mind then, Alla, that you had a boyfriend? Was it okay with him, paying for you living it up with Sergei? Because I don't think when he decided to bring you over here and support you that he had any idea what he was getting himself into."

Alla stayed quiet. She knew only too well there were prisons all over the world full of people with big mouths who had put themselves there.

Chendrill leaned in so close to her that she could smell

on his breath the cheap coffee he'd been drinking at her husband's place not less than an hour before.

"And I haven't even got started yet about your brother," he said, "and how he burned Bernado Gomez to death in Dennis's home with his flame trick and then torched the house to make it look like an accident."

Fuck, Alla thought and closed her eyes as she felt a wave of terror rip up her chest from her medicated stomach.

Chendrill watched as this beautiful girl who was rotten inside closed her eyes and tried to hide the panic washing through her body.

"That's the way it is, is it not? Your brother Illya with his special trick, producing fire out of nowhere. He used to do it when he lost his temper to get his own way, didn't he? But it went too far, and he killed the young kid—burned him to death just like he did my friend Daltrey, the cop. He surprised her with his little fire game, and he did the same thing to the guy they found on the boat. Who was that Alla? Was it Sergei, the blond, good-looking boyfriend you brought over here on your husband's coin? Or was it someone else, maybe another lover I haven't found out about yet? How many other lovers has your brother destroyed, Alla? Are you going to tell me what's been going on, or am I going to have to let you be transferred to a secure hospital where you'll be questioned incessantly about everything I already know? They will continue to do so until they find out where your brother is hiding."

Alla opened her eyes again and looked for the button she could press to summon a nurse who had the authority to tell this fucker in the flowery shirt to go. But God, he was on to her and her brother. How much did Dennis know for this guy to have found out Sergei was her lover, and it was possibly him who had burned on the creek?

It was not Illya's style to put on a display. He was a "there and then" type of personality. The burning boat out on the creek had to be the work of the guy who had hit her and put her in the hospital.

Chendrill leaned back in his chair, waited a moment, then said, "Was it your brother who put on the show, Alla, and put you in here, was it him who did all these things? Maybe you were just an innocent young girl who got caught up with bad blood, who only left to keep her husband safe?"

What was he after? Alla thought. He knew the work she'd been doing—he'd already told her that—but what was this? Was he offering her a deal, saying she had two possible ways to go—the hard way or the easy way—but he'd take her down either way? But he wasn't a cop. He'd told her that.

"I'm after the person who killed my friend," Chendrill said, "and it couldn't have been you, Alla, because you were here. The way I see it, you had it good with Dennis, but when Illya came along, things got pretty bad. If you tell me what I need to know about where Illya is, you may find I keep my mouth closed to everyone, including Dennis, about your whoring, because from what I can see, you've suffered enough. So maybe, and I mean maybe, there's a chance you can get your life in order and Dennis can be the one who helps you do this. He can be the good guy who pushes you around in your chair and takes care of you for the rest of your life. Otherwise, you'd better get some gloves because those lovely hands of yours are going to be pretty sore."

Alla lay still and thought about what the private eye wearing the bright red shirt with palm trees on it had said. She looked at the card he'd left on the bedside table conveniently propped up against the water jug for her to see.

She didn't have a lot of options—in fact, she had none. She'd been there when the kid Bernado had died, and it had been the worst day of her life, until now. But if Dennis had known that, then so would this prick. The only people who truly knew were her, Illya, Sergei, and the girl, wherever she'd ended up. And if Sergei was now dead, then sad as it was, she'd take it as a blessing and get over it. The fewer people who knew, the better.

Chapter Twenty-Seven

Chendrill pulled up Mazzi Hegan's Ferrari outside Dan's house. Walking up to the door, he pressed the button on the key fob and heard the little beep that let him know his new ride was safe and secure.

Tricia greeted him inside, holding him tightly, her delicate arms wrapped around his strong, broad shoulders. As he looked down at her, she reached up and kissed him gently on the lips.

"Wow, I was not expecting that! I'm sorry it's a little late," Chendrill whispered, looking toward Dan's doorway at the bottom of the stairway that led to the basement.

"It's fine," said Tricia as she led him to the kitchen. "Thanks for such a nice lunch. That's what the kiss was for."

"How's the supermodel in training?"

Tricia looked down through the floorboards to the basement below and said, "He's doing something electrical again. I can smell the soldering he does whenever he's making something. What have you been up to?"

"Just stuff."

"Work?"

"Kind of. It was for free. *This* is work."

Tricia looked at him and smiled. "So you wouldn't be here if you weren't on the payroll?"

Chendrill slung his head to the side and said, "Maybe, maybe not."

Tricia moved in close to him again and slowly put her hand around the back of his neck. "So you have to be paid to keep coming around here to keep an eye on my terribly naughty son in the basement?"

Chendrill put his arm around her back and pulled her into him. He kissed her on the lips, pressing his big Thomas Magnum moustache hard into the soft skin at the base of her nostrils. "I don't need to be paid to be close to a woman like you, Tricia," he said then pulled back, and she kissed him again.

Dan listened as the talking went quiet in the kitchen above. It was always the same—the kitchen was where she always seduced them. Just like the baker guy a few months back, coming in with his tray of croissants, he thought. Fuck, how could his mum still be getting more action than him? Looking up, he listened as the footsteps moved from the kitchen to his mother's bedroom. And then, on cue, as with the baker, her nervous giggle started.

******

Chendrill lay next to Dan's mother on her bed. Pulling his head back from her, he watched as Tricia's giggle came to a halt.

"I'm sorry, I'm nervous," she said to him, smiling. "It's not every day I'm in here like this with a stranger."

"So I'm a stranger now?"

"You know what I mean. We've only just met."

Chendrill leaned in and kissed her again, soft at first, then harder. Slowly, he pulled his head away and began kissing her cheek, her neck, and then gently stroking her shoulders, letting his hand slip down to her breasts. They undressed each other, one button at a time, their lips barely parting until they were both naked. Moving above her, Charles Chuck Chendrill parted Tricia's legs and gently pushed himself against her, feeling her warmth surround him as he entered her. Then he heard the familiar sound—the gentle gasp of a woman feeling herself suddenly filled from within by a man—and then the other familiar sound of Mazzi Hegan's Ferrari starting up and being slowly driven away.

******

Dan made it to the end of his road as silently as he possibly could, then pulled out onto the main road and took off as fast as the Ferrari could go.

He was back! Just as he noticed the traffic lights were there, they went green. He gunned it quickly through and took a left. Fuck, it felt good! This was the car for him, and when he'd made his first paycheck, he was going to buy one for himself and another for his mum, along with the fridge. That would stop the neighbors from frowning at her when she brought her shopping home on the bus. Fuck 'em, they could sit and watch as she came home in a Ferrari while they washed their Hyundais.

Within a couple of minutes, Dan took another left, passed under the Golden Arches, and parked the Ferrari diagonally right outside McDonald's, just as he had before. With another fierce rev of the engine before turning the car off, he got out and locked the door by pressing the button he'd taped to the top of a shoebox containing the circuitry he'd thrown together as he'd cooled off his balls that made fools of an entire team of anti-theft technicians working at the plant at Maranello.

The first thing Melissa asked him as he stood behind the counter was, "Why didn't you leave your new shoes in the car?"

Dan looked at the shoebox tucked under his right arm. "Not shoes," he said, "I've just got some important stuff in here, that's all."

"Really?"

"Yeah. It's crucial stuff, real crucial. Can't lose it or anything like that."

"Wow. What would you like?"

You, Dan thought but instead said, "I'll have a double Big Mac, please."

"Fries?"

Dan nodded. "Of course—but I also wondered if you wanted to go dancing again after work?"

And she did, and an hour later and fully fed, Dan passed back under the Golden Arches, sped out across the road with an almighty roar, and headed into town with Melissa in the passenger seat.

"Why do you keep asking me out if you're gay," she asked, "or are you one of those guys who can't make up his mind?"

Dan pulled the Ferrari over to the side of the road.

"No," he said.

Melissa frowned and then smiled in a teasing way as Dan struggled with his words.

"I mean, I'm not. You think I'm gay because of the pad I was staying in, but that place is owned by the gay guy I work for."

"Oh yeah, in electronics research?"

"No," Dan answered again, "not that. I've got other interests. I'm actually a male model now. I'm contracted to Slave."

Melissa shook her head and said, "Don't know them."

Dan looked into the Ferrari's mirror, pulled away again,

and said, "They're global." He took the car past a bunch of people who drove shit cars and said, "Yeah, I just finished up doing a shoot on a yacht out at Deep Cove."

Impressed, Melissa looked at him. "How'd it go?" she asked.

"Great, really great. In and out really, wasn't there long. They got what they needed inside, but one of the important guys had to be rushed to the hospital, so you know, once he was gone, they couldn't do a lot."

"Nothing bad, I hope?"

Dan shook his head and frowned. "No, don't worry. Nothing life-threatening. Nothing a bit of cream won't sort out."

******

Charles Chuck Chendrill lay with Dan's mother's head on his chest and listened to her breathing as she unconsciously toyed with the hair on his chest. She was a keeper, this one, there was no doubt about it. They connected, and when they made love, it felt as though they'd known each other forever.

Without looking up, Tricia asked, "What did you mean earlier when we were kissing, and you said *fuck*?"

Chendrill lifted his head. "Nothing… It was just Dan. He stole the Ferrari," Chendrill said quietly.

Tricia sat up quickly, leaped off the bed, and looked out the window to see the empty space where the Ferrari had been parked. Worried and confused, she turned back to him.

"Oh my God!" she said. "How do you know it was Dan?"

Chendrill smiled. "It was Dan."

Tricia covered herself and walked quietly to the bedroom door. She opened it and called out her son's name. Nothing.

"I told you, he's stolen it."

Horrified, Tricia paced back to the window, looked up the road, and then turned back to Chendrill. "I didn't bring my son up to steal cars," she said.

Chendrill smiled again and motioned with his hand for her to come back toward the bed. "He's borrowed it then," he said.

Tricia sat back down on the bed and placed both arms by her side, perplexed. Then, propping herself up, she asked, "How? Where are the keys? He's going to be in trouble."

Chendrill leaned off the edge of the bed to reach his jeans that had been strewn on the floor and pulled the car keys from his pocket. "I don't know how he did it," he said. "The keys are here, but he got past the alarm system easily, and off he went."

Tricia took a deep breath. "Well, I apologize. This is so embarrassing. I'm telling you, I know we're not a well-off family, but I really didn't bring my son up to do such a thing."

Chendrill laughed. "Tricia, I didn't think you did, and I'm not pointing fingers. You're more upset about it all than I am."

"You don't care?"

"I do care because if he smashes it up, he may hurt himself or someone else. But I doubt that will happen. He's driven it before."

Tricia stood up again and then turned around to face Chendrill. "What? He's driven it before? When?"

"Like I said, you are worrying more than me."

******

Dan drove the Ferrari up the center of Robson Street, listening to the engine roar through the wide-open windows as he came downshifted and pulled up to the lights. He looked over at Melissa, who was truly loving it, and then to his phone as it began to ring. Magnum PI, the name he'd attached to Chendrill's number, came up on the screen.

"What?" Dan said when he answered.

Chendrill leaned back on the bed. "What are you doing with my car?" he asked.

"What are you doing with my mother?" Dan answered right back. "Besides, it's not your car. It's Mazzi's."

"Mazzi gave me the keys, not you."

"Yeah, but like I said, you've got an electronics genius sitting in the basement, and in this day and age of electronic instruments, keys mean fuck all."

Chendrill was intrigued now. "How did you get around the key?"

"You're the detective! You work it out."

"Could you bring the car back, please."

"When I've finished with it, I will. Melissa and I are going dancing."

Chendrill smiled and looked at Dan's mother listening, her head now resting on his thighs, her eyes gazing toward the window. "So I take it you've stuffed your face with burgers then?" he asked.

Dan laughed and pulled away from the light with enough roar to get Chendrill worried. "You remember Melissa then."

"Like you said, I'm the detective."

Chapter Twenty-Eight

At one time, Skip Nolan had been the most famous paparazzi ever. He was the guy who could get the impossible shots, the shots beyond the reach of the hundreds of fellow colleagues who besieged the clubs late at night waiting for the chance to snap off a shot of one of the beautiful people, those who became a part of people's lives through the pages of glossy magazines littering the waiting room of Dennis's former dental office.

In his time, Skip Nolan had hired planes, helicopters, hang gliders, and balloons. He'd scaled trees, hills, and small mountains, carrying huge telescopic lenses to get that million-dollar shot. He had been responsible for and proud of causing more breakups of the rich and famous than anyone he knew.

The reason for his incredible success rate was his network of insiders and his reputation for paying well for information that brought him the scoop that would go on to hit the covers of almost all the kiss-and-tell magazines throughout the Western world.

And it was through one of these sources he'd heard rumor of the new secret love in Marsha's life long before the rest of the media had somehow gotten word. For the life of him, he couldn't fathom exactly who Dan was and how the hell Marsha had managed to keep her secret love a secret for so long.

He'd arrived in town on the first flight out of LA that afternoon, and for five hundred American dollars and a bit of sweet talk, he picked up a photo and address from the receptionist at Slave's offices in Vancouver. An hour later, after sitting outside this model's stucco-coated home and wishing he'd eaten on the plane, a big guy with a Hawaiian shirt had pulled up in a Ferrari. Almost an hour after that, just as he'd ordered a pizza to be delivered to the rental car, Dan had appeared outside, playing around with a shoebox next to the Ferrari.

What the fuck Marsha saw in this guy with a broken nose who lived in a shithole, he couldn't figure out. It certainly wasn't his driving skills, Skip Nolan thought as his stomach rumbled while tailing Dan up and down Robson Street for the twentieth time that evening. So far, he had about ten usable long-lens shots of this guy eating burgers, but then a woman at McDonald's had come on the scene, and as soon as that happened, instinct told him that as the night wore on, and as long as his rental car didn't run out of fuel, he'd have his money shot.

******

Marsha was outraged. She couldn't believe it. Not three hours had gone by since she'd given the interviews in her private booth at Langham's Brassiere while eating lunch, laughed off the accusations of the sexual disease issue, and proclaimed her love for this guy in Vancouver. Come the afternoon, just after she'd finished making herself sick, the press were banging on her door, asking her about what she thought about the photographs of Dan out on the town with another girl.

What the hell was her agent thinking? she wondered as she opened the door to her suite.

She screamed down the corridor of the Ritz, "Buffy!"

Seconds later, Buffy appeared from her room and scuttled down the corridor, curious as to why after all this time, Marsha was suddenly using her name. She wiped the sugar from her lips and knocked quietly on the door. Opening it, she said, "Can I help?"

Marsha looked at this girl with fat little arms and said, "I need to speak with my agent. Now."

Buffy stared at the phone sitting on the dresser right next to where this prima donna was standing and said quite innocently, "Is your phone broken?"

"No, it's fucking not. Get her on the phone. And if you want to keep your job, get over to your bank and pay back the twenty-five thousand dollars you wasted on that private jet you treated yourself to getting over here while I was roughing it with all the fucking cattle."

Roughing it? Buffy thought. Sipping champagne and eating lobster in the ten-thousand-dollar fold-down bed she'd booked for her in first class?

She picked up the phone and began to dial the number for Marsha's agent, the same number she'd left for her, placing it right next to the phone in every room of the suite when she'd arrived. Chances were high the dippy bitch didn't even know she hadn't been on the plane with her.

It wasn't the first time Buffy had been threatened with her job. In fact, it was a weekly occurrence, and the truth was that they both knew if she did go, even of her own accord, Marsha wouldn't even know how to get to the airport on her own.

Gill was still naked at her Bel Air home and had only slept an hour after going to bed and answering three emails, having four orgasms, two of which were huge, and taking six phone calls so far throughout the night.

Burn

"I thought you said the pair of us were in love" were the first words she heard from Marsha on the seventh call that woke her and her young man from Venezuela.

Gill sat up and looked at the young Venezuelan man lying beside her, wondering how the hell he kept himself so hairless and managed to look perpetually oiled.

"No," Gill said, "you said he was a jerk. And let's just get this straight—you couldn't even remember the guy's name, and now you're all cut up about him being with another woman?"

All the emails and calls Gill had taken throughout the night had had to do with this idiot from Vancouver who'd apparently been out with a girl driving around in a Ferrari like a crazy man and causing chaos on the dance floor in some club. All well and good, but the timing could have been better. Now this airhead was swearing at the person who was the only reason she, in this world full of skinny and beautiful women, was commanding so much attention and staying at the Ritz.

"But I've just gone and humiliated myself with the British press, saying I'm with this guy at the same time he's going down on some chick on the dance floor!" Marsha said. Her head was spinning. Somehow she'd managed to find her way up onto the glass coffee table that was now beginning to wobble beneath her, and she was on the verge of ordering up a half dozen peanut butter and jelly sandwiches and then taking herself to the bathroom to be sick again.

Gill took a deep breath. Trying to calm the situation down, she said, "Don't worry—I'm on it. It could be his sister."

"It's not his sister! Have you seen the photos? You don't dance like that with your sister."

Gill leaned back and began to rub her toes along the Venezuelan's calves. She had seen the photos. In fact, she was one of the first to see them as they began to be sold and distributed throughout the local and foreign press. Spinning herself around, she reached her foot all the way up to the young man's backside and slid her toe into the crack of his ass.

"Anyway," Gill asked, "who's this girl he's dating? Did he mention anything to you about her?"

Marsha went silent and got down off of the coffee table. This was really starting to piss her off. Her last flame, an Eskimo she'd met while doing a shoot someplace where there was a lot of snow and it was so cold that they had to keep her in a hot tub for almost the whole day, had left her for an actress, and two on the trot was not going to look good. She said, "How the hell am I ever going to be taken seriously as an actress if everyone keeps stealing my boyfriends?"

"But you're not an actress, Marsha, you're a model."

"But I might want to be one day."

Gill had heard enough, and had had enough. The clock by her bed said it was five in the morning, and her man, whose name for the moment she couldn't remember, was now fully erect again.

"Marsha," she asked, "what time is it there in London?"

"One o'clock, why?"

"Because it's five in the morning here."

Marsha stayed quiet on the end of the phone for a moment, then asked, "Why's that?"

"It's because of the Earth's rotation, Marsha."

And Marsha answered, "Yeah, I know all about that. We did it at school—it's what makes it get windy."

******

It was around the same time that Chendrill awoke to the slam of the door on Mazzi Hegan's Ferrari.

Dan came in, still smarting from a slap on the face from Melissa. He disappeared into the basement, oblivious of the fact he'd made the morning gossip papers' headlines in Europe due to his antics some five hours earlier on the dance floor.

Chendrill lay still for a moment and thought about getting up and sneaking off, but something inside him said no. Go home to what? he thought. Tricia felt nice lying naked beside him, warm and smooth, her hair smelling clean and tickling his face as he snuggled up closer to listen to her faint, almost silent breath.

Slowly, he lifted his arm and began to softly touch her shoulders, gently stroking them, noticing the almost invisible blond hairs that were lit up by the faint light creeping through the opening of the curtain.

Then Tricia turned to him, her eyes dazed in that wonderful state between sleep and wake. "Make love to me, Mr. Bodyguard. Please," she said.

Chendrill moved closer and kissed her gently, feeling the softness of her lips as they barely touched. His hand moved down, touching and slowly stroking her breasts as she let out the slightest of moans. Then he moved lower, caressing her tight stomach, and still lower, feeling her, stirring her.

Her nipples grew larger as he teased them gently—first one, then the other. They felt pert and hard beneath his tongue. He moved down, kissing and licking her stomach inch by inch until his mouth at last tasted the warmth of her love below.

Slowly, he slipped his head down between her legs, feeling her soft thighs against his ears and her legs crossed at her ankles across the small of his back. He felt her tighten as the sensation of his tongue against her sent shivers of ecstasy through her body. Her hands clasped whatever they could grab. He moved his tongue around and around her moistness, and Tricia began to breathe deeper and harder. Her mouth began to open to draw in each breath.

Then out of nowhere, the urge came sweeping through Tricia and she had to see him, needed to watch him down below, watch what he was doing to her. She lifted her head up from the pillow, opened her eyes and watched as the Thomas Magnum moustache on Chendrill's upper lip moved up and down like a hungry, hairy caterpillar.

******

Chendrill woke up just after six, moved slowly off the bed, and quietly began to get dressed. Tricia looked almost childlike in her sleep, her soft breath purring out from within. Leaning down, he kissed her gently on the top of her head and silently left the room.

He looked at the Ferrari as he stepped outside into the cool morning air and then to the bread van alongside it, its driver, with olive skin and slicked back hair, pulling a tray of pastries and bread loaves from its rear. He stared at Chendrill as he closed the front door and began to walk down the front steps toward the road.

Chendrill nodded and smiled as he reached the side of Mazzi Hegan's Ferrari and didn't see anything more of the man until after he felt the baseball bat crank into the side of his ribs, knocking the wind completely from his body.

Chendrill went down onto the road, his knees buckling beneath him as the Italian baker walked back quickly toward his van, pulled out the tray of the pastries and French loaves he'd brought for his girl, and cracked the tray down on top of Chendrill's head. Moving quickly before the baker could strike again, Chendrill whipped his left leg out, catching the baker on the outside of his knee with a hard kick, ripping the ligaments and destroying the man's knee.

Screaming out in pain, the baker fell to the ground, his elbow cracking on the tarmac, the sharp stones cutting deep into his forearm. He tried to stand again on his one good leg, but Chendrill got to his feet quicker. Turning with a twist of his hip, he struck the baker hard in the stomach with his fist. Again the baker went down, he rolled, gasping, across the tight road toward his bread van, and Chendrill followed, picking up a French loaf along the way.

When the baker reached the back of his van and tried to stand, Chendrill whipped the French loaf down, breaking it across the top of the baker's head. He reached in through the open back door of the van and pulled out one tray full of delicacies, then the next, and the next, crashing each of them down on top of the man's raised arms and head.

Chendrill stepped back, away from the now empty van, and stared for a moment at the baker covered in flour, pastries, jam, three-layer cakes, and sticky chocolate muffins. Turning, he walked back to the Ferrari. Now it all made sense, he thought as he opened the door and Dan and his mother's earlier conversation played back through his mind.

How'd you get a yeast infection, son? You tell me, mum... She likes Italian.

The cocky fuck.

Putting the car into gear, he pulled away, glancing at the mess he'd made of the baker and running over a couple of whole wheat loaves as he went.

So his new girl had been fucking the baker, that was obvious, and the thought of it saddened him for a moment. He looked at himself in the Ferrari's rear-view mirror and wiped a couple of sticky currants from his hair and some flour from his huge moustache.

He took a deep breath, and it sent a shiver of intense pain through his ribs in the area where the guy had hit him with the bat. Fuck, he thought, it wasn't the first time in his life his ribs had taken a hit. Bruised or broken, the pain was the same, and as the adrenaline began to leave his body, the pain was already beginning to set in. He had about four to six sleepless weeks ahead as they took their time to heal, that was a given.

The fucking prick, he thought, sucker punching him like that with a bat to the ribs. The vision of the baker sitting at the back of his van, covered in its contents, began to make him laugh, and the pain got worse.

Taking his hand off the wheel, he held his side and thought of taking himself to the hospital, but what would they do? He'd just sit there with a bunch of junkies at this time in the morning, listening to them screaming for ice water and a medicated hit of something to get them through the next few hours until the dealers could pull themselves out of bed. He'd wait, he thought, as he turned out onto the main road and took it slow around a corner, trying to ease the pain in his side.

So was she fucking this guy now, Chendrill wondered, or was he an ex? She didn't seem like the kind of girl to be a player, but you sometimes couldn't tell.

Then the phone rang, and it was Tricia, and the first thing she said was, "I'm so sorry. Are you okay?"

And Chendrill got straight to the point. "Is this baker your man?"

Tricia answered quickly, "No, absolutely not. I'm not that way."

"Well, when he saw me coming out the house with a smile on my face, it looked as though you and him were in for a feast."

Tricia was silent for few seconds, then she said, "That's not the case. I finished with him just after you surprised me and took me for our first meal, and now he won't take no for an answer."

Chendrill stared out the window to the road ahead and remembered the tray of fresh croissants he'd seen each time he'd been to their home when he'd first met Dan. There had been none in the kitchen since that first afternoon they'd shared at the restaurant.

"No worries," he said. "How is he?"

"He's just stood up, and he's limping badly. He's trying to put his load back in the van."

"Where's Dan?"

"Where do you think? Sleeping. You could have put a hand grenade into the back of that van, and he'd still not have woken."

Chendrill moved in the car's small seat, trying to get comfortable. "Are you going outside to help him?"

"Do you think I should?"

"If you want him out of your life, then its best you don't, but I'm not your dad, so please do as you feel necessary."

"Thanks." Then she said, "Chuck? I hope that what happened this morning hasn't ruined it for us, because I really enjoy you, and I especially enjoyed last night very much. To be honest, I'm actually glad Dan stole the car and you stayed—but please don't ever tell him I said that."

Chendrill smiled. He understood why the baker had lost his doughnuts over her—all's fair in love and war as they say.

"I feel the same way," he said, "so don't go worrying about it at all. Just let me know if he keeps pestering you, okay? That's all I ask."

He made it home and stepped into the shower, washed the breadcrumbs out of his hair, then stepped back out and looked in the mirror at the slight bruise on the side of his ribs. Fuck, it looked like nothing, but hurt like hell.

It hurt, but it was nothing compared to the pain Daltrey must have gone through or that poor kid Bernado who was haunting Dennis's world. This brother of the gorgeous whore was out there somewhere, burning people without a care.

Fuck, what if the Russian came for me now, he thought, with this special trick Dennis said he did with flame. He couldn't even stop a baker from getting the better of him when he was fighting fit, let alone some psychopath whilst he was in this condition. Slowly, he moved from the bathroom and sat on his bed. He could hear the police sirens and ambulances passing by in the city, seemingly filling his room with their screaming noise, assaulting his ears as they headed out toward Vancouver's east side.

It had been nice with Dan's mum, a good night, and she'd said to him the same. Apart from the end bit, he thought. But what was the deal with Dan? How the fuck had he managed to steal the car?

Wincing, he put his hands behind his head, closed his eyes, and thought about Dennis sitting in his small basement, his dentistry degree hidden away in a drawer. Fuck, those guys had really done him, the poor bastard, but what should he do now?

First, he figured he'd go back and put the squeeze on his beautiful wife again, but harder this time, tell her she'll be going to prison for theft and possibly murder once he finds out the truth about this Bernado kid and Daltrey. Then he'd go find her brother, this Illya, and when he did, he'd make sure he had a fire extinguisher with him.

Three hours later, Chendrill woke to the sound of his phone ringing just before ten a.m. Wincing in agony as the pain ripped through him, he tried to get up and answered. It was Sebastian, who without any pleasantries said straight out, "I've got Dan here, and it's an emergency—I need to see you ASAP,"

An hour later, leaving the Ferrari at a meter outside, Chendrill entered the offices of Slave. As soon as he entered the boardroom, Mazzi Hegan snapped at him.

"What was Dan doing driving my car last night?"

Chendrill looked around the room that was almost full of assistants.

Sebastian stood and shook Chendrill's hand. "Please pardon my colleague," he said, "There were none of his favorite pastries available this morning, and he loves his sticky chocolate muffins, so he's been in a bad mood ever since."

Turning, Chendrill looked at Dan, who was looking back at him, smiling. He sat in a corner with his shirt undone and his feet up, copies of the British and European tabloids laying open on the boardroom table.

Chendrill picked one up and looked at the front cover picture of Dan outside a club, sitting in the driver's seat of Mazzi Hegan's Ferrari with Melissa beside him.

The headline above read:

Exclusive: Marsha's Secret Love Caught Cheating with Canadian Porn Queen

Chendrill stared at the photo for a moment then turned to Dan and said, "I thought she worked at McDonald's?"

Dan didn't answer, just shrugged as Chendrill opened another paper to see pictures of Dan looking incredibly handsome with his shirt off, whipping up a storm on the dance floor, on a podium, one of him on top of a speaker, another of him diving out, body surfing into the crowd, and then one of him leaning backward on the dance floor, his face right up inside Melissa's short skirt.

Chendrill stared at the lewd picture for a second and then turned back to Dan. "What are you doing here?" he asked.

Dan smiled. "The limbo," he said. "I wanted to see if she was wearing any panties."

Chendrill shook his head. "You shouldn't be doing that with a young girl in a club."

Quick as a flash, Dan said, "And you shouldn't be doing that with my mum."

Mazzi Hegan had heard enough. My God, these people, he thought. He was going to be sick, he knew it. He'd tasted fish once before as a younger man, and once was enough! The thought of this guy, who was stuck in the seventies, doing the same thing with Dan's mother, who probably looked like some old washerwoman, was way too much.

"What was he doing in my car last night? He has no right to be using my car," Mazzi said.

Charles Chuck Chendrill stared at Mazzi Hegan for a moment, then shrugged. His ribs hurt, and he could care less. All he wanted to do was lie down again for a while.

Sebastian lifted his hand from his fluffy dog and said

calmly, "Everybody calm down, calm down. Mazzi, the car is not important. What we have to realize is that as crazy as all this is, we really have something special here, and I'm going to let you all know that everyone is going to have to act fast."

Gesturing at Chendrill, he continued, "Chuck, I'll fill you in. We all know Dan is an unknown. It's crazy that, for some reason, he's getting all this press. I've spoken to Dan and told him the clients are wildly ready to ride on the back of this controversy. They want to blitz right now all of Europe and North America with our advertising campaign."

Chendrill couldn't believe his ears. He sat down, gazing at Sebastian and then Mazzi sitting on the other side of the table. Looking back to Sebastian, he said, "And this is the big emergency you dragged me down here for?"

Chapter Twenty-Nine

Charles Chuck Chendrill carefully squeezed back into the driver's seat of Mazzi Hegan's Ferrari, dropped one of the printed versions of the British tabloids on the passenger seat, and pulled away. What a load of nonsense, he thought, bringing him all the way here just for that.

"It's an emergency! We need you!" he mimicked.

They were going to put him up on billboards all over Europe. Big deal. They could put Dan on a billboard on the moon, and Chendrill could care less. Neither would Dan, come to think of it. He laughed to himself. Those photos in the paper were priceless. Taking his hand off the steering wheel, he held his ribs as he felt the pain shoot through him.

Dan had been funny in there, though, sitting there with his broken nose and his feet up, oozing out this I-couldn't-give-a-fuck rebel attitude that made them want him even more. That in itself was worth the trip. He was a funny kid, Chendrill thought, a real character, he'd give him that.

Making it home, he went straight to his bedroom and lay on the bed. He turned onto one side, couldn't get comfortable, and then turned onto his other side. Fuck, this was bad. That fucking baker. What did she see in that guy, apart from fresh pastries? Chendrill wondered. Dan would definitely miss him, although with his eating habits being somewhat similar to a dog, he doubted he could tell the difference between freshly baked and store-bought croissants. His food barely touched the sides of his mouth, let alone his taste buds.

Chendrill closed his eyes and tried not to breathe too

deeply. He thought of Dan's mum lying next to him a few hours earlier, her whispers and the tenderness as she kissed him.

Just as he felt the blood begin to flow, the phone rang. It was the office of Inspector Ditcon of the Vancouver Police Department telling Chendrill that the Thief wanted to talk to him immediately.

"Tell him to wait right there," Chendrill said. "I'm coming right over. I'll be there in ten minutes." Then he closed his eyes and went to sleep.

Two hours later, the phone rang again. This time, it was Ditcon in person.

"You're supposed to be here," he said.

Chendrill sat up, holding his side. "And you're supposed to be a detective. Besides, when did you get the right to tell me what to do?"

Ten minutes later, there was a squad car waiting for him outside his apartment building.

"We need to know everything you know about Daltrey," Ditcon said as soon as Chendrill entered the office.

"I thought you were the brains around here," Chendrill said, wondering if the subject of the Ferrari being driven at three hundred kilometers per hour or the shortage of bread and delicacies downtown was going to be brought up.

"I am, but I know you've been going to the hospital to see that girl who was assaulted several days ago, the same girl Daltrey had been talking to. I need you to tell me what she's been saying."

"Why don't you ask her yourself?"

"We have, but she's not communicating. The nurse said she's been talking to a man of your description."

Great police work, Chendrill thought. This clown didn't

have a clue. Out loud, he said, "She was telling me she didn't like the food."

"We're not playing games here! We're talking about a policewoman's life!" Ditcon said.

Chendrill stared at the charts on the wall. Dennis's name wasn't anywhere to be seen. Turning to Ditcon, he said, "If I find out anything of importance, don't worry, the first thing I'll do is rush over here and fill you in."

Ditcon ignored him and walked to the other side of his office. He stared at a chart, thinking it was obvious that Chendrill, a guy who couldn't even dress properly, had a grudge against the Vancouver Police Department. He knew he was holding back information. Deciding to try a different approach, he said, "I know you're a great detective. The force could use someone with your keen mind and experience. Maybe you'd like to come back in with us on this one, perhaps as a consultant?"

Chendrill stared at him for a moment. What a crock of shit. This guy was one hell of a weasel. He'd use him, have him here working it all out, then fire him the moment they had this prick of a brother he was certain had killed Daltrey, and who knew how many others, so he said to Ditcon, "I'd rather stick needles in my eyes." Turning, Chendrill headed for the door and just as he opened it, Ditcon called out. "Just one more thing?" Reaching into an envelope, he pulled out Dan's now charred electronic infrared door and lift opening device. "Does this mean anything to you?"

Chendrill walked back across the room to the desk and looked at the device a little more closely, its circuitry held together with tape and wrapped in wire as though it had been thrown together at the last minute by someone in their basement. "What is it?" he asked.

"That's what we're trying to work out," Ditcon said. "We have a specialist flying in from Ottawa to let us know. We think that this electronic device is something Daltrey came across in the course of her inquiries and is possibly of key importance to the investigation."

******

Well, nothing's changed there, Ditcon still had fuck all. Chendrill thought as he sat in the front seat of the squad car. At least he hadn't been arrested for dangerous driving or assault. He looked at the kid driving the car, his hair cut short and his shirt freshly starched.

"You're Chuck Chendrill, aren't you?" the kid said.

Chendrill smiled, surprised. "Is that a good thing or a bad thing?"

The kid laughed. "Don't worry. It's a good thing. You know, there's a sweep running at the station, they're saying you're running as favorite to finding whoever killed Daltrey."

Chendrill looked at the kid and said, "Really?"

"You're like a legend around here."

Chendrill laughed. "Is that right?"

"Yeah, the rumor is you're driving a Ferrari now."

"It's not mine."

Then the kid said, "You know, I knew Daltrey. She called me the same day she was killed and asked me to follow this guy. I did it—but I fucked up and lost him."

Chendrill looked out the window for a moment, watching nothing. He took a deep breath, the kid having his full attention now. "It happens." He looked at the road again, wondering who the kid had been following for Daltrey. "Was the guy Russian with tattoos?" he asked.

"I didn't get that close."

"How old?"

"Late twenties early thirties, short brown hair. She had me pick him up outside the casino at BC Place."

"In the afternoon?"

"Yeah, but like I say, I screwed up. He was wearing track pants, you know, the whole suit. Looked like an athlete."

Great, Chendrill thought, that really helped. Daltrey had been on to Illya, no doubt about it, but something wasn't right within the kid's psyche. He could hear it in his voice. "Do you feel responsible?" he asked.

The kid nodded.

"Well, don't," Chendrill said. "She was a big girl, and there's nothing you could have done to have stopped what happened. Whoever got the better of her did, and that's the way it goes."

The kid was silent for a while, then said, "That's not what Ditcon said to me."

Chendrill frowned and looked back out the window at the traffic. "Well," he said, "don't worry about that. He doesn't know his ass from his elbow. If he did, he wouldn't have been quizzing me. The guy could be sitting next to him on the bus, and he wouldn't know it. But you would, so keep your eyes open and be careful. Remember, you've seen him, and he knows you've seen him, so you need to be aware of who's around—and especially behind you—all the time."

The kid laughed, but Chendrill was thinking about how he had been so loved up this morning that he didn't put two and two together, and a baseball bat in the ribs was the result.

"What's your name?" he asked the kid.

"Williams."

Nice to meet you."

"Thanks. I told Ditcon and gave him a description of the guy, but that's as far as it went. I was thinking of finding you and telling you."

"Well, you should have."

"I just did—today's my day off!"

Chendrill smiled. Another cocky fuck, he thought, then taking a deep breath that hurt, he said, "So what have you done to ease your mind?"

Williams slowed the car. He knew Chendrill's apartment was coming up soon and wanted to get his time in. Turning, he looked at Chendrill. "I was the one who swam out into the creek and pulled the charred body in, and I think that the same guy who did that was the guy who killed Daltrey."

Chendrill shrugged. "Maybe." He paused for a moment, staring out the window to the world passing by, then he asked, "What else?"

Williams pulled the car over and turned completely toward Chendrill. "I'm certain the guy in the boat didn't set himself on fire by accident, because if so, why didn't he just jump in the water?.... And there were no oars in the boat. The girl who was assaulted around the same time could be involved. She's Russian, and you asked me if the guy I was following was as well, so there's a chance I'm right. Also, I know Daltrey had also been to see her a few times. The rumor mill says you have, too."

Chendrill smiled and thought about the rumor mill, loads of cops sitting around in coffee shops on their breaks, shooting the shit about Daltrey, and this kid was out there instead, thinking, moving, looking, and actually doing. The young lad would no doubt do well unless the system broke him down as it had Chendrill. He liked him, this kid

Williams, and he was obviously trying to find out what had happened, just as Chendrill himself was, but fuck he wished he'd get to it quickly as his rib was hurting something fierce. All he wanted to do was lie down for a while.

"You've been doing your homework. That's good," he said to the rookie policeman who was going to go far. "Do you know the name of this girl in the hospital?"

Williams shook his head. "They don't know yet, and I shouldn't say this, but Ditcon's trying to find out."

Chendrill let out a deep breath. God, they were way behind him. For a moment, he wondered if the kid was a plant. If so, he should be up for an Oscar because the iron and determination in his words were strong.

"I went around to the apartment where they found the girl to see if I could find out who's name was on the lease," said Williams, "but it's registered to a third-party numbered company and subleased short term for cash. I also found out where the boat that was found burned up outside the apartment was from—it was stolen from the boathouse at the end of the creek. But whoever put the body on it did it from the marina close by the same apartment."

Chendrill nodded. "How do you know this?"

"I asked. One of the guys who lives on a boat there had a fuel can stolen. I'd say the guy in the boat was murdered on the boat, set on fire, then pushed out onto the creek."

Chendrill was impressed—the kid had been really busy. He asked, "What makes you think he was already dead on the boat?"

"I'm just trying to think about how I would have done it. You know, think like the killer. You'd have to be really strong to get a body down the gangplank, along the dock, and into that little boat. It would be easier to have walked the guy there, have him sit in it, then kill him."

Chendrill gave it some thought. He had a good idea that it was the boyfriend, this Sergei character, who had been burned in the boat, but he hadn't really put a lot of time into working out how he'd ended up there. When he was a cop, he'd have gotten those details later in the interrogation room, staring at a guy for days sometimes until he got so bored he started talking. But now he looked for dogs and babysat kids for a grand a day.

He looked straight at Williams and said with concern in his voice, "You're right, but don't ever forget what I said. Daltrey was killed less than a block from the place, so be careful. It's all good going out there doing the right thing, but never forget why you're there in the first place."

Williams dropped Chendrill off at his apartment on the water at the edge of Stanley Park and took the long way back through the park to the station. He was single now—for the moment anyway—so what else did he have to do? The news of Daltrey's death had hit him hard, and he'd taken full responsibility for her untimely end and had hardly slept since. The moment he'd heard through the grapevine that Ditcon had Chendrill in his office, he'd put his best uniform on and rushed in and made sure he would be the one to drive him home.

He knew deep down that the guy in the track pants was responsible for Daltrey's death, but how the hell could he find him and then prove it? And where did he start? He'd staked out the same casino every day and night since, but nothing. Who the fuck was the guy? Daltrey had worked it out. Why couldn't he?

Williams continued driving along the shoreline until he found himself parked in a corner, watching the front of the casino again, just as he had done almost every spare minute of his days since he'd heard the bad news.

Chapter Thirty

Illya walked along the seawall and looked back toward the casino and then to the cop who'd just pulled his unmarked car up in the distance. He'd spent so much time there with his sister and her boyfriend that the place now felt like home, and it was tempting to go in, but he'd picked up a tail there, and the guy in the car could just be that person. Anyway, fuck his sister and fuck her boyfriend. They were gone from his life, and he would move on. If they did show up, he'd make them both pay and see how things went afterward with Sergei, if he was still alive.

He'd given the girl a drink that was full of knockout drugs. She would be sleeping for a few hours, which he knew she needed because work had been so hard. If she thought he did not care and wasn't looking out for her, then she was stupid. After all, they were partners now. They both needed to eat and sleep, and he needed some new things to wear since the money was now coming back in.

He turned right and stopped in front of the high-end lingerie shop where Alla had bought her work clothes and stared at the mannequins dressed in lace in the window. This girl, who called herself Saucy Mary in her ad, was a bit bigger than Alla, and the stuff he'd made her put on was tight, which worked out fine, even if she continued to not eat.

He turned his gaze to the 'For Him' section on one side of the window. It was a place he liked to stare at and lose himself in for a while, then think about later.

The male mannequins stared back at him in their small,

tight, glitzy underwear. It was tempting, Illya thought, to just go in there and buy a pair, but then fuck, he'd have to pay for them over the counter, and then the people in there would know the way he was. He walked on, embarrassed that someone may have seen him looking at the men's section for so long. But God, it made him feel sexy.

Illya reached the end of the road, then stopped and looked back. Fuck those looked good, real good. He'd be able to strut about that fancy apartment with its designer leather furniture from Italy half-naked the way he liked, staring at his tattoo-covered body in the mirror. Turning around, he walked the short distance back to the shop, and without looking at the window again, stepped inside.

The girl behind the counter smiled widely as Illya entered. He walked straight to the women's lingerie section and heard her call out to him, "Let me know if you have any questions."

Not wanting to make eye contact, Illya nodded and wandered around looking at the women's Basques, matching knickers and bras he had no interest in. He reached the section where the clothing especially designed for guys hung. Spotting the pair of the glitzy designer underwear he'd seen in the window, he walked away, stopped, took a deep breath, turned back, and picked up a pair from the rack. Turning quickly, he walked back across the shop, plopped them on the counter, and wished he'd walked straight out the door, when he heard the girl say, "Nice choice. These are incredible, just in from Milan. They're really sexy. You'll look great in them."

Illya nodded and felt a flush of warmth through his body as he imagined being caught wearing them back home in Russia. "They're not for me, they're for a friend," he said.

The pretty girl smiling back innocently saying, "Your boyfriend? Oh wow—he's going to love them." Illya stared at her, feeling the need to escape fill his whole being as beads of sweat appeared upon his scalp and across his back. Fuck, this was not good, he thought, really wishing now he'd never come into the store in the first place. Then just as he thought it couldn't get any worse, the girl said, "I've got a friend who's gay too—he just loves these."

******

He made it home, back to the fancy pad that wasn't his, with its leather sofa in front of the windows that looked out across the small city park, and its Egyptian cotton sheets in the bedrooms. Mary was still knocked out when he unlocked her door and came into the room. He stood at the bottom of the bed, listening to her soft, shallow breathing as she slept in a drugged-out stupor.

She was good-looking for a girl, and he liked the way she did her hair, keeping it blond but staggering the roots so it didn't look bad as her hair grew out. She was starting to smell, though.

He untied her hands then went into the kitchen to fix himself a clubhouse sandwich with turkey, bacon, and a little bit of lettuce, just the way his sister used to make them for him. When he went back to the room, Mary was just waking. She sat up slowly, staring at him in a drugged daze.

"Are you hungry?" Illya asked.

Mary stared back at him, her eyes barely focusing.

"You're starting to smell. You need to clean yourself up. There'll be another guy here in half an hour for you to play with."

Mary continued to stare. She closed her eyes and opened them again. She looked to the door and then back to Illya.

"Would you like a sandwich or not?" Illya asked. "And if you try to run, I'll catch you and burn you to death."

Mary nodded. She understood. She'd take the sandwich.

"When can I go, or are you going to keep me here and then kill me?" she asked.

Illya stood there, looking down at her. "I'll not kill you as long as you are good. You will be okay. Work hard for us, and in the end, you'll be so rich you'll not ever want to leave."

******

Chendrill got himself back up to his apartment and with great effort moved himself slowly so as he could lay himself down on the bed. The kid had him worried. He was upset and had obviously taken the burden of what had happened on his own shoulders. But at least he was trying, which was more than some—and more than he himself was doing right now. Closing his eyes, he thought of the pastry chef lying there on the road covered in his wares, this guy who made buns for a living and still had a hard-on for his girl. One thing was for certain, Dan was going to miss him.

Then the phone rang, and it was Dennis.

Chendrill got up again and made his way to the hospital. He parked the Ferrari at a meter opposite, took the elevator to the sixth floor, and opened the door to Alla's room to see Dennis sitting on a chair next to her, holding her hand. Walking over, Chendrill held his hand out to shake and said to him, "I thought you'd be working on some big movie somewhere?"

Dennis laughed, and Chendrill could see there was a lightness to him now, almost as if the world had been lifted from his shoulders.

"Alla called me," said Dennis, "and we've been talking and have something to tell you. When I get my license back, and Alla gets out of the hospital, she's coming back to live with me. We're going to move up to the northern territories where we can get our marriage and my dental career back in order."

"What are you going to do when your brother turns up again?"

Dennis took a deep breath. "This is what we called you for," he said. "Alla's told me how you two have already spoken, you know, about how she offered to help you find him because she doesn't want him interfering in our life together again."

Chendrill remembered the conversation differently.

Alla looked up at him, and for the first time, Chendrill saw her beautiful smile, and looking into her green eyes, he understood why Dennis, although having been stripped bare by this siren, was still in love.

"There's a guy," she said, her silky voice flowing with an accent reminiscent of sunnier places, "who knows him. They were in contact many times throughout the day. He works as a concierge at one of the big hotels by the water, where the cruise ships dock. He may have my brother's number."

Chendrill nodded, quickly putting two and two together. Illya was the pimp, and the concierge sent guys his way. The concierge met him once a week or so for a cut. They were known for it, and a fancy little treat like Dennis's wife would pay back good dividends.

"I take it he has a few other friends he's gotten to know since he's been here?" Chendrill asked.

Alla nodded, but then said, "There are other friends, but this is his best friend."

"Does he meet with any of these guys at a set time every week?"

Alla shook her head. "My brother does nothing by routine."

"But there are more?"

Alla nodded slightly, her beautiful eyes burning into his. "But all you need is the man I spoke of," she said. "His name is Jimmy."

"Can you get me a photo of your brother?"

Alla shook her head. "There are no photographs of him that I know of. He does not allow it. Like an African bushman, he thinks it will steal his soul."

Steal his liberty, more like, Chendrill thought.

Then Alla reached out, touching Chendrill's hand with hers. The drips in her arm and the wires that connected her to the machines above swayed. Her voice now tender, she said, "If you speak to anyone, please don't tell them you were here with us."

Chendrill closed his eyes slightly and with his head gave the smallest of nods. His response was obvious. He would not break this unspoken vow.

So Illya was obviously going for the big money and keeping himself unidentifiable in the process. The only hotels around that area were high-end, and enough wealthy tourists and businessmen passed through on the conference circuit to have kept Dennis's wife busy.

"Anything else?" Chendrill asked. "Does he put himself out there in the papers for work, doing whatever he does?"

Alla shook her head and lied. "No."

She knew there was the ad in the paper with the photo Sergei had taken of her looking beautiful in the lobby of the Grand for the world to see, her there in the back pages of the local rag with her face fuzzed out, showing off her long legs and ass, but she didn't need Dennis to start looking.

"My brother," she said, "he's gay. He does not think I know, but I always have. He hates it and hides it well. There's a place he goes sometimes, late at night after the bars close, at the back of the porn shops on the main drag off Granville. I know because I've followed him there."

Chendrill sat back, surprised. This was a new angle for him. He knew of the place. It had been there for years and was part of the gay stroll circuit in Vancouver. A place to go that was nice and dark, where you could watch movies and get sucked off by a stranger when it was raining if that was your thing.

"And what's his deal with the fire?" Chendrill asked.

Alla Bragin took a deep breath and closed her eyes. Then she said, "It started when he was a kid, and you need to be careful."

"Do you have any idea where he could be now?"

Alla shook her head. "I stayed in one place, but he moves all the time," she said. "Has new places lined up weeks ahead, overlaps them in case someone is getting close, you know, like cops or immigration officials or the other people he deals with in his world. Suddenly he up and moves, and when he does, even I don't know where he is until he suddenly appears again. I don't even know his phone number, but like I said, this Jimmy guy does."

Then she went quiet, staring at the floor as tears began to well up in her beautiful eyes. Looking up again, she stared back at Chendrill and said, "Dennis and I had something special that Illya ruined. If I knew more, I'd tell you, I promise. I can tell you he'll be somewhere close to downtown. That's where he likes to be, hiding among the people. And please be careful. He fears nothing and no one."

******

Chendrill headed back to Mazzi Hegan's Ferrari and tried his best to squeeze inside without passing out from the pain in his ribs. He thought again how the baker had sneaked up on him and clubbed him with the bat.

Dennis's wife came across lovely now, but evil people were sometimes lovely and charming, that was a fact. There was an appeal about them, something that set them apart from everyone else, and just when you weren't looking, they'd stab you and kill you.

Dennis had been bitten once, but was happy to jump back in now that Alla had been hobbled. Chendrill hoped for Dennis's sake she was worth the risk.

Charles Chuck Chendrill pulled the Ferrari up outside the Grand Hotel situated on the pier at Canada Place where the cruise ships docked and asked the doorman to watch it for him for a moment while he went inside. As soon as he did so, he was greeted by Jimmy, the concierge, at his station.

Going straight for the jugular, Chendrill said, "I hear you've been delivering guys to the Russian?"

The concierge stared back at this man who was on him without even saying good afternoon. "Are you a guest here at the hotel, sir?" he asked in a whisper.

"No," Chendrill answered.

"Then fuck off, and mind your own business."

Perfect response, Chendrill thought. Alla's information had been correct. The guy's confidence proved that.

"You're Chuck Chendrill, aren't you?" the concierge asked. "The private eye, the one who found the dog?"

Jesus Christ, Chendrill thought, is that all I'm known for in this town? Then he asked aloud, "How do you know that?"

The concierge came right back at him. "How did you know I knew the Russian?"

******

They walked along the quay and sat in a bar along the way that looked out at the cruise ships and listened to the horns blowing loud so that everyone across the entire city knew the ship was leaving and whoever was sailing with it had an hour to get back on board.

"Most of the guys know him," the concierge said, "but not as well. Sadly, to do my job, I have to get to know these people and others like this guy you're looking for. For me, it's not all about the best seat in the restaurant and front row center tickets when Sting's in town. I have to delve into the shady side of life."

And he did it well. Well enough, even, to go tell some smart ass asking questions where to go. Jimmy Tucker knew everyone, it seemed, and was the man to see. With a smile, and for a fee, he could get you what you wanted or where you wanted to be, as long as you were staying at his hotel. No questions asked.

"I've never actually seen the guy," Jimmy said as he took another sip from his beer. "He called up a year back and offered the first couple of times for free. So I sent some guy I owed a favor to, and he came back in a daze. Then for round two, I sent a regular who stays here over to give it a shot, and soon after, you know, this Russian was a regular."

"And what about now?"

Jimmy shook his head. "No—I called a few days back and didn't get an answer, so I gave up."

Then Chendrill asked, "Do you know the place he operated out of?"

Jimmy shook his head. "No."

Chendrill smiled. The guy knew. It was obvious, and chances were high he was the "guy" or the "regular" or both who'd been over. At some stage, he'd met the brother. How else would he be getting his bonuses?

"Do you mean no, you don't know, or no, you aren't going to say?" Chendrill asked.

"I mean no."

Chendrill continued, "So if you were me, and you wanted to find him, what would you do?"

Jimmy stared out at a ship, its huge anchor chain having left a line of rust down the hull. A bunch of its crew members needed to get off their asses and swing down on a boson's chair with scrubbing brushes and some paint.

Jimmy thought for a moment, and then said, "Go ask elsewhere, like I said. I don't know, but I do know he's changed addresses."

"But you don't know where?"

"That's right."

"But you have his phone number?"

Jimmy shook his head again and stared back at the ship as the horn blew again, scaring the gulls and the tourists passing along the quay. With a smile on his face, he looked Chendrill straight in the eye, and lied. "No."

Fuck, why give half the info and get clever with the rest?

It was a power thing, Chendrill thought as he looked at the guy who had the keys to the city and a dozen season tickets to the Canucks in his back pocket. He was saying, without saying, "Yeah, I know, and now you know I know, but what the fuck are you going to do about it?"

The guy he was protecting had killed a policewoman a few days back and a few others scattered about. With the whore he'd been sending horny hotel guests to now lying in the hospital, this cocky prick could be on the list of potential burn victims. But if he told him that, he knew he wouldn't care, so he just said, "Thanks, Jimmy. You're a good guy," and then bought him a huge meal and some beers for his trouble, stole his phone, and left him there to eat.

Chendrill walked around the corner toward the Grand and sat back down carefully into the driver's seat of the Ferrari. He pulled out his phone and watched the short video he'd recorded of Jimmy punching the password on his own phone, then he pulled it out of his pocket and unlocked it. Taking a lead out of his pocket, he connected it to a small palm computer he'd left sitting in the Ferrari's glove box and downloaded Jimmy's phone's contents until he had every message and every number Jimmy possessed.

Reaching out the car window, Chendrill handed the phone to the doorman, and said, "Your friend Jimmy dropped this, tell him he owes me one for finding it for him." Then he pulled away. He kind of liked Jimmy, even if he was an arrogant prick, plus he knew a concierge with his hand on the pulse of entertainment in Vancouver would appreciate the trick he'd just pulled. And if he didn't, then fuck him— that's what you got for being smug.

He drove along through Vancouver, people staring at him in his car as he cruised by. Dennis was worrying him still.

271

Seeing him in the hospital, so back in love with this Russian woman who was using him again, Chendrill wondered if the man had ever been out of love with her. Deep down, though, Chendrill knew in a strange way he was guilty also, using him like he was.

He pulled away again into the steady flow of traffic, telling himself he'd look out for this man and his woman. As long as Dennis was happy, and so was she, he'd leave it be, but as soon as trouble presented itself, and he felt the guy who'd been saved from suicide by cold water was being played again, he'd step in and do his best to straighten things out.

Chapter Thirty-One

Sebastian was as happy as could be and was thinking about getting himself a new bicycle. It had been a while since his firm had had a hit, and without a doubt, they had a real big one coming with BlueBoy. This would be his present to himself.

The whole campaign was crazy and had been born from nothing. Where was the pre-planning, the late night brainstorming sessions with clients and creative producers? All it was was just a strange situation and some crazy photos shot on instinct by Mazzi. All Sebastian had done was not take it too seriously and call in Chendrill. He'd given him the Ferrari because he liked him—and liked to see him in it just as much—and even that had worked out, with Dan stealing the supercar and making the papers. And boy, the guy was funny. The pictures of Dan up on the stage, his shirt off, and then on top of the speakers with his shirt waving around his head, were priceless. And then there were those of him being dragged out by the bouncers in a fit of sweat, testosterone, and punches.

There was so much more to come. He could just feel it, the whole bizarre situation growing the way it was with a force of its own, each new chaotic element Dan brought to the table pushing the young lad further and further into the spotlight. From the chaos that ensued, Sebastian knew other contracts would begin to flow in from across the globe. It would be sensational.

Not bad for doing nothing apart from making a couple of phone calls, Sebastian thought as he looked around the bike store for one that looked as though it had the comfiest saddle and gears that were not too complicated. There was a time he'd have given blood or a kidney to a campaign and gotten nowhere, but that was what happened when you were young, he thought. But when you had your shit together and had experience, the ease of work comes along. It was certainly coming now, and all he needed to do was guide the reins and make sure it happened fast.

Sebastian was essentially a decent man who had only ever loved once, and that was a love that had lasted for twenty years of his life in a physical sense and would remain with him forever spiritually. They'd met as young men at art school in London in the '70s, their love blossoming as they moved into a small flat together in Richmond on the outskirts of London, a beautiful place with a view of the River Thames and a small garden that led out to a short walkway up the hill toward the park, where herds of deer roamed free among huge oaks, and children ran feral. The pair remained happy and untroubled by society's bigoted irreverence to their persuasion—until Alan died.

By then, Sebastian had made his name and more money than he could ever spend, and he would have thrown it all away, along with his fancy car and silk shirts and scarves, for just another day with his man. There was no one like Alan in this world. His partner's warmth, his heart, and the compassion in his touch made him so special, and in the days since he passed, Sebastian had never wanted or longed for another.

He'd looked. Of course he would. Nature's way was nature's way, after all. Why else would he keep Chendrill around if it wasn't partly for eye candy and having someone to call with his worries and know they'd be fixed with a word or an action? He was expensive, yes, but who cared? Sebastian was rich, very rich, and he was shrewd, soon discovering that taking percentage points on a new product was risky, but lucrative if they hit home. And how very lucrative this philosophy had become.

A few years before Alan had died, Sebastian decided to move to Vancouver, the place they both loved and where they had holidayed and played in the ocean and the mountains, breathing in the fresh air and sheltering from the rains when they came. It was a place of acceptance, and in that acceptance came freedom—the freedom to hold, the freedom to steal a kiss, the freedom to be who you were and wanted to be without fear of violent words or saliva spat in anger.

And now he was here living alone in Vancouver with only memories to hold onto almost everywhere he went. He ran his firm, lived his life, brought multinational corporations from London, Paris, and New York to the beautiful small city he now called home, and spotted talent and nurtured it to a level of success they'd have never achieved on their own. A man with his little dog, happy with himself as he whiled away his days, playing with time until he could see Alan again.

******

Charles Chuck Chendrill reached Dan's mother's house and pulled up outside, squashing remnants of pastries left from his scrap earlier in the day. Wary of a second attack, he carefully stepped out of the Ferrari.

Tricia came to the door, and Chendrill was relieved that she was happy to see him.

The first thing he said when he entered the kitchen was, "I'm sorry about this morning."

Stopping in her tracks, Tricia turned and spoke to him. Chendrill could tell by her voice she was still upset by the incident. "No, I'm sorry. I'm really embarrassed. Are you okay?"

"Don't worry about it. I'm a big boy. Where's the superstar fashion model?"

Tricia laughed then said, "He's in the basement. He came in, complained that you made him get the bus again, said he was going international, then disappeared into his cave with a huge piece of pizza."

Tricia pulled two cups out of the cupboard and placed them on the counter. There was something about this guy that she really liked, a sense of comfort she'd never felt before with any other man. He had this ability to make her feel at ease when she was around him, and there was never the awkwardness she'd felt with other men. He was, without a doubt, special, and as she handed him his drink, she saw the sparkle in his eye as he looked at her, and then the twinge of pain as he moved.

"You're hurt?" she asked.

"It's nothing. My rib hurts a bit, that's all."

"A bit?"

Chendrill nodded then said, "I must have twisted and pulled it."

Tricia knew that was bullshit from the moment he started to speak and wondered about the baseball bat she'd seen sitting behind the baker's seat in the bread van the one time he did take her to a place way out of town.

"Did he hit you with a bat?"

Chendrill shook his head and said, "No, a French loaf."

Tricia laughed. He was a funny guy. Obviously, she was never going to get a straight answer. "I think Dan may have gone to sleep," she said. "He gets pretty tired sometimes. Why don't you and I go and have a little lay down ourselves, and I'll have a look at whatever's bothering you."

Taking his hand, Tricia led Chendrill to the bedroom and watched him grimace as he lay down. Leaning over, she kissed him on the lips and stroked his forehead.

"I'm sorry about this morning," she said. "I really am. I promise you that there is nothing between me and that guy anymore—and the truth is, there never really was."

She sat down next to him on the bed and stroked his head and then his neck. Slowly, she began to slip her hand down his shirt. She combed her fingers through the hair on his chest as she unbuttoned, one by one, the front of his bright red Hawaiian shirt. Opening it fully, she moved herself down the bed a little and placed both hands on his chest, the palms of her hands tingling as they gently moved around and around. She felt his nipples grow harder with her touch. Moving her hands up, she reached the top of his shoulders with her fingertips, then brought them lower, flattening her fingers against his chest and pushing down hard, feeling his tight, strong chest muscles beneath his skin.

Leaning forward, she kissed Chendrill again on his lips, then moved her hands lower to his stomach as she began to kiss his chest. Then, heading south, she kept going, moving lower, inch by inch, kissing him, biting him, teasing him with her lips.

She reached his stomach with her mouth and dug her tongue hard down into Chendrill's belly button, then moved lower, biting and digging her teeth into the fabric of his jeans as she sunk her mouth down on his crotch. Sitting up, Tricia looked at him, her eyes wide and excited as they connected with his. She felt the arousal in his groin, and still looking him in the eye, she unfastened his jeans button by button, exposing his cock laying tight and hard below his shorts. She touched it, caressing it, feeling its hardness and strength.

Chendrill watched as Dan's mum took it out, pulling his clothing down off him and releasing his manhood into the open. Without speaking, she leaned down and took him deep into her mouth. He closed his eyes while she held it there, pushing down. He could feel himself in the back of her throat, tight and full. Then she pulled up slowly, licking his shaft, her tongue touching, stroking, teasing its way up and down and over and over his sensitive tip.

Tricia carried on as she felt his hand rubbing the smoothness of her legs underneath her skirt. Slowly she opened them, letting his fingers enter her and move further inside, filling her, feeling her, and making her moan as he gently caressed her.

She felt Chendrill tightening up more and more as her tongue worked its way around his penis, and just as she knew it was impossible for him to take any more, his phone rang, and it was Sebastian.

Stopping exactly where she was, Tricia looked up at Chendrill as he stared at the phone, then giving up and answering, he let go of her leg and heard Sebastian say. "Chuck! What are you doing?" Chendrill looked to Tricia, looking back at him with his cock in her mouth, and said, "I'm working."

"You're keeping an eye on Dan, right?"

"I'm at his place now."

"Good, good. I have an emergency! And we don't need any more trouble. I want him to appear mysterious, not act like an idiot."

"What's the emergency?"

"Mazzi Hegan wants his car back."

That's the emergency? Chendrill thought. "Well, tell him he can't have it," he said.

"You know how he was this morning, not getting his pastry? Well, he's just getting worse. I'm not sure what to do with him these days. The other day, he made me so angry that I went home and smashed his plate against the wall."

"His plate?"

"Yes, I secretly mark plates with people's initials. Everyone's got one—even you—and when I get really mad at them, I smash their plate."

"You devil, you!"

"Anyway, today he said he's going to quit. He said that after I'd told him the reason I'd taken the car off him was because I'd gotten a bill from Belinda saying he'd been calling her out at all hours just because he needed her to parallel park the car."

"He's been doing what?"

"Getting Belinda to come out and park the Ferrari."

"Why?"

"Because he can take an amazing photo, but he can't parallel park. And now he wants to quit!"

"Where else is he going to go where he can smash up yachts and starve people and nail them to the stage? Anyway, I thought you were the boss down there. Tell him he can't have it. You need it to be with me right now, and who's more important? What do you want me to do? Tell Dan to get the bus? We can't do that. He needs to appear mysterious."

Chapter Thirty-Two

Sebastian put the phone down and stared at the new bicycle he doubted he'd ever ride propped up against the wall of his huge office.

Chendrill was right. God, the guy was good. Dan needed to be seen in a performance car, and yes, he was the boss. He'd had enough of putting up with Mazzi's bullshit mood all day just because he didn't get his fucking Italian sticky whatever chocolate fucking thing he liked to have in the morning.

Walking out of his huge office decorated exclusively in purple grape vines, he opened Mazzi Hegan's office door without knocking and said, "I don't care what you say. Go get a taxi or some other car—I don't care. Chendrill's keeping yours. You can't park it anyway, and he needs it to make your new superstar look good. Do you want some paparazzi prick spotting him sitting on the back of a number 22 bus and ruin all your good work by snapping him?"

Through the swirling smoky glass door he'd asked for when he first joined the firm, Mazzi Hegan watched Sebastian close the door to his office and head back down the corridor to his own. Well, fuck him! Why should that prick get to drive his company car just because Sebastian fancied him, and the guy wanted to look like Thomas Magnum? I mean, why? It was Sebastian's car, yes, but what difference did that make? Dan didn't have to get the bus. There were limos out there.

Opening his door, he bellowed out across the open office, "Go get Belinda! She can chauffer him about!"

He slammed the glass door with enough force to make noise but not smash it, then he sat down. It was a power thing, and he knew it—keeping him down like this, taking away the Ferrari he liked to stand next to but couldn't drive. He should quit and move to Milan.

"Fuck it, I will. I'm going to Milan!" he shouted out loud so all the people who sat in those little booths in the office would hear him and know he was angry. He'd go there and live it up and learn to speak Italian, the language of lovers. He'd meet a nice guy or two and take holidays every month in all the European capitals he'd always wanted to go to. After all, who was the talent around here?

Mazzi stood and walked to the window and looked out at the advertising hoarding across the road. Tonight the crew would be coming in and changing it over. In the morning, he'd go out, get his breakfast, get a haircut, have his tips frosted, and come back looking sexy. And when Sebastian or any other motherfucker who worked here wanted to come in here and fuck with him, they could stare over his shoulder, look past his new hair, and see his work in all its glory. Then he'd say, 'Go beat that, go get someone else who can produce shit like that.' He'd nod and say, 'Keep the car you promised I could use. Go and give it permanently to that cretin with the shirts who thinks he's got style, because…I'm …Going…To…Milan!'

******

Chendrill sat on Tricia's bed with his shirt open, listening to her singing to herself in the kitchen as he read through the contents of Jimmy's phone. There were hundreds of numbers, all with single names or just letters and abbreviations that meant nothing to anyone except Jimmy who had it all dialed in somewhere in his lofty brain.

Jimmy had told him he'd been trying to call the Russian, then stopped. He looked at the calls made and the numbers, then looked at the numbers called late at night when some Japanese guy might have been drunk and horny and wanting to try out a Western girl. There were a lot of numbers—too many—but one of them was Illya's. His sister would know it, but she'd said enough, betraying her kin without going all the way, enough to get rid of her brother who was her pimp. but not enough to finish him off quickly. He'd have to work harder, go downtown later and snoop around, take a look inside the sex film booths used by the boys in town as a stroll, and bribe the people behind the desk to keep an eye out. He looked back at the phone and began to dial, waiting to hear the accent of whoever answered. When they did answer, he asked for the Russian every time regardless.

By the time he'd had a back rub from his new girl, another kiss and cuddle, and a nice sandwich and drink, he was halfway through the lists and still getting nowhere. And by the time he'd left Tricia's house, reached downtown Granville, and sat in the Ferrari for half an hour, working his way through the numbers he thought could be Illya, he still had nothing. Plenty of restaurants, bars, clubs, scalpers, helicopter rides, travel agents, drug dealers, and S and M specialists, but no Russian pimps.

******

Chendrill opened the car door outside a café, doing his best to peel himself out without causing too much pain. He straightened slowly and still felt the jarring pain rip through his side. He crossed Granville Street, heading up its sleazier side and passing drunks and homeless kids living in temporary camps erected in the odd empty shop doorway that smelled of piss. He reached the sex shop and looked at the window full of tacky, lipsticked mannequin girls with bad wigs and big tits, stretching their skimpy clothing to the limit.

Opening the door, he stepped inside and stared at the entranceway leading to the rear where the video booths were. Chendrill looked at the young girl behind the desk, rings through her nose and lips and ears, her arms covered in gaudy tattoos that meant nothing other than rebellion.

Looking up, the girl stared at Chendrill for a moment, taking in his size and his bright red Hawaiian shirt, then she said, "You have to buy the tokens here if you want to use the booths."

Chendrill shook his head and said, "I don't need to go in there. I just want to know if you've ever seen a Russian guy covered in tattoos, in his early thirties, with short brown hair."

The girl shook her head as Chendrill tried to make out the lyrics to the punk song she was listening to on her headphones. She sat there staring at him, her head bobbing to the music's rasping chords. "You going in or not?" she asked.

"If you ever get a guy like that come through here, I'll give you a hundred bucks if you call me and let me know."

The girl looked at Chendrill again. With that bright red and yellow shirt and his big hair, she thought he looked like one of those cockatoos her grandmother used to keep before they starved in the cage after she died and wasn't found for three weeks.

She only had another hour to go, and then she was going home to wait for her boyfriend to come over with some dope. Then they'd get totally wasted, completely fucked up, and she'd sit with him all night and talk about stuff they couldn't remember the next day, like Astral circles and the moons that surround Pluto—Charon, Styx, Nix, Kerberos, and Hydra. Charon was her favorite because it reminded her of her boyfriend's head when he shaved it. She knew he was special from the day they'd met at a party, and he'd slipped his hand down the back of her pants while she puked.

She pulled her black buds from her ears, and Chendrill could hear the lyrics burst out. "Give me a hundred bucks now," she said, "and I'll keep an eye on the customers who come through here. Otherwise, I've got a lot of work to do, and it ain't worth getting into trouble. Nothing's worth being fired for."

Chendrill nodded. *What a crock of shit*, he thought. You have to look anyway to see if they're junkies coming in to rob you or shoot up out back or take money from your usual good God-fearing customers. Then he smiled and said to the punk rock chick trying to fleece him, "I'll tell you what. I'll make it one hundred now, and I'll give you another two if you let me know if he shows."

That was a good deal, he thought, probably three days' money for paying attention and then picking up the phone— she'd do it. It was a lot, but who cared? Sebastian would be paying.

Then the girl said, "Give me a minute." She looked down to the catalog full of sexual aides and wares she'd been looking through, and without looking up asked, "You a cop?"

"No."

"You a queer?"

"Maybe."

"What you want him for?"

Fuck me, what difference does it make to you? Chendrill thought as the girl looked up at him, her hair gelled into a pointed row along the center of her head, all colored red with yellow bleached streaks sticking up, reminding Chendrill of a cockatoo.

"I owe him money," he said.

"I doubt that. You got a photo?"

Chendrill shook his head. "Sorry."

"Hang on a minute," she said and got up from her desk, leaving through a doorway toward the shop's office.

Chendrill watched her as she went, her tight jeans stopping just above her big black boots with their four-inch black soles. Then he looked around. The place was a sea of whips, lubes, DVDs, and dildos that made him feel small. He didn't need to use this shit, all neatly wrapped in plastic and covered with pictures of sluts of both genders trying to look horny.

He thought back to the afternoon where he and Dan's mother had used only themselves to please each other, lost in their own world of passion and interrupted only by Sebastian and a strange banging from the basement.

He looked to the office door and wondered where the hell that mess of a woman had gone. Then he turned and leaned against the counter, pulled out his phone, and dialed the next number on his list. It was another restaurant, Greek this time, then another one straight after, then another. Then he hit the next number and heard a phone ring along the hallway that led to the back.

Fuck me, Chendrill thought, was that him in there, or was

it a coincidence? He hit end, stopping the call, and the ringing ceased. Then he dialed again, and seconds later, a faint ringing started up again in the distance. Turning it off quickly, Chendrill left the counter and began to walk quietly down the hall into the darkness.

He reached the end and stopped, the inside now pitch black, faint lights coming through the doorways from the TV screens of the booths that had yet to be filled. Chendrill stood to the side in the gloom, listening to the moans and groans of the fucking and bad movie dialogue coming from the booths containing men in their own private little worlds.

Slowly, he moved further into the labyrinth of booths. It was darker now, and in the blackness, he saw men standing silently, waiting in the shadowy corners and alcoves for something. Chendrill stared at them as his eyes adjusted to the dark, his eyes discreetly scanning them for tattoos on their arms or Russian features on their faces. *Fuck.* These guys were creepy, he thought, and moved further toward the end as fucking noises and odd words crept out from the small plywood cabins.

Moving back, Chendrill waited, his eyes now fully adjusted to the dark. Pulling out his phone, he sank back further into a corner and dialed the number again. Seconds, later the phone rang and then turned off. Chendrill searched the darkness with his eyes. Somewhere out there, hidden within about a dozen cabins all clumped together in the center of this cesspool, was Illya.

Quickly, Chendrill checked his phone and flicked it to silent. If whoever was in the booths called him back, he didn't want them to know he was there waiting. Then a door opened, and a man was exposed in the light coming from the porno movie still playing in the booth. Turning, the man walked out into the darkness, briefly stopping to look to Chendrill, hidden in the corner in his tight jeans and cowboy boots.

As the man disappeared into the darkness toward the shop front, Chendrill looked back toward the booths. Another door opened, and a man moved toward it out of the darkness, quickly joining its occupant and closing the flimsy door quickly behind him. Muffled voices spoke briefly, then there was silence before more coins hit the slots, and the movie started playing.

Fuck, Chendrill thought, what a place this was. A perverse world occupied by creepy people slipping around in the darkness like moles while the sun was shining outside. Another booth door opened, and a man stood in its doorway, faintly silhouetted by the dim light of the TV. Chendrill stared hard from his corner, trying to pick out the man's features. The man turned and looked back into his booth, and as the light from the TV changed from a static flickering to brighter light, it lit up the man's brown track pants and tattoos. Chendrill knew he had found Illya.

******

Illya hated this bit. It was nice in the booth, in his tiny room alone with his secret, watching guys kiss and fuck the way he liked and wished he could do himself. The room was dark and dirty with holes in the walls clawed out with pen knives or keys so that men could slip their cocks through and he could feel them and sometimes put his mouth around them like he used to while locked in the cell in Moscow.

But now the magic had been ruined by some prick who kept calling. He'd have to leave, get out, step outside onto the street without anyone seeing his face and knowing he visited this place. Nighttime was the best for cover, but soon the next loser would be coming over to give him his money, and the new girl would be working. He needed to wake her before that and get her to wash.

Illya turned and began to walk through the darkness, passing the tall gay guy with a big moustache wearing a come fuck me red shirt who'd been staring at him, hoping for an invite to come in so Illya could suck him off or fuck him in the darkness while they watched a movie. He passed into the brightness of the store without looking at the punk girl with the strange boots and hair, stepped into the real world, and began to walk back to his new place with the fancy leather furniture and Egyptian cotton-lined beds. He felt good, free now, his tracksuit hanging just right, still crease-free and styling after putting it back on in the darkness and tight confines of his booth.

He crossed the road and again saw the gay guy in the red shirt, leaving now, coming through the door, giving up on a sword fight in the darkness. He followed behind him, heading back in the same direction toward the city center.

Illya crossed another road, looking through a streetside window at the women in the hairdresser's getting ready to go out for the evening and talking bullshit. The guy was still there in the background—walking, not fast and not slow, but just heading along on his way somewhere—not looking at Illya, but both knowing where they'd just been.

Stopping, Illya looked around at the guy, glancing to the fancy red Ferrari parked on the curbside outside the café. Illya opened the door to the café and went inside, ordered a drink, and sat down. The guy was now standing next to the Ferrari with the door open, staring right at him, inviting him in with a smile. *Fuck*, he thought, this was all he needed, some big homosexual guy hitting on him. He was good-looking, though, and that was a real nice car, the kind the gangsters used to get picked up in outside of the prison after being holed up in a damp pit of a cell for God knows how long. Illya, lifting himself up by the bars so he could see them through the small window covered in shit and slime, had watched them being greeted by a fancy car and a woman as pretty as his sister.

Illya looked at the guy as he slammed the door and hit the alarm, showing off with the beep-beep-bop. He could see him clearly now in the daylight. The guy was definitely good-looking. He had a nice big moustache, kind of sexy in a camp way.

What he'd have to do is just stare back at him as he had at other times when guys in town had had a hard-on for him and give his head a shake, saying no, and the guy would leave, realizing he was straight and wasn't like that.

Illya looked at his watch. He still had an hour to kill. The guy hadn't been pushy in the store, had just stood waiting quietly, knowing what he wanted. Now he was out there staring at him, going for it. Illya thought it was cool. Why wouldn't the guy want him? The guy probably thought he was a professional athlete after all. He was styling in his new tracksuit that hung just right, its creases hitting just above his expensive sports shoes.

The guy crossed the road and came toward him, not averting his gaze from Illya's eyes for a second. Illya watched him as he came into the café and walked to the counter, buying a large caramel coffee, extra hot and marbled. Then the guy walked with confidence back across the café and sat at the table right next to him. He looked Illya in the eyes, smiled, and said, "Hi!"

Illya stared at the gay guy, who obviously wanted him, coming on to him like this.

"What's happening? You busy?" asked Chendrill.

"I'm not gay," said Illya, trying as hard as he could for once to get his English right.

"I'm sorry. I was just being friendly. I didn't mean to upset you. Hey, you know I saw you back there in that place. I thought, well, maybe…you know. You look hot, and I thought you might want to go for a spin in the Ferrari, you know, maybe around Stanley Park?"

"It's all cool," Illya said. He loved this, sitting here playing with this guy who wanted him and was trying so hard to get it on.

Then the guy in the flowery red shirt asked, "Are you Russian?"

Illya shook his head. "No, Croatian, from Zagreb."

"You live downtown?"

Illya nodded, getting into it. "I'm actor here, working on a movie."

"Really? Wow, a movie star! Hey, who'd have thought? That's really cool." Then he leaned in and whispered, "You know, like I said, I've got my Ferrari here. What do you say you and I go for a spin and get to know each other a little better? Then maybe we could go somewhere quiet, or even to my place? No one needs to know. I don't kiss and tell. Your secret is safe with me."

Illya's heart began to pound, and he felt a rush of blood give a little stiffness to his pants. *Fuck, he should go with the guy*, he thought. And then after that, he should start experimenting more, go to some of the bars down on Davie Street where the heavy bass music blares out, boom-diddly-boom-boom. Maybe meet some of those free-spirited guys who liked to stare, hitting on him with their eyes when he'd cruise by pretending not to be interested.

Then panicking, Illya felt the blood rush to his head instead as the embarrassment of being found out swept through him. He could hear his mother and father and friends laughing and his sister and her pretty boyfriend talking behind his back, both here and back at the housing project where men were real men back home. He looked up at Chendrill and said, "I have to go."

Chendrill smiled and held out his hand. "That's cool. My name's Charlie."

Illya smiled and held out his hand in turn, saying, "Zadenko."

And the moment Chendrill had his hand in Illya's, he was on him like lightning, grabbing it firm like a vice. He lifted it in the air and ducked under his arm, spinning around behind him and wrapping his left arm around Illya's throat in one fluid motion. Violently, he thrust his left knee into the Russian pimp's back, pulling Illya off his chair and onto the floor with enough force to take out another two tables as they fell.

In complete shock, Illya struggled, whipping his feet around and kicking tables and chairs all over the place. He felt Chendrill's arm pull tighter and tighter on his windpipe. This guy was fucking holding him, pinning him to the floor with incredible strength. His right hand was stuck solidly between them both, held tight at an angle that immobilized it completely.

Desperately needing to free his hand, Illya kicked, lashing out with his left hand—punching, grabbing, scratching, but unable to release himself. Then with all his might, he began to wriggle vigorously, moving them both across the coffee shop floor. Pushing down, he got one knee to the ground and then the other. He lifted Chendrill, still glued to his back, and using his own weight against him, crashed him to the floor and heard the man cry out in pain as he released his grip on Illya's hand for the split second he needed to give it movement.

Suddenly from nowhere, a flame shot out between them, burning them both, sending a searing pain over Chendrill's abdomen and across Illya's back and side. Instantly, Chendrill let go and quickly stood, banging out the flames burning through his red Hawaiian with his hand. Illya, staying down, lay there, breathing heavy, spraying flame from his right hand toward Chendrill's face as he put out the flames on his own shirt.

Chendrill quickly stepped to one side of the flames. He picked up a chair and threw it at Illya, then quickly picked up another to shield himself from the flame. As Illya started to get to his feet, Chendrill went for him again. Suddenly, a small vial of glass shattered at Chendrill's feet, and flame erupted below him. The chair he was holding caught on fire. Another vial smashed, and then another. Flame burst out, ignited by the vial's now free and highly combustible accelerant.

Backing up, Illya kept up the pressure. Flames now came from both hands as he made his way toward the door. Reaching it, he opened it with a kick, stepped outside, and was gone.

Chendrill felt his face and could tell his moustache, eyebrows, and hair were badly singed. His face stung from the flames that had reached his skin. The fall to the floor and the full weight of this Russian madman hitting his ribs had almost knocked him out cold and had caused him to release his grip when he had the man pinned.

He looked around, the shocked baristas now steering clear of him as they threw water down, stamping out the fire with their feet. Pretty soon, the fire brigade and ambulance crews would be in here like the heroes they were, followed by the police, moving themselves from one coffee shop to another.

Without a word, Chendrill opened the door and left the shop. He was in real pain now, not just bearable pain, and the difference was clear in his breathing. Fuck, he nearly had him, he thought. The fucking guy was quick. He wondered if Daltrey had fought him, too, before he got the better of her. Leaving the Ferrari, Chendrill walked a couple of blocks, his eyes squinting with the pain from his ribs. He looked at himself in a store window. His moustache was badly singed, and his red Hawaiian shirt had been burned around his waist. He hurt everywhere. Jesus, that had been one hell of a scrap, fast and furious with no punches thrown.

He'd been too cocky, he thought, chastising himself, trying to be clever like that and letting his ego get the better of him, thinking he could use the gay angle, talk the Russian into getting into the Ferrari, then drive him straight to the police station compound like a hero. Nonetheless he'd nearly got him, and had the Russian gotten into the car to get to know him better, his plan would have worked, and if it had, it would have been legendary.

Chapter Thirty-Three

Well, I won't be able to go back there, Illya thought as he entered his apartment building. He could see in the elevator's mirror that his new brown tracksuit was melted on one side. Who the fuck was that guy, and how had he managed to find him in his secret place?

He certainly wasn't a cop, not in that shirt. Maybe the guy had something to do with his sister and Sergei's disappearance from his world, or maybe he was just a madman. Most people liked to announce who they were and what they were doing when they went for an arrest or were out for vengeance. They'd say something like the Moscow Police had when they'd come for him in the early hours, or like the guy from the next housing block had done when he confronted Illya after he had killed his cat. But this fucking weirdo had just seemed to want to suck his dick.

He stepped back into the apartment and unlocked the door to Mary's room. He looked inside and saw that she was still out. Checking his watch, he knew he had time to clean himself up and then her before the guy from the hotel was due over. He walked into the bathroom and stripped off his ruined tracksuit.

Fuck, that guy had been strong, Illya thought as he stared at himself in the mirror. Reaching up, he felt his neck and then his bad wrist that was aching again like a motherfucker. The guy was quick and had got him good. It was the first time in his life he'd been hit on properly by a real gay guy, and the guy had tried to kill him just because he'd rejected him, telling him he didn't want to go for a ride in the park.

294

They were a touchier and tougher bunch than he'd thought. God, it was all so odd.

He looked at his stomach and then his side. They were red and sore, but in his day in prison, he'd had worse and stronger men attack him. The difference was that they hadn't lived.

"Whatever!" he said out loud. The guy was a madman, and if he saw him again, he'd kill him, burn the fucker to death like he should have done in the café and watch his eyes bubble up and melt. That's what he would do, and that was that.

He rubbed some of the cream he'd taken from his sister's bathroom on his side then walked naked into his bedroom and stared at his reflection in the mirror. He'd been really looking forward this evening to putting on his new designer undies and admiring himself for an hour or so in the mirror while listening to whoever it was fucking the girl in the next room, letting his imagination run away with itself.

He changed into his white tracksuit and a tight, black T-shirt and looked at himself some more in the mirror. Shit, he thought, it wasn't as good as the brown suit the fag in the shirt had ruined, but once upon a time, the one he had on now had been his favorite. Then his phone rang, and it was Jimmy saying he had another guy coming over soon. He also told him he should watch out as he'd heard there was this big guy, a private investigator, out there looking for him, but he didn't know why.

******

Chendrill sat on the hospital bed as the nurse dressed his burns. When the doctor returned with the X-rays of his chest an hour later, they both looked at the screen to see that Chendrill had three cracked ribs.

Fuck, Chendrill thought. *Three?* No wonder he'd been in so much pain. If it hadn't been for that jealous fuck of a boyfriend, he'd have been able to keep the Russian in the chokehold for just a moment longer, and he would have passed out. Now he was injured even worse, and had to keep watch over his shoulder to boot.

He left the hospital and checked his phone. There were several calls from Ditcon's department, insisting he come speak to them. No doubt they'd heard about the fight and the flames involving a big guy with a loud shirt and put two and two together.

There were five more from Sebastian with an emergency and two from Tricia telling him he was the sexiest guy in the world and how much she'd enjoyed his visit earlier in the day.

He reached Mazzi Hegan's Ferrari, took the parking ticket off the windshield, balled it up, and threw it in the garbage can sitting on the sidewalk by the front of the car. *Fucking pricks,* he thought as he looked at the ticket now crumpled and sitting at the bottom of the garbage can, *giving a ticket to Mazzi Hegan like that.*

The café was now back to normal as though nothing had ever gone down. He got in the car, feeling the pain in his side with every twist and turn, then pulled away into the flow of traffic and headed home.

******

The first to call as soon he tried to lie down to rest his ribs was the man who was paying his wages at the moment.

"What have you been doing all day? I have an absolute emergency," Sebastian said.

Another? Chendrill thought but said, "Go on."

"The dinner party tomorrow night—we've got an extra guest."

"And?"

"Well, you remember me telling you I'd accidentally dropped the plate of my favorite Royal Dalton dinner service?"

"Yeah, I remember. You said you smashed it on purpose. So what's the problem?"

"Well, we're celebrating, aren't we? I told you, there are twelve people coming over."

"And now you've got only eleven plates because Mazzi Hegan's was broken in some sort of accident?"

"Exactly."

"And there're no new sets of this type anywhere in the world, and you need me to track some down?"

"Correct."

"And that's an emergency?"

"Absolutely! What the hell am I going to do?"

Chendrill closed his eyes and breathed in deeply, but stopped just before the pain in his ribs became too much. "Why don't you use another plate?" he asked.

Sebastian stayed silent for a moment, then spat back, "I don't pay you a grand a day plus expenses to state the obvious."

"I thought I was just supposed to be keeping Dan out of trouble."

"Don't go there."

"Why the anger? I thought you were supposed to be celebrating?"

"I am, that's why I'm so anxious. You took all day to call me back, and I've got a dinner party."

Four hours later, it was one in the morning, and he had barely slept. Chendrill sat up and took another hit of the painkillers the doctor had given him, then lay back and tried to get comfortable. The thought of Daltrey—and even that kid he'd never met—getting burned by that monster was haunting his mind. *Call the cops,* he told himself. *Do the right thing. Tell them this is the guy, and this is what he looks like, and call it a day. And tell them to get Jimmy the dickhead concierge at the Grand to spill the beans and be done with it.*

But what if they fucked it up and someone else got burned in the process? What if they went in guns blazing like they do, and the wrong guy got hurt? There was a reason Daltrey operated alone, and Ditcon was not the only reason.

He closed his eyes again and thought of Tricia and wondered if the baker had come over again to cause trouble. And Dan? What if he was out there somewhere doing the limbo and making headlines again? *Fuck*, he thought, *it was no good lying here like this, barely able to move from one side to the other.* He remembered Muhammed Ali talking about his ribs after taking a pounding from Joe Frazier back in the glory days of boxing, before it became eclipsed by tough muscle guys locked together like limpets on the floor of an octagon cage.

******

At four in the morning, Chendrill was awake again. He lay for a while in the darkness of his room, thinking and listening to the night, then got up, took a shower, had a cup of tea, and got dressed. Half an hour later, he was sitting back outside the Grand.

Chapter Thirty-Four

Mazzi Hegan couldn't sleep, either, and lay in his bed looking at the ceiling and the masterpiece he'd had painted there after being inspired by a trip to the Sistine Chapel a few years back. He was excited, and his excitement had nothing to do with anything that lay seven feet above him. He was excited because his photos were not only going national, but international. They would be displayed at bus stops, on trains, on billboards all over the world. They would be seen in London, Paris, Rome, Rio, New York, Sydney, Tokyo, and more, and it was all starting here in Vancouver this morning. Oh my God, he could not keep the excitement in check. He had to go full blast into the day—have himself a shower with all the jets on, dress in something super stylish and satiny, and get himself down to the Grand.

The sun was just breaking as Mazzi Hegan stepped out into the cool morning air and listened to the dawn's chorus of birds. The Grand was the place to be on a day like this, having an early morning tea like the British and a patisserie or two, so fresh from the oven they melted in your mouth, their delicious filling oozing out as you bit down. What could be better?

He walked the next two blocks and crossed the road and then continued along the waterfront, listening to the water splashing up against the side of the seawall. He passed the small float planes getting ready for their first runs out to the islands, then went up the small hill to the Grand. Glancing briefly at a Ferrari that looked just like his, he stepped through magnificent doors built for a king to take a seat in the Grand's restaurant.

I'll spend some time here, get nice and comfy in one of the big leather chairs, and when I get out, the billboard should be up, he thought. He couldn't believe his work would be up there on the hoarding across the road, a board purposely designed and perfectly positioned by Sebastian himself to capture the minds, hearts, and wallets of every hungry-to-spend tourist that came to the conference centers or walked out along the gangplanks of the world's top cruise liners to admire this magnificent city. Today was going to be one of the greatest in his life and career so far.

Then he saw Chendrill standing at the concierge desk, holding the concierge's hand and whispering in the guy's ear.

"I knew it!" Mazzi said out loud, putting his tea down and staring at Chendrill, who was still holding the guy's hand tenderly and smiling. "Busted! Outed!" he said as he stood and walked over slowly, slipping in closer to try to see what was going on and maybe get an idea of what was being said. He stood close behind Chendrill's back, and looking over his shoulder, he saw the concierge's fingers twisted back almost to the breaking point.

"Tell me, or I'll be taking you out back, beating you, then bringing you around the front and showing you to the doormen," Chendrill whispered.

My God, Mazzi thought, as he backed off slowly and went back to his chair to watch from a distance. Chendrill let go of the concierge's hand long enough for him to write something on a piece of hotel paper. The concierge nodded cautiously as the two exchanged words and looked around to see if anyone in the hotel had seen the exchange.

Then Chendrill turned and walked straight over to Mazzi. Uninvited, he sat down next to him.

"Morning, Mazzi," he said.

Mazzi Hegan nodded. He wanted to say something about his car, but after seeing what Chendrill had just done to the concierge's fingers, he thought better of it. There was something different about the guy now. He wasn't the soft, blow-dried, big-moustached teddy bear with an edge he was used to. His face appeared to be burned, and he was obviously in pain, but trying not to show it.

"What brings you here so early?" Chendrill asked.

Mazzi took a deep breath and decided to ignore what he'd just witnessed at the concierge desk. He smiled. Nothing—not even this guy who'd stolen his car and just broken the concierge's fingers—was going to ruin this day. Taking another deep breath, and barely able to contain his excitement, he said, "Very soon, the electronic billboard outside is going to display my work for the whole world to see, and when it turns on, I want to be the first to see it."

Chendrill nodded and smiled. "Really?"

Mazzi's eyes lit up like a kid on Christmas morning. "Yes, really! I'm so excited!" Then Mazzi looked at his brand new Rolex and said, "Oh my God, it's almost six already. Let's go look together!"

And as the doorman opened the huge doors to the Grand, they both stepped outside and looked up to the billboard. There, above the city, was Dan with a broken nose in all his glory, naked save for Mazzi Hegan's shining silver underpants.

Mazzi couldn't believe it. It looked better than he'd ever imagined. He jumped up and down and clapped his hands with glee. He stared at it, taking it all in. It was the first time anything he'd done was going global. He never wanted to lose this feeling.

"Oh my God, oh my God! It's going to be a wonderful day!" Mazzi said.

And he wasn't wrong, for as he turned to look at Chendrill, all he saw was the man passing by him in the Ferrari, on his way to see Illya, holding the Russian pimp's new address that the concierge had just given him.

It was late for Jimmy and early for Chendrill when he'd arrived at the Grand. At first, the concierge had been cocky and threatened to have Chendrill thrown out.

"Why don't you fuck off out of here," said Jimmy, "before I call the security guard over and have him throw you out and make you look stupid."

Then Chendrill had seen Mazzi come in and wondered what the fuck he was he doing there. He'd grabbed the guy's fingers and whispered in his ear that the Russian fuck he'd been dealing with had been killing people.

There was a guy going there soon, the concierge had told him as he felt his fingers on the verge of breaking. Another Asian businessman, the type that always seemed happy when they were sent the Russian's way and seemed to tip well on top.

******

Chendrill waited for the hardware store to open, then drove back through town, pulling the Ferrari up on the other side of the park from Illya's swanky pad. He looked up at the building. Judging from the address—suite 408—the place had to be on the far right corner of the fourth floor. Either that or the apartment before it. Looking to his right, he saw another huge billboard of Dan, smiling and full of insolence. The idiot looked like he had something to say but couldn't be bothered, when in reality Chendrill knew all Dan wanted to do was sit in his room, jerk off, and eat.

He looked back at the building. It was only a block or two from where he and Illya had had their fight the day before. The sneaky bastard had pulled his flame gag on him and got the upper hand, then gone around the corner to his place and had a lay down. The guy that Jimmy the concierge had sent over must be up there now, he thought, up there fucking some whore the Russian had teamed up with since his sister could no longer perform.

Chendrill sat and stared at the building and took a deep breath. His ribs still hurt, but the painkillers were working, thank God, taking the edge off at least. Soon, though, he knew they'd be hurting again real bad. There was no doubt about that.

Chapter Thirty-Five

Illya had been surprised to get a call so early in the morning. When Alla had been at her prime and working with him, he got calls almost twenty-four seven. No doubt things were starting to pick up now. The girl, Luscious Mary or whatever she called herself, was doing well and trying her hardest to work her way out the door. He thought that soon he'd have to give her the option of staying or cut her loose once he'd secured a replacement from Moscow.

The Asian guy had come around and, as usual, had not made eye contact. He'd handed over the five hundred dollars in cash and gone into the room. The girl, though, was really starting to smell, and her hair was getting greasier.

Who the fuck was that fag prick yesterday? he wondered. He had been thinking about it for most of the night. It sounded like he might be the private detective, the guy Jimmy with the attitude from the hotel had called him about. *What would a private eye want him for? Maybe it was because of this new whore*, he thought. Could be a few things, though, when he thought it through. *Who the fuck knows?* he thought, and walked back into the huge living room. He looked outside across the park. If that guy showed up again, like he'd decided yesterday, he'd just kill him this time and be done with it, that was certain.

Then he saw him standing on the other side of the park, looking back at him, calling to him, saying to him, "You want it…you know I got it."

Fuck, the guy was hot. Fuck, he was so hot. Jesus, his stomach was so tight. There was sweat on his chest, and his nose was obviously broken, but he still looked good. Sexy, sexy, sexy like he'd never seen before.

Illya stood and stared at the billboard as Dan looked right back at him, full of attitude. He could feel himself getting harder inside his tracksuit pants. He continued to stare into Dan's eyes as the inside of his pants tightened. This guy out there staring at him, wanting him. He said out loud, "Yeah you, guy, you want it. Yeah, you want it, don't you?"

Putting his hand down his pants, he began to touch himself, rubbing his cock and staring at the guy's dick in those tight silver underpants, just like the ones he'd just bought.

Illya looked toward the corridor and listened for Mary and the Asian guy. They'd be another hour, guaranteed. Slowly, Illya began to strip off his jacket and then his T-shirt. Next, he dropped his track pants around his ankles to the floor and stood there naked in exactly the same underpants this guy out there who wanted him so bad was wearing.

"You want me, don't you?" Illya said quietly as he spat saliva down and stroked it into his cock, getting himself harder and harder. He'd meet the guy in the street down there or across the road in the park and he'd say, "Hi guy, my name's Illya. What's yours?"

Then the guy would say to him, "You're really hot. I like your track pants. Are you an athlete?"

Illya would tell him he's an actor in a TV series, then invite him up. They'd stand there in the middle of the room, and he'd tell the guy to strip. Then he'd grab him by the hair and pull his face toward him and kiss him hard just like the older guys had made him do when he first went to prison. He'd drag the guy's head down to his waist and pull his cock out and ram it hard into his mouth, and the guy would love it and stare up at him, wanting him to—

Then Illya turned around. The Asian man was standing on the other side of the room staring at him, holding a huge-bladed knife in his hand.

"I killed your friend Sergei, the flashy blond guy with the fancy shoes," Padam Bahadur said quietly in perfect English. "I burned him to death out on the creek, and then afterward, I went up to your apartment, and I hit your sister so hard I felt her spine break beneath my fist. And now I'm here, and I'm going to kill you."

Illya stood there, still holding his dick, staring at the little man with his huge knife and unable to comprehend what he'd just heard. He saw a can of compressed oil and a lighter sitting close to him on the cabinet, and very slowly, shuffling his feet with his track pants around his ankles, he moved toward it, saying in his best English as he went, "Get the fuck out of here, you little slant-eyed cunt."

Then Padam Bahadur moved toward him fast, raising the huge blade as the fire erupted from Illya's right hand and shot out toward the man as he came. Illya moved again, back to the side, holding the flame out at the guy. He quickly leaned down, grabbing another canister from the tracksuit pants around his ankles, then with both hands blasting flame, he shuffled toward the man with full force.

Padam Bahadur retreated across the living room as the flame from the canisters sent out scorching heat, pinning him against the wall. He ducked and dove to one side as Illya moved in on him. Then he threw himself down to the floor, disappearing behind the leather sofa.

Illya kept the flame going, moving forward and looking to his side for the accelerants in the left-hand pocket of his track bottoms, which had slipped away from his feet and were now on the floor.

Fuck, he thought, wishing he'd kept his clothes on instead of stripping them off like he had, leaving himself naked and vulnerable. If he hadn't been naked, he would have hit this Asian prick with some fuel by now, and that would have been the end of him in a matter of about a minute.

Backing off, he moved quickly to his pants and bent over. He dropped one of the cans, and reaching down into the pocket, he fumbled for the glass vials. Suddenly, the man came at him again, this time even faster, like lightning, spinning himself through the one flame Illya still held at him. Illya moved to the side and grabbed the fallen can again with his left hand. He ignited it with the flame in his right, but as quickly as it was lit, the flame in his left hand went out as he felt warm liquid running down his legs. Then, looking to the floor, he saw someone's hand there, holding the canister.

The man backed away, nursing his face, keeping away from the flame Illya kept pouring out from his right hand. Then the man came at him again, spinning and twisting through Illya's now solitary flame. Then as quickly as the last time, the flame disappeared as another hand hit the floor and Illya felt a searing pain rush through his abdomen.

Illya stood there and looked at his hands below him on the floor. Blood poured from both of his wrists, and he realized that the water he'd felt on his legs was his own life force pouring from his now open stomach. He tried to close the wound but couldn't with his hands no longer connected to his body. His intestines fell out of his abdomen and hung over his tattooed skin. As he looked down at it all in disbelief, the man's shadow approached again, and then his head began to spin, going around and around until it fell to the floor and stopped, and he saw his tattooed, blood-covered torso crumple before him as everything went black.

******

Padam Bahadur stood over Illya's body with the Gurkha knife in his hand, quietly paying his respects to the man he'd just killed. He could feel the burns about his face and had been surprised at the tattooed man's speed and cunning. Why he was wearing such a ridiculous pair of underpants, however, was something he would for the rest of his life have difficulty understanding. The glass vials of accelerant lay out in the open next to the man's track pants. If he'd reached them as he'd wanted and hit him with the fuel, he knew his days would have been over.

Walking away, he headed to the kitchen and turned on the taps at the sink. He washed the blood from the ceremonial blade that had been in his family for just over a century. Cupping his hands, he bathed his burned face in the cold, soothing water before tearing off a couple of sheets of paper towel and cleaning the blood and char from the fire off the knife. He walked back into the living room and placed it at the Russian's feet.

It was not the first time Padam Bahadur had killed with a Kuri knife, and it would not be his last. His brother's Gurkha blade was as sharp and as strong now as it had been the day it had been forged at the rear of a craftsman's home at the edge of his village in Nepal. It was a blade that had served him well and given the Russian man an honorable death. The Russian's friend and his sister's boyfriend Sergei had died by flame as he had deserved, while the Russian's sister watched as she lay in agony with her spinal cord severed.

His work here was done.

Chapter Thirty-Six

Chendrill made his way across the road, carrying the heavy-duty fire extinguisher he'd picked up at the hardware store. Timing it just right, he entered the building, nipping in just as the door to the lobby closed behind him and Padam Bahadur stepped out. He walked forward toward the elevators, but catching the slightest scent of burned hair and clothing, he stopped and sniffed the air for a moment. Turning, Chendrill looked around to the Asian man, watching as he closed the cab door and disappeared down the road.

Pulling out the card the concierge had given him for the elevator, he made it up to the fourth floor and walked cautiously along its length, the scent of burning stronger now as he neared the corridor's end. He reached 408, the last apartment on the right as he'd predicted, and stopped outside, listening at the door. If there was someone there waiting to burn him to death with a mini flamethrower, he'd be a sitting duck as soon as the door opened. Lifting the fire extinguisher up with his right hand, he tried the door with his left, slowly turning the handle. As the door opened, Chendrill quickly stepped back and lifted his right leg. In one almighty kick, he blasted the door open at the same time as he hit the trigger to the fire extinguisher, sending a whoosh of white cloud into the apartment's hallway.

He crept inside and moved silently along the corridor, inhaling the stench of burned air as the cloud of white mist dissipated. Holding the large funnel from the fire extinguisher in front of him like a shield, he reached the end

310

of the hall. Slowly he crept around the corner into the living room, and there he saw Illya there in the center of the room, decapitated and handless, his naked body lying in a pool of his own blood on the floor.

Somewhat relieved, Chendrill walked over, thinking about the small man who'd passed him at the door. He looked at Illya's torso again, frowning at the guy's underpants now soaked red in the blood from his gaping stomach, and then to the ceremonial knife at his feet. Tapping the vials of accelerant with his foot, he stared at Illya's hands and decapitated head lying to the side of his tattoo-covered body, tattoos depicting his life that was now over.

Chendrill moved away, checking the rooms. The suitcase and runners he'd seen only days ago on the convenience store CCTV tapes were there now, sitting by the side of Illya's bed.

The cheeky fucker, Chendrill thought as he looked back at Illya's butchered remains. The guy's gall was incredible— to kill a police officer and have the nerve to just walk away as if he was on his way to the airport.

Chendrill made his way to the main bedroom and opened the door. The girl was lying on the bed, out cold, her hair greasy and her clothes in a heap in a corner of the room. Looking up, he saw the thin rope tied to the bedposts and the slight cut marks they had made upon her wrists.

"You deserve to be dead, you fucking monster," he said aloud.

Carefully, he lifted the girl and tried to bring her around. Whatever she'd been given, she was out, but from what Chendrill could tell from her breathing, she would be okay. Placing her back down gently on the bed, he took his phone from his pocket and called Williams.

Chapter Thirty-Seven

Padam Bahadur made his way to the airport in the taxi and thought about what he had just done. It had been a long journey, starting in his family home at the foot of the mountains in Nepal where he'd held the hand of his niece, Sushma, listening as she'd cried.

"This girl Alla from Russia," she'd told him, "who was so beautiful and gentle and her boyfriend Sergei with his blond hair, so handsome and funny…"

They'd been out for drinks and to a concert, dancing barefoot in the park, and as the weeks went on, their friendship had blossomed. Sushma told him about Alla's brother, who wore track pants but didn't run, showing up uninvited, taking off his shirt when he drank, saying things in a way that scared her boyfriend Bernado, and showing off his tattoos of rats and flames. And then one day at Alla's ex-husband's house, he'd said to her, "You have to work now."

"I didn't know what he meant," Sushma had told him as Padam sat by the window in his brother's home in the Himalayan foothills, quietly nodding, understanding everything, watching her tears create small rivers that ran down her beautiful cheeks as she sat in her chair with wheels.

She told him the Russian had followed her inside from the outside patio and had then come into the washroom with his top off. As she'd stood there looking at him, frightened and confused, he'd said, "It's time to use yourself for what God made you for."

Her tears continued to flow, and she looked to the floor, saying to her uncle, "He told me it was time for a beautiful girl like me to use my pussy. I didn't know what he meant. He didn't look like he wanted sex, not like that. He scared me. I thought about Alla, Sergei, and Bernado outside drinking beer, and I tried to leave, to push past him, but he grabbed me by the hair and dragged me to the bedroom. And I was screaming and screaming, and then he hit me with a big book they use for the telephone. He kept on beating me and shouting at Alla and her boyfriend Sergei, who was holding Bernado back at the door. He kept saying, 'I'll make her like you. I'll make her like you.' Then Bernado broke free and came rushing in."

Padam had watched as Sushma cried deep agonizing tears, tormented by the memory of a night that had destroyed her world. She'd looked up, and taking a deep breath, she continued.

"Bernado ran across the bedroom. And Alla's brother shot flames at him, burning his face as he reached me. Bernado had his hands to his eyes, he was screaming, and Alla's brother stood above him, spitting flame down, burning him more. Bernado spun around, trying to escape, crawling and screaming in pain to the window. The curtains went up in flames, and they quickly spread across the ceiling. I tried to get up, tried to get off the bed, but I couldn't move my legs. I laid there helpless, holding my hands up to Alla and her man for help, but they just left me there. I was calling and calling for Alla—and then she came back."

Sushma looked at the floor, her eyes red and bloodshot from the tears as she cried at the memory of how her Bernado had died and how for the first time she'd realized the Russian man with the tattoos had broken her back.

"She came back," she said again as she lifted her head and looked into Padam's eyes. "She came back, and she saved me, Uncle. She dragged me through the flames, down the stairs, and left me by the door, and that's where the firemen found me."

******

Padam sat in the rear of the cab, staring at the hairs on the back of the driver's neck, and knew he had only just survived. All his years as a Gurkha soldier and the special training he'd received from the British Army Special Air Services in Hereford, England could never have prepared him for the speed of the Russian who fought with fire.

It had been a little over a week now since he'd arrived. Finding Illya had been easy. He'd been sitting there at the blackjack table of the casino by the water just as his niece had said he liked to do, his tattoos showing through the white sleeve of his tracksuit top, his eyes the eyes of a man to be feared. But a Ghurkha fears nothing, let alone death. His sister had been next to him, prettier than Sushma had described, living in dread not just of him, but of what she knew she was and was incapable of not being. Her sponging boyfriend leached off of them both, not caring and without repentance.

Killing the blonde freeloader had been easy, for it was clear as he sat there with the others, drinking and eating for free, that he was not strong and had never killed nor harmed a soul himself, but Padam knew he had been there, watching, indifferent to the young lives he knew were being cut short and shattered beyond comprehension.

He'd left the casino that night, passing the man on the bench who was about to end his life. He had walked his girl back through the night air to her apartment where she would suck the cock of a stranger, and had kissed her lips tenderly. Wondering if the beer he'd left on the bar would still be there, he had wandered back. Rounding the corner, he'd felt the pain of Padam's fist. It had rendered him unconscious, striking his heart with such force that it stopped momentarily. In the darkness, Padam carried him over his shoulder down the gangplank and along the small wooden dock.

He'd had ten minutes to reach Alla's apartment as he walked away from her boyfriend, who lay unconscious in the boat out there on the creek, his blond hair, designer clothes, and Mauri slow movers shoes covered in fuel, and as Alla stood there naked by the window, waiting for Padam to come to her from behind, Padam waited for the fuses to ignite and torch her man. As the flames rose up into the night, he thought of his niece and her fiancé, robbed of a life so precious, and how this beautiful and perfect woman had watched and done nothing as her brother had destroyed their lives.

As he'd stood and walked toward the naked woman, he'd told her it was her boyfriend out there burning in the boat. She'd looked back at him, confused by his words, and he'd stepped to the right, his clenched fist snapping out like a whip, striking her hard and fast with a blow to her lower back. The bones splintered as the twist of his knuckles recoiled away from her soft skin, and she had fallen, her face pressing hard against the long plate-glass window overlooking the creek. Her hands clung to it, but could not hold. The pain in her lower back took over, slowly rendering her unconscious as she looked out at the burning boat on the water, the flames lighting up the night sky.

Many lights had been on in the apartments surrounding the creek as Padam walked back along the seawall toward the casino. Lovers out on moonlit strolls, watching the spectacle of the funeral pyre as it shone across the water, were oblivious to the small Asian who'd just killed a man as he made his way back to the Russian who would be sitting at the bar in the casino, awaiting a similar fate. Bored with drinking beer, and waiting in vain for his blond-haired friend to return, Padam knew Illya would make his exit, wandering home drunk, passing the quiet place under the bridge as he always did, and it would be there where Padam would take him and burn him alive as Illya himself had done to so many.

But it wouldn't be that night, for when Padam arrived, discreetly slipping into the casino fresh from burning Illya's friend and destroying his sister's spine, Illya had gone. And as Padam gave up the wait and walked back along the seawall through the warm night air, he turned away from the fire trucks and police now busy at the water's edge and headed toward the now empty apartment where the Russian, his sister, and her boyfriend had once slept. He passed through the city streets until he hit Granville Street, where he stopped and listened to the distant sirens only feet from where the Russian now sat after his urge had come again— an urge which had called as it had so many times before. An urge which had unknowingly given Illya a stay of execution, drawing him back to the place where he could find refuge, a place where he could be himself at the back of a sleazy store, locked in a murky booth, drunk and half-naked, listening to the groans of the men around him, hoping and waiting for another man, just as lost as he, to stick his dick through the booth's jagged wooden hole and put himself at the mercy of the Russian psychopath sitting on the other side.

Chapter Thirty-Eight

The taxi pulled up at the departure gate of the airport, and Padam stepped out, his face burned. Now that the adrenaline from the fight was beginning to dissipate, he could feel the tenderness in his skin with every facial expression.

He walked through the terminal and entered the toilet and looked at himself in the mirror. His clothes were singed. They could be replaced, but his hair was now gone at the front, and he knew from the spray of fire coming from the cans the Russian had so artfully held that the hair on his right eyebrow might never return. Leaning forward, he turned on the cold tap and filled the basin. He placed both hands into the water and splashed his face with the cool water to soothe his hot skin. The burn hurt, and it needed treatment, but despite being a long way from home, he was a soldier, and he was still standing.

After dabbing his face with a towel, Padam left the toilet. He stopped outside and looked up at the sign listing departures. The next flight out was an afternoon flight to London. Going to the States was his best bet, but he didn't want to have to answer questions with the U.S. Customs stationed here at the airport with regard to his burns. He figured he should keep his head down and get to London, where he could show his status as a special services soldier and whip through.

His training in the army had taught him to get out as quickly as he could, long before the decapitated body was found and while the police were still scratching their heads as they had been since they found Sergei burned to a crisp

317

out on the creek. He looked toward the check-in for the British Airways flight and for the second time that day saw Chendrill staring at him from across the terminal.

******

Chendrill watched as the Asian man who had just decapitated the Russian stared at the departure board, trying to figure out just which way to get out before Ditcon got his act together and had the entire city locked down.

It hadn't taken long for Chendrill to track the cab after calling the company and telling them he'd left his wallet in the one he'd seen Padam get into. Then he'd ripped the Ferrari as fast as he could toward the airport immediately after he'd made the call. Williams would be there by now, he thought, caring for the girl, calling an ambulance and letting the station know he and Chendrill had tracked down Daltrey's killer all on their own. *But what do I do now?* Chendrill thought as he looked at the small Asian man standing there, dabbing his burned face with a damp paper towel. The guy—a hero in Chendrill's eyes, who'd gone in there obviously armed with only a short sword and taken on a guy with a flamethrower and won.

Then Padam looked at him and gave a nod of respect in a way only a fellow warrior could understand. Chendrill watched as the man began to cross the busy terminal. Arriving in front of him, Padam said to him in a quiet voice, "I am a Gurkha, and I have killed many people at war. The Russian and his friend deserved their fate and I have no problem with you, I wish you no harm—Now I ask you, man to man, to let this to continue to be the case!"

Chendrill stared at this little man who showed no fear,

318

and he smiled. "Why'd you come all this way to kill him?" he asked.

Padam shook his head, not taking his eyes off Chendrill for a single second. "The moment he laid a hand on my brother's only daughter," he said, "he was as good as dead."

"You're referring to Bernado's girlfriend?"

Padam nodded. "The Russian broke her spine as his sister and her boyfriend Sergei watched. Bernado tried to stop him. The girl, Alla, saved my niece's life, dragging her out of the room when the place caught fire. This is why she is still alive."

Chendrill relaxed and awkwardly propped himself up on a small glass railing. He stared at the floor, thinking about the young kid struggling to save his girl and how Daltrey and the young man must have felt as this Russian's flame got the better of them. Then he looked up at Padam and said, "I feel for your niece and her boyfriend, and for my friend, the woman detective who tried to catch him and died in the process."

Padam nodded. He had heard the sirens that night from the small alcove he'd waited in across from the apartment Illya had walked away from on the night he should have died. He remembered the smell of burning flesh that had filled his nostrils.

"This is my biggest regret," he said. "I should have taken him out conventionally the first day I arrived instead of making a statement the way I did."

Turning, Padam looked instinctively through the crowds of people moving to and fro as a tow truck pulled up at the entranceway to the terminal.

"If I had done so," Padam said, "your friend would still be here, and you'd have been spared your burns and the broken ribs you are now suffering."

Chendrill laughed. Looking to the floor, he shook his head and said, "No, I got the damaged ribs from a baker."

He looked up and saw that Ditcon and his guys were entering the building, and the Gurkha who had travelled halfway around the world to avenge his family was gone.

Chapter Thirty-Nine

Chendrill looked around the terminal. Padam was nowhere to be seen. He had disappeared into the ether of people like a ghost as Ditcon descended on him. Then, through the crowd, Chendrill saw him. Padam raised his hand in thanks from a line of commuters he'd blended into so perfectly before disappearing again like a ghost, the way the Special Air Services in Britain had no doubt trained him to do.

Ditcon arrived at his side. "We've been monitoring your car. You've been speeding, so it's being towed."

Chendrill shook his head. *The man's a fucking idiot*, he thought. "Good police work," he said, "but it's not my car."

"Where is he?" Ditcon asked.

"Where's who?"

"The one who murdered Daltrey—the guy you're looking for."

Chendrill looked at the ground again, then discreetly scanned the terminal for Padam, now long gone. Looking up again, he said, "Daltrey's murderer is downtown. One of your police officers by the name of Williams is guarding him. Go see for yourself. He's all cut up about what he did."

"Where?"

And with that, Chendrill stood, took a deep breath that pained his ribs, and began to walk away. Turning back, he called out, "You're supposed to be the detective!"

******

Chendrill walked outside into the sunshine and recognized

the smug face of the tow truck driver smiling at him. Slamming the door to his truck, the guy stared back at Chendrill, the Ferrari he'd been searching for now his once again, strung up on the back of his dirty oil-laden tow truck like a prize deer. With a smile that said it all, he pulled the truck away along the airport concourse.

Fuck me, Chendrill thought as he watched the Ferrari being dragged away. I solve that prick Ditcon's case for him, and the only bit of true police work he's done throughout the whole investigation is to track my car and have it towed. He watched as Mazzi Hegan's Ferrari disappeared in the distance and then strolled toward the sky train.

******

The train was full when he got to the station. He squeezed himself inside and stood in among the travelers. God, he was tired, he thought as he wondered where the Gurkha who had no fear of death was right now. Nowhere near Ditcon, that was for sure. The guy was tough, small but solid, and Chendrill could only imagine the conflicts he'd been through in his career as a soldier. There was no doubt about it, killer or not, he was a good man and had come here to set the record straight.

Leaning up against a partition in the train, Chendrill closed his eyes and relaxed for a moment, feeling the train's motion as it headed driverless along its concrete runway back into town. It had been a busy morning so far. All he needed to do now was get on with the real investigative work he still needed to deal with, like hunting down a dinner plate that was no doubt sitting on an obscure shelf in a department store somewhere downtown. Maybe after that, he'd go see

Dan's mum to be sure her son was behaving himself in the basement. He opened his eyes again to see Dan looking down at him from the advertising board laid out across the top of the train's center doors. A group of Japanese students stood below giggling at the photo of Dan, naked save for Mazzi Hegan's silver underpants. The girls looking up at Dan as Dan's smoldering eyes looked down at them, the girls unconsciously shuffling from one foot to the next, their cheeks reddening, as their insides began to…Burn.

The End

Paul Slatter grew up in London, England and now lives in both Canada and Thailand. He is married and has four children.